THE LITTLE THEATRE ON HALFPENNY LANE

HALFPENNY LANE
BOOK 1

CLODAGH MURPHY

THE LITTLE THEATRE ON HALFPENNY LANE
CLODAGH MURPHY
Clodagh Murphy © 2022

ISBN: 9781915369055

Published by Balally Books

Cover design by Books Covered

OLGA: Only one desire grows and gains in strength …

IRINA: To go away to Moscow. To sell the house, drop everything here, and go to Moscow …

OLGA: Yes! To Moscow, and as soon as possible.

—Chekhov, *Three Sisters*

A NOTE ON NAMES

Some of the characters and places in this book have Irish names that might be unfamiliar. Here's a quick guide on pronunciation.

Aoife
    Pronounced: EE-fa

Sive
    Pronounced: SYVE (rhymes with 'Five')

Ranelagh
    A Dublin suburb
    Pronounced: REN-el-a

1

'Is your other sister coming?' Patrick Hanrahan looked at Aoife and Sive across the width of the polished board-room table, bushy eyebrows raised over the top of his horn-rimmed glasses. His eyes flicked to the document in front of him. 'Miriam?'

'Mimi,' Aoife automatically corrected him. 'Yes, she should be here shortly.' She glanced up at the big clock on the wall, acutely aware of it loudly ticking off the minutes, then hit the button on her phone to light up the screen. Mimi had messaged on their Weird Sisters WhatsApp group that she'd been delayed and would be a few minutes late, but there was nothing since, and Aoife and Sive had already been sitting here sweating it out for ten minutes, which to Aoife's mind counted as more than a 'few'. She gave Sive a furtive eye-roll across the empty seat between them, but Sive merely shrugged placidly in response. Aoife turned her attention back to the door, willing Mimi to appear.

She told herself to relax. It wasn't her fault, after all. She wasn't responsible for Mimi's behaviour. But having acted as a parent to her younger sisters for so many years, she couldn't seem to shake the habit – even though Sive, the baby of the family, was twenty-two now. She smiled apologetically at the two men sitting opposite them, but Patrick did nothing to hide his irritation, tapping his expensive pen impatiently on the papers in front of him, and Jonathan Hunt kept his eyes down, glowering at the table from beneath his long dark lashes.

She looked up at the ornate cornicing, trying to distract herself by imagining the people who would have lived here in former times and the lovely lives they must have led in these elegant rooms. Situated on Merrion Square in the heart of Georgian Dublin, the building that was now home to the offices of Hanrahan & Co solicitors would once have been the townhouse of a wealthy, genteel family. She thought of the parties they might have hosted, the distinguished people who would have been their neighbours. They could have been on nodding acquaintance with Yeats or the Wildes …

'Perhaps we should get started—'

Patrick's words shook her out of her reverie, but as he spoke the door was thrust open and Mimi burst through it. She entered the room like she was walking onto a stage, immediately commanding her audience's attention.

'Sorry, sorry, sorry!' she said breezily, looking around at everyone as she strode over to take the chair between Aoife and Sive. Aoife caught her slight frown as her gaze landed on Jonathan Hunt seated beside Patrick. 'The first two buses were full,' she said as she shrugged out of her purple teddy coat, 'and then when I finally got on one, it crawled through town.'

Aoife wondered if the excuse was genuine. Mimi had gone on a date last night and not come home, so Aoife had no idea where she was coming from this morning.

'Anyway, I'm here now.' Mimi pulled out the chair and threw herself into it with a hearty sigh and a waft of cool outside air and perfume.

Patrick gave her what Aoife supposed was intended as a smile, but came out as more of a pained grimace. 'You know Jonathan,' he said to Mimi, nodding to the man on his left.

'Yes. Hello.'

As a young woman entered with a tray of tea, drawing Patrick's attention away, Mimi leaned close to Aoife and whispered, 'What's *he* doing here?', rolling her eyes in Jonathan's direction.

Aoife shrugged and Mimi turned to Sive, who did the same. They'd both been equally surprised to find Jonathan here when they'd arrived. He was their Great-aunt Detta's godson, the eldest grandson of her best friend, and they'd crossed paths with him occasionally over the years – waving hello across the green room of Halfpenny Lane Theatre, or exchanging small talk at family parties. As a teen, Aoife had had a bit of a crush on Jonathan, lusting after him from afar. But they'd had very little personal interaction with him, and then he'd moved to London and disappeared from their lives completely until Detta's funeral a couple of weeks ago. He'd been solemn and distant as he'd sympathised with them on their loss, but with a kindness in his green eyes that touched Aoife more deeply than any sentimental words and brought her teenage romantic fantasies slamming to the front of her brain.

She'd been disappointed when he'd turned down their invitation to the lunch they'd arranged after the funeral at Detta's favourite pub. She thought it would have been nice to reconnect as adults. But she'd never expected him to be here, when Patrick had called them in for the reading of their great-aunt's will. They'd assumed it would just be the three of them.

Aoife wondered now if perhaps he worked here. Detta had taken a keen interest in Jonathan's career, as proud of his achievements as if he was her own grandson, so Aoife always knew what he was up to, whether it was graduating top of his class from Trinity, acing his Law Society exams or winning a Fulbright Scholar Award to do postgraduate studies at Harvard. Last she'd heard he was taking London by storm, working in some prestigious law firm there. But Detta had been rambling and incoherent in her final years, and it was a while since Aoife had heard any news about Jonathan from her. It was possible he'd moved back to Dublin and joined Patrick's firm. It still seemed strange that he'd sit in on this, though.

'Well, thank you for coming,' Patrick said when they'd all been served with tea and a plate of shortbread biscuits had been passed around.

'Oh, thank god!' Mimi said when they came to her, taking the remaining three before she placed the empty plate in the centre of the table. 'I didn't have time for breakfast.'

After explaining a few preliminaries, Patrick turned his attention to the document on the table and began reading. 'This is the Last Will and Testament of me, Bernadette Josephine Carroll of 15 Swift Lane, Dublin 8 ...'

Detta had appointed 'my godson Jonathan James Hunt of 24 Sycamore Avenue, Sandymount, Dublin 4' as her sole executor, which explained his presence here, and Aoife zoned out as Patrick continued reading through the legalese. Detta had loved making wills, and had changed hers often, delighting in making lots of small, specific bequests – leaving a piece of jewellery to a friend who'd admired it, or a favourite painting to an artist who she

4

knew would appreciate it – and updating it over the years as friends and family pre-deceased her.

As children, whenever Aoife and her sisters had fallen in love with something belonging to her, she'd say 'I'll leave it to you in my will'. They'd thought it was just an expression, but later they came to realise she meant it. However, it was only the small bequests that constantly changed. Aoife, Mimi and Sive already knew the bulk of Detta's estate would be left to them, her sole surviving blood relatives – a stark reminder that the three sisters now constituted the entire Carroll family and at twenty-seven, Aoife was its matriarch.

So she was only half listening as Patrick intoned 'The Halfpenny Lane Theatre at 1 Halfpenny Lane, Dublin 8 and all contents thereof unto my grand-nieces Aoife Bernadette Carroll, Miriam Therese Carroll and Sive Louise Carroll and my godson Jonathan James Hunt ...'

Wait, what? Did he say—

She was jolted to attention by Sive nudging her elbow at the same time as the words penetrated her brain.

On her other side, Mimi surged to her feet, her chair scraping back so suddenly it tipped over. 'Objection!' she roared, slapping the table.

'I beg your pardon?' Patrick looked at her in astonishment, while beside him, Jonathan suppressed a startled snigger.

'Sit down!' Aoife hissed at her. She bent and pulled the chair back up, then grabbed a handful of her sister's jumper and yanked her down into it. 'You're not on *Kelly's Law* now.' Mimi had an occasional recurring role as an up-and-coming barrister on the popular TV drama, and sometimes let it spill over into real life.

'Well, we can't just sit here and do nothing,' Mimi said, looking between her sisters, 'while this – this – *imposter*' –

she waved a hand at Jonathan – 'steals Halfpenny Lane from us.' She turned to Patrick, who looked like he was seriously regretting coming to work today. 'I—I declare the existence of an impediment,' she announced.

'Excuse me?'

Jonathan snorted.

'That's for bigamists who are trying to get married,' Sive whispered to her.

'Well, what do you say when someone's trying to falsely claim an inheritance?' Mimi demanded, eyeballing Patrick. 'I'm sorry, we didn't cover this on *Kelly's Law.*'

'I can assure you there's nothing untoward going on here,' Patrick told her calmly, unmoved by the determined set of her little heart-shaped face. 'These are your great-aunt's instructions. I made this will for her myself.'

'Um … sorry,' Aoife said to him. 'Could you read that bit again, please?'

He gave her an impatient look before doing as she asked. But there was no mistake – it said exactly the same thing the second time.

'What's the date on that?' Mimi asked.

Patrick flicked back to the front page and read a date in March two years previously.

'Detta was in the nursing home then,' Aoife said. She'd moved there in January of that year, when doctors had decided she could no longer live at home.

'Yes, I visited her there because she wanted to make some changes to her will.'

'Let me see it.' Mimi extended a hand to Patrick. He frowned, but passed the will across the table to her.

Mimi slid the document in front of her, and they all leaned in to study it together. It was all there in black and white – the name and address of the theatre, and the three of them listed as beneficiaries, their names standing out in block capitals … and Jonathan Hunt's name alongside them in the same type. Holy hell!

'There must be some mistake,' Mimi said, her eyes flicking up at Patrick. 'How do we contest this?'

'We can't,' Sive said to her in an agonised whisper. 'This is Detta's will.'

'Is it, though? We've always known what her intentions were for the theatre. How many times did she tell us she was leaving Halfpenny Lane to us? She never mentioned … this guy.' She waved vaguely at Jonathan as if he wasn't right there in the room, and Aoife cringed.

But even though the evidence was there before them in print, she couldn't help thinking Mimi had a point.

'I guess she changed her mind,' Sive said.

'Oh, don't be so defeatist,' Mimi snapped. 'There must be something we can do about this,' she said to Patrick, her eyes gleaming with defiance. 'People contest wills, don't they?'

'She'd started having … episodes when she went into the nursing home,' Aoife said, glancing at Jonathan. Had he somehow persuaded Detta to change her will in his favour when she wasn't in her right mind? High on medication, perhaps?

'She had that UTI,' Mimi said urgently, turning to her. 'People go doolally when they have those. When was that?'

'And when did she have the first stroke?' Aoife whispered back.

Patrick sighed. 'I can assure you your great-aunt was of perfectly sound mind when she made this will.'

Aoife slumped in her chair and nodded, acknowledging that they were being fanciful. 'I'm sure she was.' She could sense Mimi bristling beside her, and she turned to her to give her a warning look. They were just going to have to accept it – this will was real. For whatever reason, Detta had decided to give Jonathan Hunt a share in Halfpenny Lane. But *why*? She wanted to howl at the unfairness of it, as the implications started to sink in and she saw all their hopes and dreams for the future evaporate.

Halfpenny Lane was always meant to be theirs – hers and her sisters'. They'd talked so often about what they'd do when this day came. She would quit her job and finally go to acting school; they'd revive the theatre and do *Three Sisters* together. The play was one of their favourites, and they were perfect for the roles of Olga, Masha and Irina – orphans like them, and similar in age. She'd play the eldest, Olga – the sensible, pragmatic one with the responsible teaching job who mothered the others. Mimi would be the witty and tempestuous middle sister Masha, and Sive would play the youngest Irina, naive and optimistic, still full of hope for a bright future when they'd return to their beloved Moscow and the life they'd lived there.

How could Detta have done this to them? If she'd wanted to leave Jonathan something, why her beloved theatre of all things? What were the chances of a corporate type like him carrying on its tradition?

'May I?' Patrick nodded to the will and held out his hand to Mimi.

'Sorry.' She handed it back to him.

'Sorry,' Aoife said meekly.

'It's quite all right. I can see this has come as a shock to you.' He cleared his throat. 'Now, where was I?' He bent over the document and resumed reading.

But Aoife didn't hear another word that was said. She sat in a daze, her mind spinning with questions. Why had Detta done this? Why hadn't she told them? How would it work? And what the hell was going to happen now?

2

____

'WELL, THAT WAS …' Aoife sank onto the step outside the offices of Hanrahan & Co. as the smartly painted yellow door shut behind them.

'Yeah. What the bally hell?'

'What do we do now?'

Sive and Mimi sat on either side of her, huddling close against the cold.

'I haven't a clue.' She put her gloved hands to her cheeks, taking comfort in the warmth.

'Well, we have to get away from here anyway before *he* comes out,' Sive said. They'd left Jonathan discussing various administrative issues relating to his executorship with Patrick.

'Okay, crisis talks,' Mimi said, standing. 'Bewley's?'

Aoife and Sive looked up at her and nodded in agreement.

'To Bewley's,' Sive said, 'and as quickly as possible.'

It was a sunny April morning, cold but bright as they cut through Merrion Square Park, surrounded on all sides by terraces of tall, elegant houses like the one they'd just been in, their doors painted a variety of cheery colours.

'We should ask Oscar for his advice,' Sive said, stopping when they reached the corner of the park where a colourful sculpture of Oscar Wilde lounged on a rock opposite the house where he was born. 'He'll know what we should do.'

Aoife smiled. 'Don't be so dramatic.'

'But I *am* dramatic. We all are. It's our thing.'

All three stood before the sculpture as if at a shrine.

'I think we know what Oscar would say,' Mimi said.

'I have nothing to declare but my genius?'

She shook her head. 'He'd say "Save the Theatre, ditch the Suit". Only, you know, in a much wittier way.'

Aoife sighed. 'I don't see how we can do either, frankly.'

All three girls hung their heads despondently.

'But come on,' Aoife said briskly. 'We'll discuss it when we get to Bewley's. I can't think straight until I have some caffeine inside me.'

'And cake,' Sive said. 'I need sugar.'

They walked in silence along the curve of Lincoln Place and onto Nassau Street, weaving through the crowds of tourists being offloaded from coaches outside Trinity College. When they reached Grafton Street, it was already bustling with mid-morning shoppers.

The delicious aroma of roasting coffee beans perfumed the air as they were shown to a table at the back of Bewley's Cafe under the high stained-glass windows. Aoife felt better already as she sank onto the plush red banquette, the cosy warmth of the cafe instantly soothing. They'd been coming here since they were children, and it gave her a reassuring sense of continuity and dependability. Today of all days, it was nice to know that some things never changed.

They removed their coats and studied menus in silence, all still shaken by this morning's sucker punch. It was almost like losing Detta all over again.

Her death had hit them hard, even though it had been expected and they'd had a long time to prepare for it. She'd been a huge part of their lives, especially since their parents died. While she'd never been able to help them out financially, she'd enriched their lives in so many ways, introducing them to the poetry of Shakespeare, the wit of Oscar Wilde, the waspish aristocrats of Noël Coward and the faded Southern belles of Tennessee Williams. She'd been a glorious cook, though not a frugal one, her repertoire stuck firmly in the seventies and relying heavily on copious amounts of butter, cream and brandy, and they'd spend every Sunday at her house eating dinner and watching old movies, while Detta shared bits of gossip about the stars, and passed on tips for their future careers.

For as long as Aoife could remember, Detta had taken it for granted that the three of them would follow in her footsteps and become actresses, and she'd doled out career advice liberally and randomly, counselling them on everything from stage etiquette to handling nudity and sex scenes. She was particularly emphatic that they should choose their roles carefully so as to avoid typecasting.

Sive was the most conventionally pretty of them, with her pale-blonde hair and big blue eyes, and according to Detta would get stuck playing an endless line of 'nincompoops and flibbertigibbets' if she wasn't careful. Mimi had a kind of old-fashioned beauty perfect for costume drama, with a cupid's bow mouth and voluminous pre-Raphaelite curls, and should steer clear of too many period pieces.

Aoife, she'd said, was lucky to have one of those faces that could transform completely and would find it easiest to disappear into a character. But versatility was key, and it was important to mix it up and choose roles as diverse from each other as possible, especially at the beginning of their careers.

Even though Detta hadn't been a real presence in their lives for some time, her passing felt like a seismic shift in their world. It was as if they'd been cut adrift, the last link to their parents' generation severed. A shiver ran through Aoife as she recalled Mimi turning to her at the graveside, her tone bleak as she whispered, 'It's just us now'.

A waitress came to take their order, shaking Aoife out of her gloomy thoughts. No one needed to say it, but there was a tacit agreement that they wouldn't broach the subject at hand until they'd all been served with steaming mugs of coffee and a plate of cakes.

Sive took a bite of a sticky cherry bun and rested her head against the back of the banquette. 'I needed that. I'm still in shock.'

'That makes three of us, I think.' Aoife looked to Mimi, who nodded in agreement, her mouth full of pistachio cake.

'So,' Mimi said when she'd swallowed, wiping her mouth with a napkin. 'What do we do?'

Aoife lifted her mug, cradling it in both hands. 'What *can* we do? It's Detta's will. She had a right to leave her property to whomever she chose.'

'Of course she did, but couldn't there be some mistake? She always told us she was leaving the theatre to us.'

'And she did.'

'But not *just* to us. She never once mentioned leaving a share of it to Jonathan Hunt, of all people. Why would she *do* that?'

Aoife shook her head. 'I don't know.'

'Do you think it was really her intention?'

'You don't seriously think he tampered with her will, do you?'

Mimi wrinkled her nose. 'I mean you have to ask yourself: what kind of man would take advantage of an old lady and three penniless orphans?'

Aoife snorted. 'I really don't think Jonathan would do anything underhand.' Detta had always spoken highly of him, and Aoife saw no reason to second-guess her opinion.

'Okay, maybe he didn't tamper with it exactly,' Mimi conceded. 'But he could have persuaded her to change it in his favour.'

Aoife couldn't deny the thought had crossed her mind, but only fleetingly. Everything Detta had said about Jonathan over the years gave her the impression he was completely honest and trustworthy.

'But *why*?' Sive asked. 'Why would he want to? Do you think he's ever even *been* to the theatre?'

Mimi gave a bitter laugh. 'Probably only to the panto at Christmas when he was a kid.'

'We've no reason to suppose he's a complete savage,' Aoife said. 'He could be a passionate theatre-goer for all we know.'

'Come on.' Mimi gave her a sceptical look. 'He's a solicitor. It's a well-known fact they have no souls.'

'Really?' Sive gave a worried frown.

'You've seen Patrick.'

'So why would Detta leave part of her precious theatre to him?' Sive said plaintively. 'To someone with no soul?'

'Oh, don't listen to her,' Aoife said. 'Of course he has a soul. You probably say the same thing about accountants when I'm not around, don't you?' She looked at Mimi accusingly.

'Well …' Mimi gave a sheepish smirk. 'But of course I don't think of you as an accountant, darling.' She leaned forward, resting a hand on Aoife's knee and giving it a reassuring pat. 'We never think of you like that, do we?' She looked to Sive, who shook her head emphatically.

'No, absolutely not.'

'Why not? That's what I am!'

'No you're not.' Mimi shook her head dismissively. 'Not deep down in your soul.'

'Oh, so you do think I have a soul?'

'Of course you do. Which just goes to prove my point.' She gave Aoife a self-satisfied smile and took another bite of cake.

Aoife didn't see how it proved anything, but she had given up trying to follow Mimi's weird logic a long time ago. She tended to twist the laws of the universe to suit herself.

'I still don't understand why she'd put him in her will,' Mimi said. 'I know his grandmother was her best friend, but she hadn't seen *him* in years, had she?'

'She had, actually,' Aoife said. 'He'd seen her a few times in the nursing home.' She'd noticed his name in the visitors' book a couple of times and had been a little disappointed she'd never run into him.

'*Had* he?' Mimi's tone was suspicious, as if this was a vital clue in a murder mystery.

Aoife nodded. 'He'd actually been to see her the day before she died.'

Mimi gasped and grabbed Aoife's arm, clutching so hard it hurt.

'Ow! What?'

'Listen to what you're saying, Aoife. He was the last person to see her alive, and now suddenly she's changed her will to put him in it.'

Aoife pulled her arm away from Mimi's death grip. 'Calm down, Miss Marple. First of all, that will was made two years ago. And secondly, he was hardly the last person to see her alive. She was in the nursing home, and then in hospital. Loads of people would have seen her after him.'

'But not people who she'd put in her will.'

'People do leave things to the care staff in nursing homes,' Sive mused. 'Or to the nurses and doctors when they've been in hospital.'

Mimi frowned at her. 'A box of chocolates or a bunch of flowers, maybe. Not property!'

Aoife turned to her. 'You're not seriously suggesting he had some hand in her death? Or doctored her will somehow?'

'No, but … well, it's something to think about, isn't it?'

'It really isn't.'

'But why wouldn't she at least *tell* us?' Sive wailed. 'If she intended to change her will, don't you think she'd have said something to us? She must have known how disappointed we'd be.'

Mimi nodded. 'She'd given us … expectations.'

Detta had always spoken matter-of-factly about them owning Halfpenny Lane one day – what it would mean for their careers; the opportunity it would give them to create their own work.

Aoife frowned, a memory suddenly coming to her. 'Maybe she intended to, but then she had the stroke. She did want to see us, remember – all three of us together? She said she had something important to tell us.'

Mimi nodded. 'We assumed it was about funeral arrangements or something.' Detta had taken as much delight in planning her own funeral as she had in making wills – choosing the music and readings, deciding who should be tasked with writing her eulogy, even making notes for her obituary so that her grand-nieces could fact-check the newspapers.

'But what if it was this? The next time we went to see her, she couldn't tell us anything.' Detta had lost the power of speech after her stroke. She'd recovered it after several months, but she was often confused and sometimes delusional, and her condition had deteriorated steadily after that. It had been heartbreaking to watch a woman who'd been so strong and independent all her life so diminished. Detta had been active and alert well into her eighties, still living alone in her little cottage in the Liberties. But shortly after her ninetieth birthday, she'd had a TIA and started having accidents and episodes of confusion. After a couple of falls at home, the doctors had decided it was no longer safe for her to live on her own and she'd gone into the nursing home. Aoife had tried to get her to move in with her and her sisters, but she wouldn't hear of it.

'Could we dispute it?' Mimi asked.

'I suppose we could, but I doubt it would get us anywhere. She was fine mentally until after the stroke. Anyway, I'm sure Patrick was circumspect about ensuring she was capable when she made it.'

'But what happened to make her change it?' Mimi said.

'You know how she loved making wills,' Sive said. 'She was changing it all the time.'

'But not radically – just small bits and pieces. Halfpenny Lane was always left to us.'

Aoife shrugged. 'I suppose we'll never know now.'

'It didn't seem to come as a surprise to Jonathan,' Mimi said.

Aoife thought back to the meeting with Patrick. She'd been too stunned to take everything in properly, but Mimi was right. Jonathan hadn't reacted at all when Patrick had read out his name along with theirs, his face remaining impassive until Mimi's little outburst.

'He's the executor, though. He might have already seen the will.'

'You must at least be suspicious that he persuaded her to change it,' Mimi persisted. 'He may have visited her occasionally, but it's not like he was a big part of her life.'

'I suppose she must have been fonder of him than we knew,' Aoife said.

'Maybe.' Mimi didn't sound convinced.

'But even so, why leave him Halfpenny Lane of all things?' Sive asked. 'He's a solicitor. What would he do with a theatre?'

'What do you think?' Aoife gave her sister a patient look. 'Sell it, of course.'

Sive gave a startled gasp and recoiled against the banquette as if she'd been slapped. 'But ... he can't!'

'It's a prime piece of real estate,' Aoife reasoned. 'Right in the centre of Dublin. It's probably worth a fortune.'

'Real estate!' Mimi made a face as if she'd got a bad smell. 'Now you *are* starting to sound like an accountant.'

'Someone would buy it and turn it into a horrible trendy bar or poncy restaurant,' Sive said, grimacing.

'We can't have that,' Mimi said with an air of finality. 'So, how do we get rid of Jonathan Hunt?'

'You said his name!' Sive exclaimed.

'So? He's not the devil. Well, not the *actual* devil.'

'We could buy him out!' Sive said, as if she'd had a light-bulb moment.

'With what?' Aoife asked.

'Oh yeah.' Sive's shoulders slumped. 'But it's not just up to him, is it? Halfpenny Lane belongs to all of us. We'd all have to agree to sell, wouldn't we?'

'Yes, and there's three of us and only one of him,' Mimi said, brightening. 'We'd outvote him.'

Aoife shook her head. 'That's not how it works, I'm afraid. He's entitled to his inheritance, and as the executor, it's also his duty to see that he gets it. The only way we can split Halfpenny Lane four ways is by selling it.'

'Then he'll just have to be our partner, like it or lump it,' Mimi said. 'Maybe that's what he'll want to do anyway. Rich people like investing in the theatre, don't they – even soulless solicitors? Being patrons of the arts makes them look well rounded and cultured, so no one suspects them of being the horrendous philistines they really are.'

'Like Batman!' Sive said.

'Exactly,' Mimi said. 'Except in reverse.'

Aoife couldn't see how the Batman analogy worked, even in reverse, but she let it slide. 'Rich people like investing in hot West End musicals that will run for years and tour all over the world. Not a tiny little run-down theatre in Dublin doing budget productions of Chekov and Ibsen.' She hated being the naysayer, but someone had to inject a note of reality into proceedings.

'Don't be so defeatist,' Mimi said. 'We can mix in some more commercial stuff – Wilde and Coward, Shakespeare's greatest hits.'

'You know as well as I do that even a run of popular shows like that in a theatre the size of Halfpenny Lane is never going to be a worthwhile prospect for an investor.'

Mimi nodded. 'You're right. What we need is a proper money-spinner – one big sure-fire hit that will put us on the map, and make enough money to buy Jonathan out.'

'Well, we have the whole sisters thing,' Sive said.

'What do you mean?' Aoife frowned.

'Our first show would be *Three Sisters*, right?'

'Of course,' Mimi said. 'What else?'

'So it's got the novelty factor – *Three Sisters* played by three actual real-life sisters. People love stuff like that.'

'Like the equivalent of a dog in a Shakespeare play,' Mimi laughed. 'We could put it on the posters.'

'I don't think that's quite the big draw you think it is,' Aoife said, picking up her cup. 'Besides, you're only two sisters.'

'Is there something you haven't told us?' Mimi said archly.

'Were you adopted? Did Mum have a love child she never told us about?'

'You know what I mean. Only you two are actors.'

'But you'd do the play with us,' Mimi said matter-of-factly. 'That was always the plan.'

'Yes, but only after I'd spent at least a year in acting school – not right away! I'm not an actress.'

'You are, though.' Mimi tilted her head to the side, regarding Aoife with something resembling pity, as if confronting her with a fundamental truth about herself that she'd tried to deny.

Sive nodded. 'It's in your bones. Same as us.' She waved a hand between her and Mimi.

'Except you're better than either of us – which is so unfair. You're a natural!'

'But that was just play-acting as kids, and amateur stuff. This is different. I'm not a professional.'

'But you could be – like that.' Mimi snapped her fingers. 'Do this play with us, get people to pay to see you in it and hey presto – you're a professional.'

'You may not be trained like us, but you're so talented,' Sive said. 'It'd be a crime to waste that.'

'Well, be that as it may, I don't think *Three Sisters* is the way to go if we want to make a big splash – even if all three of us were in it,' she added as Sive opened her mouth to protest. 'It's popular enough, but it's hardly going to set the town ablaze.'

'What we need is a big name,' Mimi mused. 'A major star, who people would go to see no matter what they were in.'

'Yes!' Sive's face lit up. 'Someone people would come from all over the world to see in the flesh – like when Benedict Cumberbatch did *Hamlet*.'

'It would be a game-changer,' Mimi said. 'But who could we get like that?'

They were all silent for a moment, concentrating. Aoife wracked her brain, but the only actor they knew personally with that kind of clout was Mimi's ex Rocco Agnew, and no one was going to mention him.

'Oh!' Sive jerked upright, her eyes sparkling. 'What about Andrew Scott?'

'Do any of us know Andrew Scott?' Aoife looked at her sisters.

'No.' They sighed in unison.

'So how do you propose we get him?'

Sive shrugged. 'I suppose we find out who his agent is and take it from there.'

'Right,' Aoife nodded. 'Problem solved, then. Let's get Andrew Scott.'

'Yeah,' Mimi said. 'As if he'd agree to come to our crummy little theatre.'

'I can see it happening,' Sive said. 'He seems lovely, and he doesn't only do mainstream stuff. He's done some very interesting roles – and he's an amazing actor, of course.'

'Also seriously hot,' Mimi put in. 'He's got a huge fan base. He could really pull in the crowds.'

'He could play Nikolai,' Sive said.

'No, Vershinin,' Mimi countered.

'You just say that because you'd get to kiss him,' Sive said with a laugh.

'I'd be willing to take one for the team.'

'Unless I fight you for the role of Masha.'

'You couldn't kiss him anyway. You're spoken for.'

'Stage kisses don't count. Ben knows that.'

It was the sort of whimsical talk Aoife had happily joined in with so many times in the past – casting their imaginary plays, choosing their dream directors and actors. But today reality was setting in hard and fast, and she found herself unable to indulge in their shared fantasy.

'Look, you don't have to sell me on Andrew Scott,' she said. 'I have as much appreciation of him as any other full-blooded human. But even if we could somehow lure him to Halfpenny Lane, there's no way we could afford him.'

'I suppose not,' Sive agreed.

'Besides, the theatre hasn't operated as a going concern for ages. It's going to take time to get it in any fit state to put on a performance – and a lot of hard work.'

'Well, at least we're not afraid of hard work, are we?' Sive appealed to her sisters with an enthusiastic expression.

Mimi made a little moue.

'What?'

'I mean, I'm not *afraid* of hard work. But it's not my favourite.'

'Oh, come on. It'll be fun. A lick of paint and some TLC and Halfpenny Lane will be back to its old self in no time. It's just been a bit neglected, poor old love. A theatre needs life – people, lights, greasepaint.'

Sive had huge let's-put-the-show-on-in-the-barn energy.

'I think it's going to need a bit more than that,' Aoife said. 'Money, for one thing – which brings us right back around to the problem that we don't have any.'

'Jonathan Hunt does, though, doesn't he?' Sive said. 'He's a fancy lawyer, and you heard where he lives.' The address that Patrick had read out from Detta's will was in Sandymount, one of the most expensive suburbs of Dublin.

'Yes, he's probably loaded,' Mimi said, looking thoughtful. 'Well off, anyway.'

'That could be why Detta left him a share in the theatre – so he could help us out financially.' Sive beamed.

'Oh, that would make sense,' Mimi said, latching onto the idea readily.

'Maybe he wants to get Halfpenny Lane back on its feet as much as we do.'

They both looked to Aoife questioningly.

'Unlikely,' she said. 'But I suppose it's possible.' She drained her coffee. 'Anyway, I've got the whole day off work. Why don't we go over to the theatre when we're finished here, and see exactly what we're dealing with?'

3

HALFPENNY LANE WAS A CURVING cobbled alleyway in the bustling Temple Bar neighbourhood on the south bank of the Liffey, a warren of winding, narrow streets packed with pubs, restaurants, galleries and quirky shops, beloved of hipsters, hen parties and tourists alike. Set slightly back from the street behind a cast-iron gate and railings, the theatre of the same name had been converted from an eighteenth-century Quaker meeting house. Its two-storey red-brick facade still boasted the elegance and grandeur of a bygone era, with twelve tall sash windows and an arched door adorned with ornate moulded surrounds and scrolled keystones.

The three sisters stood for a moment on the pavement gazing at the building, arms around each other.

'I can't believe it's ours,' Sive squealed, squeezing Aoife's waist.

Aoife banished the thought that it probably wouldn't be theirs for long. For now, it was. Today she'd allow herself to live in the moment and enjoy the dream-come-true feeling of ownership, however fleeting.

Sive got them all to turn around, then took a selfie with the building behind them to send to her boyfriend Ben, who was on a gap year, working his way around Europe as a trek leader for an adventure tour company.

They were quiet as they unlocked the door and went inside, their footsteps echoing in the empty lobby, and Aoife knew they were all thinking about their beloved Detta. Halfpenny Lane had been her life's work and her greatest achievement.

A legend of Irish theatre, she'd been a great eccentric – 'a real character' when people were being diplomatic; 'nutty as a barm brack' to those of a less sensitive disposition; 'away with the fairies' according to their father, who adored his aunt, but was wary of her influence on his impressionable daughters.

When they were little, Detta had swept into their lives occasionally, bringing with her an air of glamour and adventure that enthralled them. She told them stories about foreign cities she'd visited and famous people she'd met. She took them out for long lavish lunches at Trocadero and Chapter One, introduced them to champagne and taught them how to eat oysters.

It hadn't occurred to them at the time to wonder how she'd paid for it all. They'd always thought of her as rich, but over the years Aoife came to realise that she lived very frugally most of the time, so she could have a few spendthrift days splashing out on champagne and caviar. They'd seen the stark reality of her finances this morning when Patrick spelled out what constituted the 'rest and remainder' of her estate – a post office savings book with thirty-six euros, a bank account containing less than a year's nursing home fees, and some shares in a company that had long since gone bust. She'd been living on the proceeds from the sale of her home for the last few years, but Aoife was horrified to see how rapidly that money had been running out. If she'd lived much longer, they'd have had to sell Halfpenny Lane anyway to pay for her care.

She'd had a long and illustrious career, gracing the stages of Dublin, London and Broadway, and had even had small roles in a few Hollywood films. The girls had listened enraptured as she talked about her time in La-La Land and the weird and wonderful experiences she'd had there. She'd worked with Orson Welles and Peter O'Toole, and had once met Marilyn Monroe. She'd even hinted at some sort of fling or flirtation with Sir Peter Bradshaw, which she was unusually discreet about, and a passionate love affair with a major movie star whose name she never divulged.

But she could never stay away from Dublin or the stage for long, and Halfpenny Lane had been the great love of her life. All her energy and most of her money had gone into converting the building and she'd worked tirelessly to raise funds for its renovation. Then she'd gathered a wealth of talent around her and formed a thriving repertory company, producing important and experimental work to great acclaim. As well as running the theatre, she'd trained, mentored and nurtured a generation of actors, directors and writers, and Halfpenny Lane had gained a reputation as a training ground for Irish theatrical talent. The little theatre, like Detta, had always punched above its weight, and Aoife knew she'd left much more behind her than the meagre assets listed in her will.

'Gosh! I didn't think it'd be this bad.' Aoife looked around in dismay as they stood in the aisle of the auditorium. She felt guilty that they'd neglected the place for so long. The theatre had been ailing for years before Detta fell ill. She'd always poured whatever she had into keeping it afloat. But it became an impossible task, and she'd finally run out of money and been forced into retirement in her mid-eighties. She'd been heartbroken to admit defeat and turn out the lights on her beloved theatre for the last time. She'd kept up its licences and hired it out occasionally as a venue for events, to generate a little extra income, but it had mostly remained vacant in the intervening years.

Aoife and her sisters had checked in occasionally in the years it had lain idle, to make sure it wasn't falling into dereliction. They'd spend occasional afternoons wandering around the building, playing dress-up with the costumes and fooling around on the stage, pretending they were playing to an audience. Sometimes they'd simply sit in one of the dressing rooms with a bottle of wine, breathing in the atmosphere while they reminisced. But their visits had dwindled as time went on, and Aoife couldn't remember the last time any of them had been here.

Mimi pulled a dust sheet off a row of seats, coughing as a cloud of dust rose up. She waved a hand in front of her mouth, squeezing her eyes closed.

'It's not that bad,' Sive said cheerfully, her voice full of optimism that sounded forced to Aoife's ears. 'All it needs is a bit of love.'

'These seats are falling apart.' Mimi prodded the ripped red velvet of the seat in front of her.

'And look at the curtains,' Aoife said, nodding to the threadbare red velvet that sagged over the proscenium arch. 'They're in rag order.'

The three of them looked around despondently.

'Maybe it's beyond salvaging?' Aoife suggested tentatively, suddenly overwhelmed by the enormity of the task of restoring it. 'We might have to put it on the market anyway, regardless of what Jonathan wants to do.' She'd be as loath to let it go as her sisters, and it broke her heart to say it, but one of them had to be the voice of reason, and unfortunately, that role invariably fell to her.

'No!' Sive protested vehemently. 'We just need to repair the seats, fix the curtains—'

'Replace this carpet,' Mimi said, her foot making a tacky sound as she tapped it on the floor. 'Ugh, it's a health hazard.'

'How?' Aoife howled. 'How would we pay for all that? We don't have any money. This,' she said, spreading her arms wide, 'is our entire inheritance.'

'We'll do it ourselves,' Sive said. 'The carpet might be okay if we got it cleaned. I could upcycle the seats, and—'

'You can't upcycle a whole theatre,' Mimi said.

'Why not?' Sive said cheerfully. 'I love a project. And it's a small theatre – only a hundred and forty seats.'

'A hundred and thirty-eight,' Aoife corrected her.

'Even better!' Sive said triumphantly.

'It would take you approximately forever.' Sive loved upcycling, and she was good at it. But this was a far cry from reupholstering the odd armchair.

'So? We're not in any rush, are we?'

'Well, it would be nice if we could open some time this century,' Mimi said. 'Ideally in time for the Theatre Festival. But there's no way we could have this place ready by October.'

'Not this year, maybe,' Sive said. 'But there's always next year. Or even the year after that.'

'And what about all the rest?' Mimi asked. 'Are you going to weave a new carpet? Sew curtains? And god knows what backstage is like – a health and safety nightmare, probably. Even if you could do it, we'd be too old to play *Three Sisters* by the time you'd have finished.'

'But we can't sell!' Sive wailed.

'Of course we're not selling,' Mimi reassured her. 'I'm just saying we can't do it all ourselves. It's a job for professionals.'

'Which we can't afford,' Aoife said.

'Well, we think Jonathan Hunt is rich, remember.'

'I don't see how that helps us,' Aoife said.

'He's in this with us now, isn't he? He's a part owner.'

'Yes, but no matter how rich he is, I doubt he wants to fund a money pit like this. Besides, we can't expect him to shoulder the financial burden of renovations on his own, while we're dead weight.'

'We're not dead weight,' Mimi said. 'We're the talent, which is a far more valuable asset in a theatre than some soft furnishings.'

'I honestly think that could have been what Detta was planning all along, when she included him in her will,' Sive said.

Mimi nodded. 'She wanted the theatre to survive and she knew we wouldn't be able to do it on our own.'

They both looked to Aoife eagerly.

'Possibly,' she said with more conviction than she felt. They were both so clearly taken with the idea. Besides, there was just the glimmer of hope that Sive could be right. For all her eccentricity and scattiness, Detta could be surprisingly shrewd at times, especially when it came to finding money for her theatre.

'We'll have to talk to Jonathan and discuss what we're going to do,' Mimi said, suddenly seeming more sanguine about his involvement. 'Why don't we take a walkabout and check out what needs doing?' She pulled a notebook from her tapestry bag. 'Then we can talk it over with him.'

'Good idea.' Aoife nodded. If they were asking Jonathan to bankroll this project, it would be good to have some facts and figures to present him with, and not merely vague dreams about putting on shows. Just then her phone rang and she bent to fish it out of the depths of the satchel at her feet.

'Aoife?' The voice was deep and familiar.

'Yes?' She put a question into her voice, even though she'd known immediately who it was.

'Jonathan Hunt. We need to talk.'

'Right. Um … How did you get my number?'

'Patrick gave it to me. You three left his office so fast, I didn't get a chance to speak to you.'

That had been the general idea. 'Sorry, we were … in a rush.'

'Are you free now?'

'Yes,' she said unthinkingly. 'I mean, kind of …' She racked her brain for some excuse to put him off.

'Maybe we could have a quick chat. Obviously there are some things we need to go over.'

'Okay. But we're at the theatre at the moment. We thought we should have a look around, you know – take stock and see what kind of state it's in.'

'Good idea! I could join you there? I'm still in town.'

'Um … sure.' Damn! He'd caught her off guard. They needed more time to strategise, just the three of them, and come up with a solid plan – something they could present to Jonathan Hunt as a fait accompli. She had a feeling they'd need to have their wits about them when dealing with him.

'Great. I'll be there in ten.'

She felt dazed as she ended the call. 'Um … that was Jonathan. He's coming to meet us here.'

'What, *now*?' Mimi asked, annoyed.

'Yeah. Sorry.'

'Why did you agree to that?'

'I don't know! Aoife wailed. 'See, you're wrong about

me. You say I'm a great actress, but I totally suck at improv. He put me on the spot and I couldn't think of anything to say to put him off. Sorry.'

'Hey, it's not your fault.' Sive reached out and rubbed her arm.

Mimi was less forgiving. 'But we haven't even got started!'

'Well, it's too late now. He'll be here in a few minutes.'

'It could be good to have another pair of eyes on it,' Sive said. 'He might see things that we'd miss.'

'Besides,' Aoife said, 'he's a joint owner, so he has as much right as us to decide what we're going to do with the place. He'll have to be involved anyway.'

'Especially if he's the one who's going to pay for it all,' Sive said.

She sounded so hopeful, Aoife wanted to sob.

4

_____

AFTER WHAT SEEMED like mere seconds, the door to the auditorium was thrown open and Jonathan was striding down the aisle towards them.

'Aoife, Mimi, Sive.' He nodded hello to them in turn. 'So,' he said, rubbing his hands, 'quite a morning of surprises.'

Aoife frowned. 'You didn't know? What was in Detta's will?'

He shook his head. 'Not at all. She never told me. I was as surprised as you were when Patrick showed it to me this morning.'

That was something at least. She hated to think of Detta being in cahoots with him behind their backs.

'I gathered it was a shock to you too.' He looked around at the three of them.

'It certainly was,' Mimi said, her tone sharp. 'She'd always told us she was leaving us the theatre. But we thought—'

'That it would just be the three of you.'

'Yes. She never mentioned you.'

'No, I kind of gathered that from your performance this morning,' he said to Mimi with a sardonic smile.

'Sorry about that.' She pursed her lips, frowning. 'I was taken by surprise, that's all.'

'Well, I promise you I had nothing to do with Detta changing her will.'

'So what were you doing there this morning?' Mimi narrowed her eyes at him.

'Patrick asked me to be there, but I assumed it was just as the executor. I had no idea Detta had left me anything. I certainly didn't expect it.'

Mimi nodded grudgingly, satisfied with the explanation, but still not happy.

'So, how's it looking?' He put his hands on his hips and turned in a circle, tilting his head to the moulded ceiling.

'We hadn't got started yet,' Mimi said. 'We were going to take a walk around and make a list of what needs to be done.'

'We hadn't been here long when you rang,' Aoife told him.

'We haven't even been backstage yet,' Sive said. 'At least, not today.'

'Not today? You've been here before, then? I mean, recently?'

'Not for a while,' Aoife said. 'But we used to come down here from time to time, just to keep an eye on the place.' She felt a stab of guilt that it had been so long. They hadn't done a very good job of looking after it.

'Well, I'm free for the rest of the day. Why don't we all have a recce?'

Aoife already had a fair idea of what they'd find as they all trooped backstage. But it was worse than she remembered, and she could only imagine how it must look to Jonathan, who didn't have their emotional attachment to the place. It would take more than a lick of paint and some of Sive's make-do-and-mend to get it into working order. There were crumbling floorboards and dodgy-looking lighting rigs, and the list of everything that needed fixing or replacing grew longer and longer as they walked around – because it was basically everything. Aoife could feel her sisters getting more dejected by the second. Even Sive had fallen silent.

'We'll have to go through all this stuff and do a good clear-out,' Jonathan said, nodding to the baskets of props strewn around in the wings.

'We'll get a skip,' Aoife said, her heart sinking at the thought. They'd spent weeks clearing out Detta's little one-bedroom cottage in the Liberties when she put it on sale after moving to the nursing home. It had been sad sorting through the detritus of a lifetime, consigning what they didn't keep to charity shops, recycling or landfill. At least the stuff in Halfpenny Lane wasn't so personal.

'I love it back here.' Sive breathed in deeply as they walked into one of the tiny dressing rooms.

Aoife smiled. She did too. It had all seemed impossibly glamorous and exciting when they'd come back here as children after one of Detta's shows, despite the makeshift shabbiness of the backstage reality. Up close, you could see the frayed threads and worn brocade of a sumptuous gown, the lines and wrinkles beneath an actor's thick make-up, all the youth, beauty and opulence revealed as nothing but smoke and mirrors. But seeing behind the curtain hadn't detracted from the sense of magic and wonder the theatre had always inspired in Aoife and her sisters. In fact, it had only made what Detta did here seem more miraculous – conjuring an entire other world out of a few bolts of material, a make-up box and some clever lighting.

The evocative smell of old grease-paint and musty costumes that hung in the air brought Aoife right back to afternoons spent here playing dress-up, the thrill of walking out onto a real stage and acting out little plays in front of an audience of three – Detta and their parents. Aoife had loved it just as much as her sisters, and Detta had always lavished praise on her for her performances. Aoife was 'a natural', she'd say.

But even then, Aoife had known it wasn't a proper job for a grown-up, and that their father worried about them following in Detta's footsteps. While he appreciated his aunt's talent and her dedication to her chosen profession, her impecunious, hand-to-mouth lifestyle wasn't what he wanted for his children. Watching her sisters traipse from audition to audition and eke out a meagre living had done nothing to persuade Aoife that he'd been wrong. They were both deeply talented, but they barely managed to scrape by on what they earned from the casual minimum wage jobs they worked between acting gigs.

'You've been here before, haven't you?' Aoife asked Jonathan as he pushed open the door of the largest dressing room. 'Backstage, I mean?'

'Yes,' he said, stepping into the room. 'I came back here with my mum a couple of times on opening nights. Detta let me have some champagne.' His voice had gone husky, and there was a faraway look in his eyes.

Aoife nodded. 'Us too.' She'd felt so grown-up and sophisticated on those nights when they came to backstage parties and were allowed to mingle with the adults and sip champagne from the coupe glasses Detta always insisted on. For Aoife and her sisters it had been thrilling to know that one day this life would be theirs – they'd have their own opening nights and after-show parties, and one day all the flowers, air-kisses and adulation would be for them.

She vaguely remembered Detta pointing her great friend Marian's grandson out to her one night – a cute boy of around Aoife's own age standing across the room, beside his mother. Detta had urged her to go over and talk to him, but something stand-offish in his body language had deterred her. She wished now that she had spoken to him, that they'd got to know each other back then and developed a friendship over the intervening years. It would be so much easier if they were old friends now.

'What shows did you see?' she asked him.

He leaned against a dressing table, folding his arms. '*A Doll's House* and *Uncle Vanya* … and something else.' He frowned, thinking. '*The Duchess of Malfi*?'

'That was my first taste of champagne – after *The Duchess of Malfi*.'

'I should hope so. You'd only have been, what – eight? Nine?'

'I was ten. You weren't much older.'

'I was a very mature fourteen.'

'What did you think?'

'Of the champagne? Not a big fan, I'm sorry to say. It was wasted on me.'

'Of the show?'

'Also wasted on me. I didn't think it was a patch on *Jack and the Beanstalk*,' he said, a smile tugging at the corners of his mouth.

Aoife laughed. 'Well, *Jack and the Beanstalk* is a timeless masterpiece.'

While they were chatting, Sive and Mimi had been exploring the room, rummaging through discarded boxes of props and studying the notes and pictures still pinned to the small bulletin board by the door. Now Mimi was trying on a wig and Sive was playing with a black lace fan she'd found on one of the dressing tables.

'Look at these!' said, striding over to a rail of costumes. She pulled out a hanger and ran her hand appreciatively over the heavy fabric of a military jacket. 'We're definitely keeping all these.'

'Really?' Aoife joined her, fingering a threadbare silk and brocade gown. 'You think we can do something with them?'

'Of course! They're fantastic. They just need a good clean and a bit of work with a needle and thread. We can totally use them, and it'd save us a fortune on costumes. We could let it dictate the programme – put on whatever plays we have suitable costumes for.'

Aoife laughed. 'That'd be a hell of a USP.'

They left the dressing rooms and walked through the wings, still cluttered with bits of scenery and discarded props. Aoife experienced a familiar rush of excitement as she stepped onto the stage and looked out over the auditorium.

'So, what do you think?' Sive asked Jonathan.

'Well, it's a great building. Admittedly it's a bit of a wreck, but it's got good bones.'

Good bones! Aoife shivered, the image of a skeleton flitting across her mind. He was talking about the place as if it was already dead – which she supposed was understandable, given its present condition. But surely he remembered what it was like in the old days when it was full of life and energy.

'I don't think we need to do anything to it,' he said, to Aoife's surprise. 'Apart from clearing out the junk and cleaning up a bit.'

'Oh! But what about all this?' Aoife pointed to Mimi's notepad. The list of work that needed to be done had gone onto a second page.

'I don't think it'd be worth our while doing any of that. We'd just be throwing good money after bad.'

'What do you propose, then?' Aoife asked. She didn't really want to know, but it was only fair – he was an equal partner in this now, after all, whether they liked it or not.

'You can't knock it down!' Sive blurted out.

Jonathan turned to her, surprised by her outburst. 'We couldn't even if we wanted to. It's a protected structure.'

Aoife breathed a sigh of relief, grateful for the small reprieve. Thank goodness for building conservation regulations.

'Of course, that also means it would be a lot more costly to renovate.'

Damn conservation regulations, Aoife thought. He was right – it would make the renovations much more tricky and a lot more expensive. They'd have to get approval for everything and use special materials in keeping with the period of the building. They'd probably have to get conservation specialists to work on it. There was no way Sive would be allowed to have a go at upcycling anything, even if it was doable.

'But that would be someone else's problem,' Jonathan continued cheerfully, leading the way to the steps at the side of the stage. He didn't see their looks of dismay as they followed him.

'How so?' Mimi looked at him challengingly when they were back in the auditorium.

'Well, whoever bought it could worry about that.'

Sive's jaw dropped. 'You want to sell?'

'Of course he wants to sell,' Mimi hissed angrily to her sister.

Aoife's heart sank. She'd known this conversation was coming as soon as they'd discovered Jonathan had been left a share in the theatre, but she'd hoped they could put it off a little longer.

'Of course. What else? It's a great building in a prime location,' Jonathan said. 'It could make a great restaurant or bar – you know, a real landmark place. They could even trade on its history—'

Mimi gave Aoife a look that said: see, no soul. 'Or it could work as a theatre,' she said archly. 'Call me a visionary, but I can practically see it now.'

Jonathan gave her a confused frown, not understanding her tone.

'Yes,' Sive joined in. 'It's already set up as a performance space. It'd take much less work to turn it around as a theatre than to start converting it into something else.'

'Again, not our problem. It'd be up to the buyer to decide what they want to do with it.'

'But we don't want to sell,' Sive said.

'You don't?' Jonathan looked taken aback. 'I thought it was the obvious course of action.'

All three sisters shook their heads.

'Not to us,' Aoife said.

'What did you think all this was about?' Mimi waved her notebook at him.

'I thought we were just seeing what we need to do before putting it on the market – getting it cleared out and that sort of thing. Seeing if there was anything you wanted to take, like the costumes …' He trailed off.

'We weren't talking about *taking* the costumes,' Sive said. 'We want them to stay here, with us.'

'So … what were you planning to do with it?'

'What do you think?' Mimi said. 'We want to put on plays, of course. What else would you do with a theatre? Apart from turning it into a themed bar or landmark McDonald's, of course.'

'Oh! Really?' Jonathan looked at them, frowning. 'You want to keep it?'

'Of course,' Mimi said. 'It's a theatre. We're actresses. If you want to talk about the obvious choice ...'

'We want to restore it and carry on Detta's legacy,' Sive said more gently.

'Right. Well, that changes things.' Jonathan raked a hand through his hair. 'Sorry, I just assumed ... Patrick seemed to think we'd have to sell because Detta didn't have any other assets in her will. But if you have money of your own to buy me out and renovate it ...'

'Well, we don't really,' Sive hedged, twirling a lock of hair around her finger. 'Nothing substantial anyway.'

'So how do you propose to get this place back on its feet? It looks like you'd need to sink a lot of money into it.'

'Oh, it's not that bad,' Sive protested.

Jonathan curled his hand around the back of a seat in the front row and gave it a shake. The whole row rattled, and a cloud of dust flew up. 'Doesn't look great to me.'

'That's just superficial stuff – easily fixed,' Mimi said. 'You said yourself it just needs tidying up and a good clean.'

'That was when I thought we were selling.'

'And we can do a lot of it ourselves,' Sive said cheerfully. 'I'm very good at upcycling. I can upholster the seats and make curtains ...'

Jonathan looked at her as if she was mad, and Aoife couldn't blame him. 'I think we can all agree it needs a bit more than that. Are any of you good at carpentry? Plastering?'

'I did a beginners' carpentry course,' Sive said, putting her hand up like she was in class.

'Yes, but that chair you made ...' Aoife tried to think of a diplomatic way to say it.

'It didn't really work as a chair, did it?' Mimi said. 'As in, it wasn't something a person could actually sit on – not if they valued their arses.'

'You'd have to pay professionals,' Jonathan said. 'Get it done properly.'

'Well,' Sive began hesitantly, and Aoife willed her not to say it. 'We thought maybe that could be where you come in.'

'I don't know the first thing about plastering.'

'No, but we thought you might like to … you know … just leave everything as it is now. We keep the theatre and we all continue to own it jointly. You could be a producer.'

Jonathan gave a surprised bark of laughter. 'A producer? So you were thinking I'd put up the money for all this?' He waved to Mimi's notepad.

'Not just you. We could get other people to put money into it too.' Sive sounded more uncertain of herself by the second. 'Lots of people invest in shows, don't they? It's a whole thing.'

'A whole thing?' Jonathan smirked. 'That sounds like a solid business proposal to take to the bank.'

Ugh, you don't have to be such a dick to her! But Aoife knew he was right. The whole idea was ridiculous.

He looked around the auditorium. 'It doesn't seem like much of an investment to me. I mean, does anyone even go to the theatre anymore?'

Mimi gasped in outrage. 'You're such a philistine! Of course people go to the theatre. Just not knuckleheads like you,' she spluttered.

Jonathan broke out in a grin, whether because Mimi had risen to his bait or at the surprise of being called a 'knucklehead'. 'Hey, I'm kidding. Of course I go to the theatre. Saw the panto every year without fail as a kid.'

Mimi gave Aoife a told-you-so look.

'But you didn't know until this morning that Detta had left me a share in the theatre.' Jonathan frowned. 'How were you planning to renovate it then?'

'We've only just come from the will reading,' Mimi said, her tone verging on belligerent. 'We haven't had time to think about that.'

'You said you always knew you were going to inherit it, though. You must have thought about it before.'

Aoife realised they hadn't, not really. 'I suppose we thought we'd have time to do it at our own pace,' she said. 'We could just do the basics needed to reopen, and then once we had some money coming in, we'd do the rest bit by bit.'

'But that could take years.'

Aoife shrugged.

'Okay, this is turning out to be more complicated than I thought.' Jonathan sighed. 'Obviously this has been sprung on all of us, and we have a lot to talk about. Why don't I take you to lunch and we can discuss it?'

The three sisters consulted each other silently. Mimi already looked more well disposed towards Jonathan at the prospect of being taken for lunch.

'That would be good,' Aoife answered for all of them. 'Thanks.'

Jonathan nodded. 'Okay, let's go.'

It felt symbolic as Aoife switched off the lights on their way back out through the auditorium and into the small lobby, plunging the little theatre back into darkness. Jonathan was right – it was hopeless.

5

AOIFE SHIELDED her eyes as they stepped out into the street, the low sun painfully bright after the gloom of the theatre. Jonathan fiddled with his phone as he led the way through the narrow pedestrian streets of Temple Bar and out onto the quays.

Aoife crashed into his broad back as he stopped to drop some money into a beggar's cup, exchanging a few words with the young man before moving on.

'Did you see that?' Sive hissed when he'd strode ahead. 'That was a tenner!'

Aoife nodded. She'd noticed, and she was starting to feel more warmly towards Jonathan.

'If he'd give a tenner to some randomer in the street, he might give us the money for the theatre after all.'

'We're not a charity,' Aoife said primly. 'Anyway, it's not fair to expect him to fund the whole thing. If he doesn't want to run the theatre with us, we'll have to find some way of doing it by ourselves.'

'So, where should we go for lunch?' Sive asked as Jonathan came to a halt at the edge of the pavement.

'There's a very nice sandwich bar just opposite,' Aoife said, pointing across the Halfpenny Bridge.

Jonathan looked up from his phone. 'I've booked us a table in the Saddle Room,' he said. 'I hope that's okay?'

'Oh! Yes, that's lovely.' Aoife smiled.

Sive and Mimi both nodded enthusiastically.

'We love the Saddle Room!' Sive said.

'Not that we ever get to go there.' Mimi looked like she was warming to Jonathan by the second.

But Aoife still had PTSD from a date with a guy called Matthew who'd invited her to dinner in a Michelin-starred restaurant and then presented her with an itemised bill for her share at the end of the evening, right down to half a bottle of mineral water. Jonathan had said he was 'taking' them to lunch, which implied he'd be paying, but she needed to be sure. So: how to ask someone if they were footing the bill without asking them if they were footing the bill?

'But you're paying, right?' For once Aoife was grateful for Mimi's directness.

'Yes, of course,' he said with a slight frown. 'I invited you. I thought that was implied. But just to be clear, yes, it's on me.'

At least he had an understanding of the social niceties.

'Let's go, then!' Aoife turned to start walking in the direction of Stephen's Green, when a taxi pulled up in front of them.

'This is us,' Jonathan said, glancing at his phone before sliding it into his coat pocket. He held open the back door and the three sisters got into the back seat, then he sat in the front beside the driver.

In the taxi, Sive sat in the middle, beaming meaningfully at each of her sisters in turn. Aoife knew how her mind was working. Jonathan was obviously rich, and not averse to throwing his money around – the future of Half-penny Lane was in safe hands as far as Sive was concerned.

It was only a few minutes' drive before they were pulling up in front of the Shelbourne Hotel. The top-hatted doorman opened the door of the taxi and ushered them into the hotel.

There was something instantly calming and reassuring about the old world elegance of the marbled lobby, an air of sedate tranquility and luxury that descended as soon as you stepped inside.

Sive beamed gleefully at Aoife, her eyes sparkling as Jonathan led them through to the restaurant. It all felt comfortingly familiar as the maitre d' seated them at a round table set with sparkling crystal, polished silverware and thick linen napkins. Detta used to bring them to the Saddle Room sometimes for grand long lunches and boozy dinners when she was particularly flush. But it was far beyond their means and they hadn't been here in years.

'I thought we'd come here in honour of Detta,' Jonathan said. 'She loved this place.'

'Did she bring you here?' Aoife asked.

'Yes, she brought me and mum here a few times. All the waiters used to treat her like family and make a huge fuss of her.'

Aoife nodded. 'She knew everyone.' Detta had been so interested in people, she'd made friends everywhere. It had astonished Aoife that she not only seemed to know all the service staff by name, she also knew about their lives and would chat to them like old friends, enquiring after a wait-er's wife who was ill or sending her best wishes to a sommelier's son who had an important exam coming up.

'She and my grandmother used to come here back in the day.'

'Oh yes, I think I've seen a photograph!' There had

been lots of pictures of Detta and Marian together. Jonathan's grandmother had been Detta's best friend, and the two had been inseparable. She recalled a picture of them in the Shelbourne's Horseshoe Bar in the sixties, both looking very chic and trendy in the fashions of the day, wearing mini skirts and dramatic eye make-up, and smoking cigarettes from long, slender holders. Marian was long-legged and stunning, and according to Detta was often mistaken for a model. But was in fact a barrister, and Detta had been very proud of her clever, beautiful friend. Marian had died of cancer in her early fifties, and Detta had missed her every day since until her last.

'I wish I could have known them then,' Aoife said wistfully. 'They always seemed to be having fun.'

'Me too,' Jonathan said.

'You never knew your grandmother, did you?'

'No. She died shortly after I was born. I think that's why Mum made Detta my godmother. Her mother and Detta were so alike, it was the closest she could get to keeping my grandmother in my life.'

'And you took after her,' Aoife said. 'I guess you get your interest in law from her.' Not to mention his dark good looks. He had Marian's jet black hair and penetrating green eyes.

He nodded. 'And from Mum.' There was a slight huskiness in his voice and Aoife felt a pang of sympathy.

'Of course.' She recalled now that his mother had been a journalist, specialising in court reporting. She'd also died tragically young in her mid-fifties. His father had died a few years ago, so he was an orphan like them.

A waiter came to take their drinks order and Jonathan asked for a bottle of champagne.

'Champagne before menus,' Sive whispered to Aoife. 'Classy!'

Aoife smiled. Detta would definitely approve. Jonathan was everything their great-aunt appreciated in a man – impeccably dressed in a sharply tailored suit; well mannered, assertive and worldly, with the sheen of sophistication she'd so admired in people; respectful to service staff, but decisive and commanding at the same time. He was what Detta would have called a 'proper man'. She'd often lamented that they were a dying breed. Aoife had to admit she could see the appeal.

'A toast to Detta,' he said, lifting his glass when the waiter had poured the champagne.

'To Detta!' Aoife and her sisters chorused, in voices soft with nostalgia and love.

Aoife sipped the champagne as she bent her head to the menu. It was crisp and delicious.

'So,' Jonathan said when they'd ordered food. 'You want to keep the theatre.'

'That's what we'd always planned,' Aoife said.

'But now I've come along and put a spanner in the works.'

'Not necessarily,' Sive piped up hopefully. 'We could be partners, like I said.'

'Partners, right. With me putting up all the money for the renovations?'

'Yes, and we'd take care of everything else – the administration, the artistic direction and all of that.'

'And if I don't want to be your meal ticket? Which, by the way, I don't. Sorry to burst your bubble.'

Sive's face fell. 'In that case, I suppose we'd have to buy you out.'

'How? You said you don't have any money. And it's not a worthwhile investment for anyone,' he said flatly, pre-empting Sive's next suggestion.

'How much do you think your share would be worth?' Mimi asked.

Jonathan thought for a moment. 'It's a beautiful building, and structurally I'd say it's not in bad shape, though we'd have to get a survey done, of course. The location is fantastic, obviously. I don't know anything about the market for commercial premises like that, but at a guess I reckon it could make around two million – perhaps more.'

'Wow!' Sive's eyes widened in astonishment. 'That much?'

'I'm no estate agent, but–'

'Seriously?' Aoife hated the snark in her tone, but she couldn't help it. 'Because you sound just like one right now.'

'It's just a guess,' he said, throwing her a hard look. 'But say it got two mil, that'd be half a million each. You'd have one and a half million between you. You could buy your own theatre with that, and have plenty left over.'

For a moment Aoife let that sink in, imagining what it would mean to have that kind of money – the relief of never having to worry about paying bills, the luxury of being able to afford whatever they wanted. There'd be no more scrimping and saving, no more minimum-wage jobs for Mimi and Sive. She wouldn't have to work part-time while she was at acting school.

'But we don't want just any theatre,' Sive said. 'We want Halfpenny Lane.' Aoife wondered how Jonathan could be so impervious to her big pleading eyes.

'It's our heritage,' Mimi said.

'Detta's legacy,' Aoife chimed in, hoping to appeal to his sense of decency – though she was beginning to wonder if he had one.

'Okay, say I wasn't in the equation. If Detta had just

left the theatre to the three of you, what would you do then?'

'That's easy,' Mimi said. They'd thought about it often enough. 'We'd fix it up as quickly as we could, and hopefully have it ready to do our first show for the Dublin Theatre Festival.'

His eyebrows shot up. 'October? That's ambitious.'

'Well, we didn't know when it was going to happen or what kind of state the theatre would be in. It was just dreaming really,' Aoife said.

'And our first show would be *Three Sisters*,' Sive cut in.

'With us playing the lead roles,' Mimi added.

'Oh?' He turned to Aoife. 'I didn't know you were an actress too.'

'I'm not.'

'Oh, don't mind her.' Sive waved away Aoife's protests. 'She has the most natural talent of all of us. Detta always said so.'

'Really?' he said, his gaze intent on Aoife as if the others weren't there. It was unsettling. 'I'd like to see that.'

Aoife cleared her throat, and looked down at her menu. 'Well, you won't. No one will. I've already told my sisters I'm not doing it.'

'That's a shame.'

She glanced up at him. Did he want to save the theatre now? Had he changed his mind about selling? 'It won't be happening anyway, if you get your way, so what does it matter?' She snapped her menu shut.

'You're giving up already? I thought you'd fight harder.'

'What's the point?' Aoife said tightly. 'We can't afford to buy you out, so we'll have to sell for you to get your inheritance.'

Mimi frowned. 'Why did Detta leave you a share in

Halfpenny Lane anyway?' she said crossly to Jonathan. 'You don't care about it at all. She loved it so much, she put everything she had into it. But you don't care what happens to it. She always said she wanted it to be our theatre, for us to carry on her legacy. She must have known you'd just want to offload it to the highest bidder. What was she thinking?'

'I have no idea. I guess it was all she had to leave, and she wanted to give me something.'

'*Why*?' Mimi demanded.

He looked down at the menu in his lap, but Aoife saw the tensing of his jaw, and his voice was gruff when he said, 'Because my grandmother was her best friend. And because she loved me, I suppose.'

The three sisters looked at each other, stunned into silence. Aoife was a little ashamed that they'd never considered that, and she knew they were all feeling the same. Suddenly they were the mean girls. It hadn't occurred to her that he'd been close to Detta too – that he was also grieving her. The realisation brought a rush of empathy that took her by surprise.

'And *you* loved *her*,' she said quietly.

'Didn't everyone?' There was a softness in his green eyes that she'd never noticed before.

'Anyway, you're right. Even if we didn't need to buy you out, we still wouldn't have the money for renovations.' Perhaps they had to face the reality that owning Halfpenny Lane had been a pipe dream all along.

'But there'd be no rush,' Mimi said. 'We could do it gradually over years.'

'We'd find a way,' Sive said. 'There are Arts Council grants, and we could do a lot ourselves.'

'Maybe we could find other backers,' Mimi added.

Jonathan sighed. 'Look, I'm sure Detta didn't mean

this bequest to be a burden to you. She'd have wanted it to benefit you, to set you up in life – not to be an albatross around your necks.'

For a moment Aoife thought longingly of all the security and freedom the money would give them. Perhaps that *had* been Detta's intention after all.

'We thought that could be why she left you a share in it,' Sive said to Jonathan. 'So you could help us out financially.'

'That's out of the question,' he said flatly. 'Sorry.'

'Well, that's that, then,' Aoife said as a waiter came to take their order. 'There's nothing more to discuss.' She swallowed over the lump in her throat, irked that he seemed determined to stamp out any tiny spark of hope.

'Anyway, we don't have to decide what to do about it right now,' Jonathan said when the waiter had gone.

'You mean you might change your mind about selling?' Mimi asked.

'Or about being a producer?' Sive beamed at him. 'It'll be great fun, honestly, and it'll give you so much kudos. You'll love it!'

'Steady on,' he said with a laugh. 'I'm just saying there's no great hurry to get the place on the market. You can take some time to come to terms with the circumstances and see if you can come up with some way of funding the theatre. Either way, we need to get it cleared out. So we can organise that and, in the meantime, we can get a survey and valuation done while you explore other options. Then we can decide what to do. Fair?'

Aoife nodded. 'Fair,' she said grudgingly. She had to admit it was.

'Don't worry,' Sive said, 'we'll think of something. There's no way we can let Halfpenny Lane go out of the family.'

Aoife was glad of the temporary reprieve, but she didn't share Sive's confidence.

They were distracted by the arrival of the starters, and, as they began to eat, they turned to less contentious topics.

Lunch passed pleasantly after that. The food was sublime, and the conversation flowed with reminiscences about Detta. When Jonathan paid the bill after barely glancing at it, Aoife tried to appreciate his generosity and not resent his obdurate refusal to help finance the theatre when he obviously had no shortage of disposable income.

'I have to get back to the office,' he said, glancing at his watch when they were back on the street. 'But why don't we meet up again one day next week to arrange clearing Halfpenny Lane out? In the meantime, I'll organise a survey and get a valuer to come around. Unless you had someone in mind?' He looked around at the three of them, and they shook their heads.

'Can I drop you girls somewhere?' he asked as a cab pulled up to the kerb.

'No, thanks. We're going to head home.'

'Okay, I'll be in touch.'

'Thanks for lunch,' Aoife called as he slid into the back seat.

They stood on the pavement watching as the cab pulled away.

'Why do I feel like I've just been run over by a bulldozer?' Mimi said looking after it.

'A very handsome bulldozer,' Sive said dreamily.

'Granted,' Mimi allowed. 'A handsome, charming bulldozer with deep pockets. But a bulldozer by any other name …'

'Leaves you just as flattened,' Aoife finished.

'Lunch was amazing, though,' Mimi said as they

walked towards the tram stop on Stephen's Green. 'It was so nice to be back in the Saddle Room.'

'Yeah.' Aoife smiled at the thought of the meal she'd just eaten – silky-soft cured salmon, meltingly tender beef, creamy mashed potatoes, a smooth and rich chocolate and raspberry tart …

'So we need to start thinking about how we can save the theatre,' Sive said when they were on the tram and rattling towards Ranelagh.

'Can we talk about it tomorrow?' Mimi closed her eyes and laid her head on Aoife's shoulder. 'I need a nap.'

Aoife could do with a nap herself. None of them were used to having a big boozy meal in the middle of the day.

'Yes!' Sive beamed. 'Lunch in the Saddle Room and an afternoon nap – divine decadence, darling! And maybe a solution for the theatre will come to us in a dream.'

6

Even though it was hard to get out of bed the next morning, Aoife was glad to have work to go to. She liked having a structure to her day, and much as she longed to be an actress, she didn't envy her sisters' erratic lifestyles and unpredictable schedules. Sive and Mimi's work lives were precarious, cobbling together a living from shift work and part-time jobs in between acting gigs. Mimi waited tables in a local restaurant, and Sive had a variety of freelance side-hustles which she fitted in around auditions and acting classes – everything from cleaning to dog-walking to mystery shopping. Somehow she still found the time to work on the skills she was always learning to add to her CV – fencing, ballroom dancing, judo, horse-riding ... the list was endless and ever increasing.

Today Aoife was particularly grateful to have something to distract her from brooding over Halfpenny Lane. She hadn't slept well, still reeling from the events of yesterday. They'd all been too tired to discuss it again last night, and no solution had come to her in her dreams. She wasn't pinning her hopes on her sisters having any better luck with theirs when she left them still sleeping in their beds and padded downstairs for breakfast. The only other inhabitant of the house awake at this hour was Kit Marlowe, a chunky ginger tabby Mimi had rescued from an animal shelter and named after the Elizabethan playwright, on whom she had a very long-distance crush.

'It suits him,' she'd claimed, 'because he's smart but scrappy, and good in a fight.'

Never one to stay in bed if there was someone available to feed him, Marlowe snaked around the kitchen door as Aoife flicked the kettle on and she gave him his breakfast while she waited for it to boil.

Work and home were the twin comforts of Aoife's life, and she loved the security and familiarity of both. Even though she was a temp, she'd been working at O'Brien Sweeney for almost a year now. She'd started at the accounting firm on a six-month contract covering maternity leave, but it had been extended for another three months as the person she was replacing had subsequently gone on sick leave. She liked having somewhere to go every morning, and returning each evening to the house she and her sisters had grown up in, where they still lived together.

It was a great house – a terraced Victorian red-brick in Ranelagh, in need of some updating that they couldn't afford to do, and in a neighbourhood that would be far beyond their means if they had to pay rent. But, fortunately, their parents had had life assurance so the mortgage on the house had been paid off when they'd died ten years ago in a car crash on their way back from a weekend break in Galway.

Aoife was seventeen and in her final year of school. Detta had come to stay with the girls, guiding them through the funeral and wake, cooking beautiful food and supporting them in their mutual grief and loss. She'd offered to move in permanently to look after them, but Aoife had refused. Detta was in her eighties then and they couldn't uproot her from her little cottage in the Liberties where she loved to hold court and host her famous parties.

Instead Aoife had done her best to step up and take on the role of parent to her younger sisters. She'd cooked meals and washed clothes and saw to it that everyone got to school on time – generally carrying on as normal, apart from the huge gaping hole in their lives. She'd been thankful that they could stay in their childhood home as she'd tried to provide some semblance of stability for them all.

She hadn't felt remotely up to the task of parenting her younger siblings, and she'd fretted about letting everyone down – Sive in particular. She'd worried for all of them, of course, herself included. But Sive was the baby, only thirteen when their parents died, and the least equipped to cope. Aoife had hated seeing her sunny nature dimmed, her instinctive confidence in the world eroded as her sense of security was snatched away from her. But Sive had surprised her with her resilience, revealing an inner strength that was remarkable for someone so young.

Instead it was Mimi who'd been the most trouble, causing Aoife endless heartache and anxiety as she tried to act in loco parentis. She'd been a precocious child and was already a stroppy teenager at fifteen, but she'd gone off the rails after their parents died, acting out in every way imaginable and refusing to accept Aoife's authority as a surrogate parent instead of a slightly older sibling who wasn't the boss of her. She'd skipped school, and spent far too many nights in bars and clubs, staggering home in the small hours and crashing through the front door barely able to stand. Aoife would tiptoe into her room later to find her passed out on the bed fully clothed, checking to make sure she wasn't lying on her back before creeping back to her own room for a last few precious hours of sleep. There had been a lot of nights when Aoife had lain awake worrying where Mimi was and what she was doing, and a lot of mornings when she couldn't get her out of bed to go to school no matter how hard she tried.

There had been boys too, and not the sort of boys Mimi would have brought home to meet their parents if they'd been alive. But then Aoife suspected she wouldn't have been hanging out with those boys anyway if their parents were alive. It was just one more way she'd found to rebel – one more sign of Aoife's inadequacy as a substitute parent.

Aoife had worried about teenage pregnancies and failed exams, and she felt responsible, as if she'd failed Mimi as a parent. But sometimes, when she was alone at night, she sobbed into her pillow at the unfairness of it all. She *wasn't* a parent, and she shouldn't have to be responsible for a wayward teenager who was only a couple of years younger than her.

However, she couldn't afford to wallow too often, and she was glad of that, grateful that in the morning she'd have to brush herself off, get up and get on with another day of holding the family together – going through the motions again and again until the feelings of self-pity gradually faded away.

The only thing Mimi had never done to act out was get a tattoo. She'd claimed it was because they'd become too common and every middle-aged mum at the school gates had at least one, so now the cool thing was to not have any. But Aoife had a sneaking suspicion that she was thinking of her future acting career and wouldn't do anything that might be a bar to her getting a part, however small. It gave

Aoife hope that she still had some sense of self-preservation that would pull her back from the brink.

And so it proved. Mimi had sobered up and straightened herself out in time to catch up with her school work before the Leaving Cert exams, which she'd got through with respectable if not brilliant results. She began to behave more maturely and was kinder to her sisters, pulling together with them instead of fighting Aoife every step of the way. She acknowledged what a nightmare she'd been, and tried to make up for it in myriad ways. She'd even tried AA briefly, but decided it wasn't for her after a couple of meetings. 'They're all so self-obsessed and boring,' she'd said, 'droning on all the time about how awful they used to be and how marvellous their lives are now.' But Aoife suspected what really put her off was that she resented relinquishing centre stage to anyone else.

Somehow they'd all muddled through and made it to their twenties relatively unscathed. Aoife was proud now of how they'd rallied together and coped. Her acting career had been the only long-term casualty. She'd been accepted into the Gaiety School of Acting after two rounds of auditions, and was due to start there in October the year she finished school. But though the money left over from their parents' estate would keep them going for a while, it couldn't last indefinitely. Besides heating bills, boiler repairs and the countless dull but necessary household expenses, there were school trips, dance classes and singing lessons that she didn't want her sisters to miss out on. There wouldn't be enough to put all three of them through acting school. Besides, at least one of them needed a job with a good guaranteed income, and as the eldest Aoife decided it should be her.

So she cancelled her place at acting school and instead did an arts degree, graduating with a BA in

English Literature and Drama Studies. Then she'd taken a variety of temporary office jobs while she studied online to qualify as an accounting technician. Mimi and Sive had been appalled that she was giving up on her acting ambitions, but Aoife couldn't bring herself to risk all their livelihoods on something as fickle and precarious as an acting career. Perhaps they were simply braver than her, but she suspected there was an element of guilt too behind Mimi and Sive's protestations. They knew she was sacrificing her dreams for their sakes. But neither of them had been willing to give up on acting and take on the role of breadwinner. They just tried to persuade Aoife that none of them had to, that they'd manage somehow.

Detta had been disappointed too, though she'd been careful not to show it. She'd robustly supported Aoife's decision, and regularly added the proviso that the theatrical life 'wasn't for everyone' while she continued to extol its virtues.

Aoife hadn't quite committed entirely to the idea of a steady, pensionable job, however. She'd still always worked as a temp, and though she'd barely admitted it even to herself, deep down she knew she was still treating the work as a stop-gap, waiting for the day when she could pick up where she'd left off and go to acting school. Now, just as that seemed almost within reach, it was being pulled away again. Maybe she should accept that this was her life and it was time to look for a permanent job.

When Aoife got home from work that evening, she found her sisters in the kitchen, condensation rolling down the steamed-up windows and a delicious aroma wafting from the pan bubbling on the hob.

'We made chicken cacciatore,' Sive said as Aoife took off her coat and hung it on the back of a chair.

'We were just waiting until you came home to put the pasta on.' Mimi lit the gas under their biggest pot and grabbed a fistful of sea salt from the cellar on the worktop, crumbling it into the water.

'Oh my god! Enough with the salt!' Sive turned to Aoife. 'Did you see how much she put in?'

'That's what you're supposed to do,' Mimi said. 'You know that. Detta always told us the water you cook pasta in should be as salty as the Mediterranean.'

'Detta had a stroke,' Sive mumbled, turning back to the pan.

'It's not as if we're going to eat it all. It's just in the water.'

'Well, I know who to blame if I stroke out before I'm thirty.'

Mimi rolled her eyes and poured in the pasta. 'We've got garlic bread too,' she said to Aoife. There was parmesan grated in a little bowl on the table, Aoife noticed, and there was a bottle of red wine open. Cheering as it was to come home to, these weren't good signs. She recognised all the hallmarks of a consolation dinner.

'Did you hear back about that movie?' she asked Mimi tentatively. She'd had a callback for a part in the latest instalment of a major film franchise that was to be filmed in Ireland.

'Yes,' Mimi huffed, pouting. She shoved the spoon into the pan of bubbling sauce and turned to Aoife. 'I didn't get it.'

'Oh, I'm sorry.'

'But worse than that, bloody Catherine did.'

Aoife gave her a sympathetic grimace as she flopped down at the table. 'That sucks.'

Mimi joined her at the table and poured three glasses of wine. 'Yeah, so not only did I not get it, now I have to pretend I'm delighted that she did.'

'And you're not?'

'I mean … no,' she said after a long silence when she appeared to be tussling with her emotions. She took a gulp of wine. 'I know I *should* be. She's my friend and everything, and of course I want her to do well. But not at my expense.'

Marlowe trotted into the room and jumped up on the chair beside Mimi. She pulled him into her arms, kissing the top of his head.

'It's not fair,' she continued as she scratched his chin and he purred softly. 'Now on top of the disappointment of not getting it, I'm left with all this envy and resentment, plus the guilt of being a crappy friend and not just being happy for her.'

Aoife wanted to tell her that it wasn't a zero sum game, that Catherine's gain wasn't her loss and there was enough to go around. But they all knew it wasn't true. There were so few parts, and so many people going for them. They were all fishing in the same small pool, and if one person got cast in a role, it meant that everyone else who auditioned didn't. There were no two ways about it: Catherine's success correlated exactly with Mimi's disappointment.

'There'll be other parts,' she said, aware how inane it sounded.

'That's what I said,' Sive called from her position at the stove as she stirred pasta into the sauce. 'You didn't get this part because there's something better out there for you,' she said to Mimi, ever the optimist.

Mimi gave her a weary look. 'I was brilliant too! I'm

just as good as Catherine. Better, in fact, let's be honest about it.'

'I know you are,' Aoife said. 'But, you know, sometimes it's not just about talent.'

Mimi narrowed her eyes, intrigued. 'Oh, you think she's sleeping with someone?' she asked, perking up, happy to pounce on any nefarious explanation for Catherine winning out over her.

Aoife laughed. 'No, of course not. Just that it might be – I don't know – a certain look they want, or chemistry with the leading man. You know how it goes. It's not all about your acting.'

Mimi sighed. 'I just thought this could be it, you know – my big break.'

'I know.' Aoife reached across the table and gave her arm a squeeze.

'It would have been a game-changer. And not just for me, for all of us.' Mimi smiled wryly. 'Our chance to get back to Moscow.'

'Yeah. It could have been the answer to our prayers for Halfpenny Lane.'

Marlowe wriggled in Mimi's arms and she released him. He dropped to the floor and padded to the door, making a loud exit through the cat flap.

Sive brought the pasta and garlic bread to the table and sat beside Mimi.

'Speaking of Halfpenny Lane,' Aoife said as she helped herself to garlic bread. 'Have we had any ideas about that?'

'Apart from getting a part in a big Hollywood movie and making a fortune?' Mimi sighed, winding spaghetti onto her fork. 'No.'

'We need to think of something we can bring to Jonathan – some concrete plan.'

'A proposal you could take to the bank ...' Sive chewed her lip, recalling Jonathan's words. 'Oh, the bank! We could get a loan.'

'How? No bank's going to give us a loan with our income,' Mimi said gloomily. 'They won't even let me have a tiny overdraft.'

'What about Aoife? She's got a proper job, and a steady income.'

'Not enough to borrow the kind of money we'd need,' Aoife told her.

'Well, what about Jonathan?' Sive asked.

'What about him?'

'I know he doesn't want to invest in the theatre, but what if he gave us his share as a loan and we could buy him out over time and pay him interest?'

Mimi looked at her thoughtfully as she chewed. 'That could work.'

'That would be a hell of a lot of interest,' Aoife said. 'And it would take forever to pay him back.'

'We should ask him anyway,' Sive said. 'We've got nothing to lose. He can only say no.'

Aoife disliked the idea of asking Jonathan to bankroll them in any way. If he didn't want to be involved, they needed to find a way to buy him out, fair and square. 'If we want to keep the theatre, we have to make it pay. We're not going to be a charity case.'

'It wouldn't be charity if someone invested in it.'

'It would if they put money into that place. They'd never see a worthwhile return, no matter how successful we were. It's too small, and the audience is limited. It doesn't make financial sense as an investment.'

'There are Arts Council grants we could apply for,' Mimi said.

'Yeah. That all takes time, though. We need to get the

money to buy Jonathan out *now*. Then we could take as long as we needed to do the renovations.'

'Oh!' Sive shot up straight. 'You know who we need to see?'

'Who?'

'Conor O'Neill.'

'That's actually a good idea,' Mimi said.

'I'm sure he could tell us what to do.'

'Advise us, you mean,' Mimi said dryly.

Sive gave a little laugh. 'Yeah, right. I meant advise.' Her voice dripped with sarcasm.

Conor O'Neill was the director of one of Dublin's longest established theatres. He had a reputation as a shrewd operator with an uncanny ability to attract funding, and he'd steered the Players Theatre to international renown and consistent commercial success.

'Detta was fond of him,' Aoife mused. 'He might want to help. It's a good idea. We should make an appointment to meet with him.'

'Do we all have to go, though?' Sive asked.

'I think we should. Put on a united front.'

Mimi frowned. 'I don't think we all need to go. One of us should be enough.'

'I agree,' Sive said, looking expectantly at Aoife.

'Okay, then. Off you go.'

Sive shook her head. 'Not me. I'm kind of scared of him.'

'I'm not afraid of him,' Mimi said sulkily, 'but I could do without his unsolicited opinions.'

'You're not still bearing a grudge about that?' Mimi had run into Conor O'Neill as a teen when she was auditioning at Players, and he'd told her she'd never get anywhere until she lost the hobnail boots and the attitude. Aoife would never suggest to Mimi that she agreed with him, but he'd been right about the attitude. Thankfully, Mimi had grown out of it, though she'd never shed her beloved Dr Martens boots.

'So what if I am? I think I'm entitled.'

Aoife sighed. Why did she always have to be the grown-up? 'Fine. I'll go. I can take some time off work.'

'We'll go with you as back-up if you want,' Sive said, looking to Mimi for confirmation.

'Yeah, I don't mind going, but you have to do the talking.'

7

THE FOLLOWING MONDAY AFTERNOON, Aoife, Sive and Mimi met Conor O'Neill in his office next door to the Players Theatre.

'I remember you,' he said to Mimi as they introduced themselves. 'Still wearing the hobnail boots, I see.' Mimi looked mutinous, and Aoife blushed as they took seats in front of his desk. This was getting off to a bad start.

'Anyway, I'm glad to see they haven't held you back,' he continued, his face softening in a smile. 'I saw you in *The Threepenny Opera* last year. You were marvellous.'

'Oh! Thank you.' Mimi flushed with pleasure, mollified, and Aoife relaxed.

'So, what can I do for you?'

Aoife was itching to explore Conor's office – to get a closer look at the photographs of past productions that lined the walls, and browse through the scripts that filled the bookcases. But she focused her attention on Conor and the task at hand and explained why they were there.

'So, you're going to reopen Halfpenny Lane,' Conor said, leaning across his desk.

'Yes … hopefully.'

'Well, that's good news. It would be great to see it brought back to life. It's a shame for such a great theatre to go to rack and ruin.'

'We thought you might be able to help,' Aoife said, emboldened by his obvious regard for Halfpenny Lane.

'Of course. I'd be happy to do anything I can. Detta was a great woman!'

'She was,' Aoife said, relieved. She'd expected to have more of a fight on her hands. Conor had a formidable reputation as a tough, even ruthless impresario – straight-talking to the point of being offensive, as Mimi could attest.

'She did marvellous things for Dublin theatre. Some of our finest actors started out at Halfpenny Lane. She was a terrific actress herself too,' he said with a fond smile. 'Absolute headbanger, of course. But I'm sure I don't need to tell *you* that.'

Sive stifled a shocked laugh, and Aoife was dumb-founded, unsure how to respond. Her first instinct was to defend Detta, but Conor wasn't saying anything they hadn't all thought.

'But she was a real trooper – never let you down. One of the last of her kind. So – how can I help?'

'Well, um …' Aoife rallied, gathering her thoughts. 'We need to raise money – for the renovations. We thought you might have some ideas.'

'Of course.'

'And there's another owner we need to buy out,' Mimi added.

'Oh? Who's that?'

'Detta's godson.'

'Detta left the theatre to the four of us,' Aoife explained.

'I see.' Conor frowned. 'That's tricky. Do you have to buy him out? Couldn't you all run the theatre together?'

'He doesn't want to do that,' Aoife said. 'He wants to sell and split the proceeds.'

'What is he, some sort of philistine?'

'He's a solicitor,' Mimi said.

'Have you told him how much fun it is running a theatre?'

'We did,' Sive said. 'But he's not interested.'

'He sounds like a bit of a bollix to me. If you don't mind me saying so.'

'We don't mind at all,' Mimi said.

Aoife minded a bit. Jonathan wasn't a bollix.

'Well, you don't want to waste any funds you raise buying him out. My advice is you talk him around,' Conor said as if it was the simplest thing in the world. He was obviously used to people bending to his will. 'You're going to need to spend every penny you can get on Halfpenny Lane.'

'Well, we can try,' Aoife said, already knowing it would be futile. 'But in the meantime, we thought you might have some suggestions for fundraising ideas.'

Conor nodded, and began scribbling on a pad as she spoke. Aoife peered across at the desk and he seemed to be writing a list of names. How rude!

'We thought we'd apply to the Arts Council for a grant,' she soldiered on, on the off-chance that he was still actually listening.

He lifted his head, continuing to jot down names on his pad. 'I can help you with that. I know some people.'

'Oh! That would be great, thanks.' So he *was* paying attention. 'Maybe he was just a good multi-tasker. 'But that would take time. We need to raise money right away.'

Finally Conor lifted his head. 'So – you put on a show.'

'Oh, right. A show.' Aoife tried to hide her disappointment. 'The thing is, we're not ready for that. I mean, the theatre isn't in a fit state yet for paying customers. That's why we need to raise the money.'

'And it would take too long to produce a show anyway,' Mimi said.

Conor shook his head. 'Not at all. Get everyone to muck in and you could have a show up in three or four weeks.'

'Gosh! Do you think so?' Aoife wasn't sure who he meant by 'everyone'.

'Do bits from shows that have already run and you won't need much rehearsal time. Get people to do their tried and tested party pieces – sing a song, do a sketch, read a poem or whatever.' He stopped and added a couple of names to the list he was making. 'Do it on a Sunday, when most of the theatres are closed, so everyone's free. You can use the Players.'

'Wow, that's really kind.'

'Do one night only, charge a hundred euro a ticket – maybe two.'

'That's an awful lot!' Sive cried.

'It's for a good cause. And they'll get their money's worth. It'll be a one-off, a unique event. The hottest ticket in town.'

Aoife did some quick calculations in her head. Players was a decent size. As far as she could recall it had capacity for around six hundred. But even charging two hundred euro a ticket, that still wouldn't be close to what they needed, especially after overheads. 'It's really nice of you to offer, and it's a good idea. But it still wouldn't raise much money, after we'd paid everyone.'

Conor frowned. 'You won't be paying anyone. Get them to do it for free. Call in some favours.'

Aoife nodded as if she thought this was good advice. 'Um … we don't really have anyone who owes us favours, though.'

'Not you. Your great-aunt. Good luck finding anyone in Dublin theatre who Detta didn't help out in one way or another.' Conor tore off the page he'd been writing on and held it out to Aoife. 'Here are some names to start with – that's just off the top of my head. There'll be more.'

Aoife looked at the sheet in bewilderment. He'd listed just about every star of the Irish stage, along with some of the most gifted directors and lighting designers.

'Anne will give you the numbers,' he said, nodding to the outer office beyond the door, where his assistant sat. 'Don't look so worried.' He smiled at Aoife. 'This is just to get the ball rolling and launch your fundraising efforts with a bit of a splash. You can borrow Fran for the marketing and publicity,' he said, naming the Players' marketing manager. 'I'll tell her to liaise with you on it.'

'Gosh, thank you so much,' Aoife said. 'That's so generous.'

'You should think about ice creams,' he said, tapping his chin as he stared off into space.

'Sorry?' Aoife wondered had she missed something.

'Ice creams, for the interval. It'd be another little bit of profit. Not much, but every little helps.'

'Oh, right. Good idea.' She took a pen from her bag and scrawled 'ice cream' on the page he'd given her.

'Start rounding up that lot,' Conor nodded to the list in her hand. 'And I'll get back to you with more when I've gone through my address book.'

Aoife was already squirming at the thought of cold-calling all these eminent actors, many of whom were her idols, and asking them to work for free.

'I'll make a few calls myself too.' She knew Conor had

lots of rich friends who he could tap for money. 'Anything else you need help with, give me a call. You can mention my name when you're talking to people, if you think it'll help. Which it will,' he added. 'Okay, if that's it, I've got another appointment.'

'Oh, of course.' Aoife stood, realising they'd been dismissed. 'Thank you so much for your time. You've been really helpful.'

'Glad to do it. Detta was a force to be reckoned with. We won't see her like again.'

'No,' Aoife said sadly. 'We won't.'

'But it's good to see you girls picking up the baton. If you're anything like your great-aunt, Halfpenny Lane is in safe hands.'

The problem was she wasn't anything like Detta, Aoife thought as they walked back down the stairs and onto the street. She didn't have a fraction of her chutzpah, and she was already dreading making these calls. But if they were going to save Halfpenny Lane, she'd just have to grit her teeth and do whatever was necessary. Detta had been such a great advocate for her little theatre, and Aoife didn't want to let her down now. She'd try to channel a little of Detta's drive and determination, and throw as much energy into saving Halfpenny Lane as Detta had put into building it.

8

_____

Aoife and her sisters spent the rest of the week planning the fundraising concert. Aoife hadn't been convinced they should even go ahead with the idea – it couldn't possibly raise enough, so what was the point? But Conor had called her the very next day after they met to tell her he'd already got some big names on board. Aoife's head spun as he told her Sir Peter Bradshaw and his son Rafe were signed up, and he gave her more names to add to her list.

'I guess we're doing it then,' she said to her sisters as she ended the call.

They divided Conor's list between them and started making calls. Aoife was usually happy to take charge, but this was one task she wished she could hand off to her sisters. She was always ready to offer help, but hated asking for it, and she cringed as she tried to enlist the support of the great and good of Dublin theatre, even though everyone was very kind and seemed keen to rally round. It didn't help that she felt like a fraud because she knew the endeavour was doomed from the start.

'You never know,' Sive said when she voiced her misgivings. 'It might be more successful than you think.'

'It's just a start,' Mimi said. 'It'll get the word out.'

'Maybe we'll find some rich benefactor who'll take us under his wing.'

'You've been reading too many Dickens novels.' Mimi rolled her eyes at Sive. 'But it could turn up some rich donors who want to back us.'

'I suppose.' Aoife wasn't hopeful. 'Anyway, we can't call it off now.' Conor's assistant had been on to her earlier in the day to discuss possible dates. 'So we'll just have to do our best to make it a success.'

'We can have a tombola!' Sive said, clapping her hands gleefully. 'We could ask local businesses to donate prizes.'

'That's a good idea,' Aoife said, though her stomach churned at the thought of more begging calls. 'But we can't pin our hopes on this fundraiser, or some sponsor coming along. We need to come up with some realistic ideas for buying Jonathan out, or else we're just going to have to face facts and ... let Halfpenny Lane go.'

'Sell?' Sive cried piteously.

'What option do we have? Jonathan has to execute Detta's will. If we can't come up with the money ...'

'Why don't we try talking him around, like Conor said?'

'I can't see him changing his mind.'

'I bet *you* could change his mind,' Mimi said to Aoife with a cheeky grin. 'If you ask him nicely.' She fluttered her eyelashes flirtatiously.

'Yes!' Sive beamed. 'It's obvious he's sweet on you.' Aoife and her sisters had an antiquated way of speaking sometimes that others could think affected. But it was simply a habit they'd picked up from old movies and their cherished Noel Streatfeild novels, an arcane language they shared and slipped into naturally when they were together.

'It's true,' Mimi said. 'He's soft on you. Anyone can see it.'

'No, he's not!' Aoife felt herself flush. 'Anyway, regardless, I'm not going to … seduce him into signing his share over to us, or whatever it is you're suggesting.'

'Fine,' Mimi said. 'But we can at least make our case – try to persuade him keeping Halfpenny Lane is the right thing to do. And it'd be a good look for him. He could lord it up as a patron of the arts.'

'I can't see it working. But no harm in giving it a shot, I suppose. What have we got to lose?'

'Only Moscow!' Mimi sighed dramatically.

On Friday morning they went to meet Jonathan at his office in a tall glass building on the banks of the canal. Aoife had rung him the previous day to make an appointment, and he'd said he'd 'fit them in' at eleven between meetings, making it sound like he was doing them a huge favour.

She already felt on the back foot as they made their way up to the fourth floor in a glass lift, and it didn't help that she and her sisters looked so out of place among all the tailored suits, crisp shirts and shiny shoes. They rarely bought anything new, getting most of their clothes from vintage stores and charity shops, and what they'd salvaged from the treasure trove that Detta had left behind in her wardrobes. Mimi had a particularly eclectic style and today she resembled a walking eighties jumble sale in layers of jersey and lace accessorised with multiple necklaces and bracelets, big dangly earrings, and a bright-red scarf tied in her voluminous curls, her feet clad in an ancient pair of

DM boots. Sive was in one of her signature long floaty skirt and lace-up ankle-boot ensembles under a gorgeously embroidered Afghan coat that had once belonged to Detta.

'We probably should have dressed more conservatively,' Aoife whispered as the lift doors opened.

'Please!' Mimi sniffed. 'I'm wearing lace gloves.' She held out her hands, admiring the black fingerless gloves. 'How fecking demure can you get?'

It wasn't a good beginning when Jonathan ushered them into his office and waved them to a sofa in the corner, looking harried and glancing at his watch.

'So, what brings you here?' he asked, perching on the edge of the chair opposite them as if poised to spring up at any moment.

'It's about the theatre,' Sive said, fiddling with the sleeve of her coat.

'Yes, I thought it might be.' He nodded, indicating for her to go on.

'We don't want to sell,' Mimi said flatly.

'Right.' He nodded. 'So what do you propose?'

'We've got a few ideas.' Aoife reached into her bag for her notebook. They'd spent time brainstorming ways to save the theatre in the past week, in between organising the fundraising concert. It had occupied Aoife's every waking moment.

'Well, first of all, there's the option of keeping it,' Sive said, looking at him with big, hopeful eyes.

'All of us?'

'Yes. We'd all be equal owners, of course. It's just as much your inheritance as ours. We're not talking about cutting you out.'

'That's very decent of you.'

Sive beamed, failing to hear the sarcasm in his tone. It was all too apparent to Aoife, who itched to slap him.

'But I already told you I don't want to keep it.'

'We thought you might change your mind,' Mimi said, giving him a hard look.

'Why would you think that?'

'Because … it'd be a nice thing to do?' Sive said. 'Besides, imagine how much fun it would be, owning a theatre.'

'And think of the kudos you'd get for being involved in the arts,' Mimi said.

'Plus you'd have free tickets to all the shows,' Sive said. 'You could bring all your friends and entertain clients.'

'So I should just do it for fun, and bragging rights? Pass up half a million for the sake of free tickets to a twenty-euro show?'

'You can't put a value on a show,' Sive said solemnly.

'This is sounding like less of a viable business proposition by the minute.'

'But it's not as if you need the money, is it?' Mimi said, looking around the office. 'I mean, I'm sure you earn a decent whack here. And you have that big house in Sandymount.'

Jonathan gave her a curious look as if he was surprised Mimi knew where he lived. Had he forgotten Patrick reading his address out from Detta's will? 'Where I live or what I earn is irrelevant. I'm still not interested in running a theatre.'

'What about what Detta would have wanted?' Sive said, as if she'd landed on the perfect argument to win him around.

'What Detta wanted was for me to have a share of the worth of Halfpenny Lane. Her intentions were perfectly clear.'

The three of them exchanged worried glances. This was going even worse than Aoife had imagined. Despite how she'd admonished Sive about being unrealistic, she realised that, deep down, she'd nurtured a grain of hope that he might change his mind. As Mimi said, he obviously didn't need the money. Surely he could at least try to meet them halfway when he saw how much it meant to them.

'Don't you think it's odd, though, that she changed her will like that at the last minute?' Mimi asked. 'I mean, why then? She'd known you your whole life, and you weren't in any of her previous wills. We saw them.'

Jonathan frowned, looking down at his clasped hands. 'I suppose she had her reasons.'

'Do you know what they were?'

'No. Though I have my suspicions.'

'So?' Mimi looked at him expectantly, waiting for more.

'Detta didn't feel the need to explain herself to you, and neither do I.'

'Or you can't?'

'Look, if you're suggesting that she wasn't in her right mind, or that I did something underhand—'

'Of course she isn't,' Aoife said, giving Mimi a warning look. 'None of us thinks that.'

'Good.' His gaze lingered on Aoife. 'I'm sorry, but if you've just come here to persuade me to change my mind about selling, you're wasting your time.'

'We have lots of other ideas,' Sive said, nodding to the notebook open on Aoife's lap.

'If you insist on getting your pound of flesh,' Mimi mumbled sulkily.

'Okay, first of all, there's a loan,' Sive said, glancing at Aoife's notepad.

'You're going to get a loan to buy me out? Why didn't you say so in the first place?'

'Oh no! None of us would get approved for a loan

from a bank,' Sive said with a little laugh. 'We thought you could loan us the value of your share and we'd pay it off over time – with interest, of course.'

'No,' Jonathan said flatly. 'That's out.'

'You haven't even thought about it—'

'I don't need to. It'd take you forever to buy me out that way. I might as well just hand over my share to you right now, lock stock and barrel.'

'Oh!' Sive perked up, smiling. 'That would be–'

'Which I'm not doing. So – what else have you got?'

'Okay, well …' Aoife looked down at her notebook. 'Since you don't want to own the theatre, we thought maybe we could rent your share from you.'

Jonathan shook his head. 'No. Next.'

Aoife tried to tamp down a tremor of fury that shivered through her. She'd thought that was a perfectly fair and reasonable suggestion. 'It wouldn't cost you anything,' she said, trying to keep her tone level. 'We'd pay you proper rent. It would be an income, so it'd be an investment for you, and you'd still be getting your inheritance, just over a longer time.'

'A much longer time. I'd probably be dead before I realised a fraction of what it's worth.'

'Well, our only other option then is to find the money to buy you out,' Aoife said, looking down at her list disconsolately.

'Yes, finally! Do you have any ideas for how you might do that?'

'We're working on it. We're starting to do fundraising. We're holding a benefit concert at the Players Theatre at the end of May.'

'A benefit concert? How much do you hope to raise from that?'

'Um … well, about sixty grand.'

Jonathan gave her a dubious look.

'And there'll be more,' Sive said. 'That's just from ticket sales, but we're selling ice creams at the interval.'

'And there'll be a tombola,' Mimi added.

'Oh, well, in that case … obviously a tombola changes everything.'

Aoife had never wanted so badly to thump someone, but she gritted her teeth and tried to keep her temper. 'I know it's not nearly enough, but it's just the start. It'll get the word out about the theatre and people might make donations – big ones.'

Jonathan gave her a long, pitying look. He sighed, raking a hand through his hair. 'Look, I can see how much the theatre means to you, and I wish I could say we can just keep it. I genuinely do.'

Mimi gave him a hard, narrow-eyed glare, but there was a sincerity in his eyes when he looked up at Aoife that hit her like a punch, and to her surprise, she believed him.

'Anyway, I've arranged for an estate agent to call around on Monday and do a valuation. We can see what he says and take it from there?'

Aoife nodded. 'Does one of us need to be there?'

'No, unless you want to be. I can let him in.' He gave Aoife a weak smile. 'Maybe it won't be worth as much as we think and your sixty grand will be enough to buy me out.'

'Yeah, maybe.' She knew he was trying to be nice, but she had to swallow down another wave of resentment at the thought of handing all the hard-won money from the fundraiser over to him. She had to keep reminding herself he had every right.

He glanced at his watch. 'Well, I have another meeting to get to. But I'll be in touch about the valuation, and we can arrange clearing the place out.'

9

On Sunday morning, Aoife, Sive and Mimi sat in the front row of Halfpenny Lane waiting for people to arrive for the first meeting about the benefit concert. They'd set up a trestle table in front of the stage with tea, coffee and pastries. Sive had even baked scones specially for the occasion.

'No one's going to come, are they?' Mimi said, looking at her phone as the time ticked over to eleven thirty.

'Give it a minute,' Aoife said with more confidence than she felt. As well as calling Conor's leads personally, they'd got the word out on social media over the week, and Dublin's theatrical community had taken up the cause, enthusiastically retweeting each other and spreading the word, while reminiscing about their own memories of Detta and the glory days of Halfpenny Lane. They'd all seemed eager to help and had readily agreed to lend a hand.

Now she wondered if it was just lip service and they had no intention of giving up their valuable time for free. After all, why should they? They may have been fond of

Detta and nostalgic about Halfpenny Lane, but they didn't owe Aoife and her sisters anything. When she thought about it, she realised no one had definitely said they'd come this morning. She'd got lots of vague half-hearted promises from people that they'd 'try to make it' or 'do their best', and she hadn't had the nerve to push them for a firmer commitment. She felt guilty now for letting them fob her off and not being more pushy about enlisting their help. Detta would have been more forceful, and once more Aoife felt she was letting her down.

'I'm starving,' Mimi grumbled beside her. 'I'm going to have a scone.'

'You can't have a scone,' Sive told her. 'They're for the actors.'

'Oh, I think she could risk it,' Aoife said dryly.

As Mimi stood up, the auditorium door opened and they all turned around to look.

'Oh, it's just you,' Mimi said, her shoulders slumping as she continued over to the coffee station.

'Good morning to you too.' Jonathan strode down the aisle and joined her at the table. Aoife tried to ignore the traitorous way her heart leapt at the sight of him. She was used to seeing him in his work suits, and she thought he looked more handsome than ever in a cream crew-neck jumper and black skinny jeans.

'What's he doing here?' Sive hissed to Aoife.

'I told him this was happening and he could come if he wanted. He's one of the owners of Halfpenny Lane. He has a right to be included in whatever we're doing with it.' Nevertheless, she was as surprised as Sive to see him here this morning. She didn't think he'd be interested in coming.

'So, where is everyone?' he asked, turning back to

Aoife, a plastic cup of steaming coffee clutched in his hand. 'I thought you said eleven?'

'Maybe they're all as good at time-keeping as you.'

'I thought I'd just drop in to see how it's going. I expected it to be in full swing by now.'

Damn! Where *was* everyone? It was one thing them leaving her and her sisters in the lurch, but showing them up in front of Jonathan Hunt was a whole other clusterfuck. The entire enterprise was looking like a no-hoper before they'd even got started. It would just give him more ammunition to insist that selling was their only option. If they couldn't even get a small fundraising concert off the ground, what chance did they have of raising half a million euros?

'I'm sure they'll be here soon,' Sive called to him.

As if she'd conjured her with the words, the auditorium door opened at that moment, and Aoife turned to see Margaret Brennan hurrying down the aisle. A small, barrel-chested woman in late middle age, she was a theatrical legend, widely regarded as a national treasure.

'Sorry, am I late?' she asked breathlessly as she unwound a scarf. 'Oh!' She looked around in surprise at the empty seats.

Aoife shook her head. 'You're the first.'

'Well, that's a first. Go me!' She beamed as Aoife stood to greet her. 'Darling, it's so lovely to see you.' Aoife was dismayed as Margaret pulled her into a hug and kissed her cheek. She only had a vague recollection of having met the woman once before.

'Thank you so much for coming.'

Sive and Mimi came over to join them, and Margaret hugged them just as warmly. 'Not at all. Happy to help. Detta was a great friend of mine, you know. Ooh, scones!'

Her eyes lit on the tea station. 'May I? I didn't have time for breakfast.'

'Of course. Help yourself.'

As Margaret made her way to the table, the door swung open again and Aoife had a fan-girl moment as Sir Peter Bradshaw walked in accompanied by his elder son Rafe. Lanky, grey-haired and still devastatingly attractive, Sir Peter was a huge star, one of the old Hollywood elite, and Aoife knew he was a great friend of Conor O'Neill. His son Rafe was also a famous actor and massive heart-throb since playing Mr Darcy in a TV series of *Pride and Prejudice*.

Suddenly it was as if a bell had gone off somewhere, and a steady stream of well-known actors poured into the little theatre, like the star-studded cast appearing from the wings to take their bows at the end of a performance. Aoife looked on in astonishment as they greeted each other with hugs and kisses and congregated around the trestle table, chatting animatedly as they helped themselves to tea and coffee, and fell on the food as if they hadn't seen a bite in weeks. It was a glorious sight, and she had to blink back tears as she watched.

'Actors!' She turned to find Conor O'Neill had appeared beside her. 'They'll always turn up for a free bun.'

'Oh, hello! I didn't expect you. Thanks for coming.'

'I'm just calling in for a few minutes to help you get started. I thought it'd help if I showed my face.'

Aoife noticed several of the actors looking over, nodding at Conor with nervy smiles.

'If they think I'm involved, they'll be more inclined to behave themselves.'

'It was very good of them all to come.'

'Sure, sure. But don't let them get the upper hand.

They'll all want to do their party pieces, but you want to stick to the big hits – crowd-pleasers that will appeal to the great unwashed. Tom will want to do *Krapp*, but don't let him,' he said, nodding to Tom Clancy, a wonderful actor and Beckett expert who was chatting with Shay Murphy at the side of the stage. They'd done a gorgeous and hugely successful production of *Waiting For Godot* together that had toured the world and been showered with awards. 'If he must do Beckett, you can let him and Shay do *Godot*, but even then only the funniest bits.'

Aoife nodded. 'Okay,' she said, trying not to betray how intimidated she was at the thought of bossing around an actor of Tom's stature.

'Rafe should come on as Mr Darcy, do something from *Pride and Prejudice* – that's always a winner. Even better, get someone to throw a bucket of water over him first – it'll bring the house down.' Aoife knew he was referring to the scene in the BBC adaptation where Mr Darcy had gone skinny-dipping and appeared before Elizabeth Bennett dripping wet and half dressed. It was a scene beloved of fans the world over, and sorely missed in the series Rafe had starred in more recently. Nevertheless, she didn't think she'd be suggesting anyone throw a bucket of water over Rafe Bradshaw, even in the hope of swelling Halfpenny Lane's coffers.

'Is anyone doing poetry?' Conor asked.

'Um … we haven't made any decisions about the programme yet.'

'Well, if they are, keep it simple and again stick with the old favourites – Heaney, the Auden one from *Four Weddings* that everyone knows. Yeats, of course – anything people will remember from having it drummed into them at school. Have you thought about the ice cream?'

'Oh, yes. We're doing that.'

'I'm fond of a choc-ice myself, but you can charge more for a Magnum, or tubs of Ben and Jerry's.'

It seemed no detail was too small for Conor to take an interest in.

Margaret wandered over to them, and Conor bent to kiss her cheek. 'So what are your ideas for the show?' she asked Aoife, dipping a green tea bag in her mug.

'Well, that's what we're here to discuss. We thought you'd all have some suggestions.' Out of the corner of her eye she was aware of Conor frowning at her sternly.

'I thought I might give my Hedda,' Margaret said, looking up at Conor with a twinkly smile.

'No,' Conor said flatly. 'There'll be none of that malarkey. The girls need to make money.'

'Oh!' Margaret nodded, chastened.

'It'll be crowd-pleasers only, right?' He looked to Aoife for back-up.

'Right.' Aoife nodded, already in a sweat. She felt way out of her depth. She was the least-qualified person in the room to take charge.

'Stuff every muck savage in the street can appreciate.'

Margaret looked between Conor and Aoife, like a little bird, her eyes bright and sharp. 'I think sometimes people underestimate the appetite of the general public for–'

'You know what they say,' Conor interrupted. 'No one ever went broke underestimating the taste of the masses.' He softened his words with a warm smile. 'Darling, you know I'd walk over hot coals to see your Hedda. But there's a time and a place.'

'Right.' Margaret flushed, looking pleased.

'And this isn't the time. Or the place.'

Margaret nodded. 'Understood,' she said, without rancour.

'Well, it's my daughter's birthday, and I have to spend

the afternoon at Jumpzone,' Conor said, as Margaret drifted away. 'I envy you. I'd much rather be here with this lot.' He nodded to the crowd of actors by the table drinking coffee and chatting, an affectionate smile suffusing his features. Aoife suddenly saw why he was so good at what he did. Behind all his tough words and bully-boy attitude, he adored these people and there was nowhere he'd rather be on a cold Sunday morning than in a chilly auditorium with them.

When Conor had gone, she wound her way over to the table and approached Margaret. 'Sorry about that,' she said to her. 'Conor's been really helpful, but I didn't expect him to be here today.'

'Oh, don't mind Conor,' Margaret said with a dismissive wave of her hand. 'I'm well used to him.'

'But he's so rude!'

'He is.' Margaret nodded, unperturbed.

'You do a piece from *Hedda Gabler* if you want to.'

'Oh no.' She shook her head vehemently. 'This is about making money for Halfpenny Lane, and Conor's right.' She gave a rueful smile. 'Unfortunately, he's always right.'

As Aoife mingled with the actors, she was touched by how affectionately everyone spoke of Detta and their fond memories of her theatre. She'd always known their great-aunt was lauded as a supremely talented actress, but she hadn't realised she'd been so highly regarded as a director, producer and mentor. She'd used Halfpenny Lane to nurture the talents of so many, and given generations of young actors their first experience of performing on a professional stage.

Anxious to show her appreciation to everyone who'd come, she tried to put aside how star-struck she felt as she wound her way over to Rafe Bradshaw and approached him shyly. It was surreal to see him here, helping himself to custard creams on a Sunday morning in a disused theatre.

'Thanks for being part of this,' she said. 'It's really good of you.'

He turned to her and Aoife was overcome by how tall and handsome he was. 'Not at all. My pleasure. Detta gave me my very first part, you know.'

'Oh! I didn't know that.'

'Just a little walk-on in a production of *A Woman of No Importance*. But yes, this was where it all started for me.' He glanced around the auditorium. 'I'm glad to do whatever I can to help save the place. It'd be a tragedy to lose it.'

As they chatted, Aoife noticed Sive talking to Tom and Shay. She tried to concentrate on what Rafe was saying, but she couldn't help worrying about the conversation her sister was having and what she might be agreeing to. Mindful of Conor's advice, she itched to rush over and intervene.

'Excuse me a minute, I just need to have a word with my sister,' she said to Rafe. She immediately made a beeline for Sive, ready to diplomatically steer Tom away from his beloved Krapp.

But as she approached, she heard Sive saying firmly 'No Beckett except *Godot*, and then only the funniest bits.' Clearly, Conor had briefed her too. It was the most broadly comedic moment in the play.

'So "we'll hang ourselves tomorrow",' Tom said, smiling.

'Perfect!'

'You just want to see me with my trousers down,' Shay said, laughing good-naturedly.

Aoife smiled to herself, surprised but pleased that Sive didn't need her help. She had this in hand. As she swerved away, she spotted Mimi talking to Jonathan – badgering him, by the looks of it. She recognised Mimi's combative stance, arms folded across her chest. She decided to rescue him.

'What *are* you doing here, then?' Mimi was saying as Aoife approached.

'I thought I could help with the show.' He turned to Aoife and smiled as she joined them.

'Oh, really? I didn't know you could act. What shall we put you down for? Something from *Doctor Faustus* perhaps?'

'"Was this the face that launched a thousand ships",' Jonathan quoted.

'I was thinking more of the bit where he makes a deal with the devil.'

'Anyway, I can't act,' Jonathan said, ignoring Mimi's waspishness.

'No? What were you thinking you'd do, then? Sing a song? Do a tap dance? Do you juggle?'

Jonathan laughed. 'No, I wasn't suggesting I perform. Believe me, nobody wants to see that. But I could help in more practical ways. I thought maybe I could get some corporate sponsorship, advertising for the programme, that sort of thing. I know everyone here is working for free, but it will still cost money to put the show on.'

'It will,' Aoife interrupted before Mimi could say anything. 'We have to pay for the printing of the programme for one thing. Not to mention advertising flyers and posters …'

Mimi nodded reluctantly. 'You're right. Sponsorship is a good idea,' she said grudgingly to Jonathan. 'Well, I suppose we should call this meeting to order,' she said, as Sive came to join them.

'One of us should say something,' Sive said. 'Thank them all for coming, before we get down to business making plans for the show.'

'I'll do it,' Aoife said.

'The three of us should do it,' Mimi said. 'We're all asking for help, not just you. We're in this together.'

A hush fell over the gathering as the three sisters stepped up onto the stage. Aoife and Sive said a few words thanking everyone for their support and for giving so generously of their time and expertise. But they let Mimi do most of the talking, and everyone listened enraptured as she spoke about their hopes for reviving Halfpenny Lane and carrying on their great-aunt's legacy. There were more than a few people brushing away tears as she told them how much it would have meant to Detta to see them all there.

'Everyone here knows of Detta's lifelong devotion to this place,' she said. 'This theatre was her great love. Hopefully with your help, my sisters and I can give it a new lease of life and it'll be the dawn of a new era for Halfpenny Lane,' she finished to cheers and clapping.

'That went well,' Aoife said later that afternoon, when the last of the actors had finally trailed out of the auditorium. They'd seemed reluctant to leave and go their separate ways, so happy to be catching up with old friends and enjoying each other's company. Aoife was buoyed up by the enthusiastic response to the fundraising effort. Everyone was so keen to get stuck in and help, each of them seeming as personally invested in the project as if it was their own.

After Mimi spoke, they settled down to planning the programme for the show. They'd already worked out a schedule with performance times, and by the end of the afternoon, they'd filled every slot. They themselves were slated to do an excerpt from *Three Sisters*, which Margaret

Brennan's husband Neil, a distinguished playwright, was going to adapt especially for the occasion.

'I'm so excited!' Sive squealed, looking down at the schedule in Aoife's lap. 'It's going to be an amazing show.'

'It is.' Aoife beamed. It wouldn't be enough. They might never make enough to save the theatre. But at least if this was to be its last show, Halfpenny Lane would go out with a bang.

10

AOIFE TRUDGED home from a wearying day at work when it seemed like everything that could go wrong did go wrong. She'd slept out the alarm and had to forego a shower, so she'd felt grungy and not properly awake all day. The tram had been too full and she'd had to walk, so despite skipping breakfast, she'd been late anyway. Then she'd made a silly error on a spreadsheet and got a bollocking from her boss. It was freezing cold and sleeting, her boots were leaking, her feet were soaking wet, and she was utterly miserable. She was looking forward to a long hot shower, a warm house, a nice dinner, and an evening of vegging out in front of the fire.

At the gate, she shucked off her boots and threw them in the bin, in case she'd forget how useless they were and be tempted to wear them ever again. She knew that once she got inside, she wouldn't want to go out again, and her feet couldn't get any wetter anyway. She pulled off her sopping wet coat in the hall and hung it on the coat stand to drip onto the mat below, then padded down the hall in her socks, leaving a wet trail behind her. The kitchen door was closed, and there was an A4 sheet of paper taped to it with the words 'Enter quietly – recording in progress' scrawled on it in Sharpie. She pushed the door open slowly and tiptoed inside. Sive was standing with her back to Aoife, filming on her mobile phone while Mimi mimed … an air steward demonstrating the location of the emergency exits Aoife guessed from the way she was gesticulating with her arms. She crept over to stand beside Sive and watch as Mimi continued, an uncharacteristically placid smile on her face as she hunkered down and picked something up from the floor, handing it to an imaginary person.

'Okay, cut,' Sive said, stopping the video.

Mimi sprang to her feet, her smile vanishing.

'What are you doing?' Aoife asked.

'Audition tape,' Mimi said. 'It's just an extra job for an airline ad.'

'Is this the brief?' Aoife pointed to an email printout on the table.

Mimi nodded. 'Yeah.'

Aoife picked it up and read. The role was for an air steward, and the instructions were to mime helping passengers put luggage into the overhead bins, do part of the safety demonstration, and improvise anything else they saw fit.

'So what were you doing there?' Aoife nodded to the floor.

'A child dropped their teddy and I was handing it back to them.'

'Good idea.'

Mimi took the phone from Sive and replayed the video, and they all huddled together to watch. 'Do you think it's okay? Do I need to go again?' she asked when it ended.

Sive and Aoife both pronounced it perfect.

'You don't think I look like a lobotomised Moonie?'

'Is that what you were going for?' Sive asked, and Mimi gave her a playful shove. 'Hey, I was going to say you missed the mark, if it was. It's great.'

'The money's not bad,' Mimi said, 'especially if I get featured – and depending on how long the ad runs and where it's shown, of course.'

'She's doing it for Halfpenny Lane,' Sive told Aoife proudly.

'I know it's a drop in the ocean, but—'

'Every little helps,' Aoife said, trying to sound positive. Mimi rarely considered extra work, but ads paid well, especially if you got a featured role.

'That arrived for you.' Sive nodded to a large white envelope on the table addressed to Aoife. She knew what it was, even before she saw the estate agent's stamp on it, and her heart sank.

'I'll open it later,' she said, looking at her sisters' expectant faces. 'First I need a shower and to change out of these clothes.' She suspected she needed a lot more inner strength than she had right now to face whatever was in that envelope.

'Oh, you poor thing!' Sive exclaimed, taking one of Aoife's icy hands. 'You're frozen! You go and have a shower, and we'll have dinner ready for you when you come down.'

'There's dinner?'

'Of course there's dinner,' Mimi said. 'What do you take us for? You don't think it took me all day to research the role of trolley-dolly shoving a suitcase into the overhead bin, do you?'

'There's chicken pie,' Sive said.

Aoife was almost teary with gratitude – which confirmed it was the right decision to leave opening that envelope until she was warm and dry and had some hot food inside her. She clearly wasn't in any emotional state for dealing with it at the moment. She needed to regroup before she could take any more punches today.

Standing under a scalding hot shower for far longer than necessary worked wonders to thaw her icy skin, massage her weary limbs and lift her mood. She changed into a pair of soft joggers, a fluffy hooded sweatshirt, and a pair of slipper boots over thick socks, and returned to the kitchen revived and refreshed, and more awake than she'd been since throwing herself out of bed at seven this morning.

'Drink!' Mimi handed her a glass of red wine as soon as she stepped into the room. The table was set for three, and there were delicious smells emanating from the oven.

Aoife took a sip and closed her eyes, feeling all her muscles soften and relax. Even the envelope that still sat in the middle of the table didn't seem so threatening anymore. She pretty much already knew what was going to be in it anyway. She couldn't predict the exact figure, of course – but whatever it was, it would be too much; more than they could ever hope to raise.

Still, as she picked up the envelope and tore it open, she couldn't shake off a last faint vestige of hope that by some miracle the survey would have unearthed an underlying problem that would seriously undermine the theatre's value.

Her sisters stood either side of her as she slid out the estate agent's report, and they all read it together in silence.

'Dagnabbit!' Aoife said, as she skimmed over the contents, her eyes going straight to the bottom line. The estimated value was two million euro.

'Damn and blast!'

'Oh no!'

Aoife threw the report onto the table. 'Well,' she said dully. 'I guess that's that.'

'No! It can't be!'

'Let's not be defeatist,' Mimi said. 'We haven't even had the fundraiser yet.'

Aoife shook her head. 'It doesn't matter. You can see for yourself.' She waved to the report. 'We'd need half a million just to buy Jonathan out. There's no way we're going to make that kind of money with a fundraiser, no matter how successful it is.' She thought of all those people who were donating their services for free because they wanted to see Halfpenny Lane get back on its feet. That was never going to happen now, and she felt like a fraud for letting them think it could. She hadn't deliberately deceived anyone, but it had been wishful thinking from the start, and she shouldn't have drawn other people into their pie-in-the-sky scheme.

'There must be something else we can do,' Sive said.

'Like what?'

'Mimi is doing this ad for starters.'

'I haven't got it yet,' Mimi reminded her sister, looking dejected. Aoife felt awful for bursting their bubble. They'd both been so excited and optimistic earlier.

'Well, let's think about it later,' she said, 'after dinner. I'm starving, and that pie smells amazing.'

The pie was creamy and comforting, and Sive had made buttered carrots the way their mother used to cook them, with lots of salt and garlic. It should have been balm to her battered soul, but there was an air of despondency around the table as they ate in silence, each lost in their own gloomy thoughts.

'We could have another fundraising event,' Sive piped up eventually, and it was obvious they'd all been brooding on the same thing.

Mimi shook her head. 'Even if we had ten fundraisers, we could never make that amount.' She nodded to the valuation report that still lay on the table like a dark cloud, throwing a pall over everything.

'I think we have to face facts.' Aoife pushed her plate away as she finished eating. 'We're going to have to sell.' She hated saying it, but they had to face up to the reality. The fact was they were out of options.

'Unless we could persuade Jonathan to give us more time,' Mimi mused.

'We'd need a lifetime to earn that kind of money from the theatre.'

They all sighed as the hopelessness of the situation sank in.

'Do you think we should call off the fundraising concert?' Aoife asked tentatively.

'No!' Mimi and Sive answered in unison.

'Everyone would be so disappointed,' Sive said. 'You saw how glad they all were to help. They all want to do something to save Halfpenny Lane.'

'But if it can't be saved …'

'We can't be certain of that,' Mimi said. 'Not until we've at least tried. The concert may not raise enough on its own, but you never know what it might lead to.'

'And what about Conor O'Neill?' Sive said. 'He's been so helpful rounding up support and letting us use Players. We can't throw that back in his face.'

Aoife nodded. 'You're right. Everyone's been so generous with their time and efforts. Even if we end up losing the theatre, at least they can feel they did all they could.'

11

'I THINK we should do the concert at Halfpenny Lane,' Aoife announced to her sisters at breakfast the next morning. She'd been thinking about it last night in bed when she couldn't sleep, her mind whirring with ideas about how they could save the theatre.

'Really?' Mimi frowned.

'It was good of Conor to offer us Players,' Aoife said, 'but I think we should get people into Halfpenny Lane. It's important to remind them what's at stake – what we'll be losing if we can't save it. It's all very well people being nostalgic about the place, but we need to show them that it doesn't have to be consigned to history. It can be a vibrant, living part of the city again.' It might also be their only opportunity to perform on the stage or see the auditorium filled with an audience one last time. But she kept that thought to herself.

'But is it in any condition to hold an event like that? Is it even safe to allow the public into it?'

'And what about permits and licences?' Sive asked. 'It's been a long time since it's been used as a venue.' The last time the theatre had been open to the public had been for an interview with a panel of authors during the Dublin Book Festival a couple of years ago.

Aoife nodded. 'We need to look into all that, of course. But if we can sort out that side of it, I think we can get it into good enough shape for a one-off event like this. It doesn't have to be perfect.'

'I like the idea of doing it in Halfpenny Lane,' Mimi said. 'But it's got less than half the capacity of Players. We wouldn't be able to make as much money. Or does that not matter, because you think it's a lost cause anyway?' She narrowed her eyes at Aoife suspiciously.

'I don't think it's a lost cause,' Aoife protested. 'I admit I'm not optimistic, but I haven't given up hope.'

Mimi regarded her, chewing silently. 'It would be a more exclusive event,' she said finally. 'I suppose we could charge more for tickets.'

'Yes, it'll be unique – not just the show, but the venue. I think the whole thing will have more impact. It's all about Halfpenny Lane, so we should get people in there – show them what they've been missing.'

'You're right,' Mimi said. 'We should do it.'

'Let's put the show on in the barn!' Sive grinned.

'Come on, it's not that bad.' Mimi laughed. 'Almost, but not quite. But it would be wonderful to perform on the stage at Halfpenny Lane for real,' she said dreamily.

Her sisters had never had the chance to perform at Halfpenny Lane as professionals – only play-acting in front of their family. She knew how much it would mean to them to step out onto that stage in front of a full auditorium, and she wanted that for them – even if it was for the first and last time, which she was beginning to suspect it would be.

'It would be amazing to see it full and buzzing again, with a living, breathing audience,' Sive said.

Aoife saw the transformation already in the way they were thinking about the concert, and was convinced she'd had the right idea. Her sisters were remembering what it was like in its heyday – vital and exciting, a lively part of the cultural life of the city. Hopefully others would too once they got them through the doors.

'It would be a great tribute to Detta too,' Mimi said, and they were all silent for a moment, their eyes welling up.

'Oh!' Sive gasped suddenly. 'Who's going to tell Conor thanks but no thanks?'

'I will,' Aoife said. 'I'll call him this morning. And I'll tell Jonathan too.'

'Do we have to involve him?' Mimi's lip curled.

'Yes,' Aoife told her firmly. 'He's a co-owner, whether we like it or not.'

'Not,' Mimi said sulkily.

'Be that as it may, he's entitled to be included. He probably won't even be interested, but we should at least keep him in the loop.'

Aoife called Conor later on her morning break at work. To her relief, he was perfectly sanguine about the change of plan – even agreeing with her that it was a much better idea if they could pull it off.

'Get people into the building and pull on the old heart-strings,' he said. 'Good thinking! A picture paints a thousand words and all that. Well done.'

Aoife felt like she'd been knighted by a king. She rang Jonathan next, expecting him to be only vaguely interested at best. So she was taken aback when he immediately started talking logistics.

'We'll need to look into the regulations for holding an event like that. And have you thought about public liability insurance?'

'Yes, of course,' Aoife said, irritated that he'd assume she wouldn't have. 'I was going to start working on all that today. We only decided to go this way this morning.'

'It might take some time if we have to get any permits or licences. The Council aren't renowned for their efficiency. We should look into that as soon as possible.'

And by 'we' of course he meant her and her sisters, Aoife thought sourly. She was beginning to regret insisting that they involve him if all he was going to do was throw his weight around and dictate to them from his lofty tower.

'Anything you want me to do, let me know,' he continued. 'We should probably go through the place again with a view to what needs to be done to get it ready for a public event.'

'Of course. We're going to do that.'

'How are you fixed this week?'

Oh! He was planning to come too? 'Um … I'm at work today and tomorrow. I'm free in the evening.'

'It'd be better to go in daylight, don't you think? How about Saturday?'

'I can do Saturday. But Sive's at a workshop all weekend (she didn't have to tell him that it was an origami workshop) and Mimi's filming in Wicklow.' She'd got a small part in an episode of a TV costume drama.

'Well, the two of us could go? I think it's important to get an idea of where we stand as soon as possible. Then we can start arranging whatever work needs to be done first thing next week.'

'Yes, you're right. I'll meet you on Saturday.'

They arranged to meet at Halfpenny Lane on Saturday morning, and Aoife hung up feeling dazed.

'It was nice of him to offer,' Aoife said to her sisters the next morning at breakfast as they discussed the planned meeting, anxious to put a positive spin on it. She didn't want them to feel they were being left out or that Jonathan was muscling in and taking over. But she needn't have worried.

'Only right he should put in some work for his half a mil,' Mimi said haughtily.

Sive took a more kindly – and romantic – view of it. 'He's using it as an excuse to spend more time with you,' she said to Aoife with a sly smile. 'I told you he was sweet on you.'

'He's just looking after his investment,' Mimi said. 'No offence,' she added hastily, grabbing Aoife's arm.

'None taken.' Aoife tried to ignore the rush of pleasure she'd felt at Sive's suggestion. She didn't want Jonathan Hunt to be 'sweet on her', she told herself, annoyed by how much she liked the idea. It was just a stupid crush, but she'd get over it. She couldn't let herself fall for someone her sisters regarded as Public Enemy Number One.

However, she was glad of his assistance. She couldn't help being irritated that it was always left to her to take care of practicalities, while her sisters could just sit back and do nothing, safe in the knowledge that everything would somehow magically turn out all right. It must be nice, she thought, to sail through life without a care in the world, knowing that there would always be food on the table and shoes on your feet without having to worry about where they came from. Just once she'd like to be able to relax and let someone else take charge.

'I have to go,' Mimi said, taking one last gulp of coffee. 'It's going to take me the best part of two hours to get to this location in the middle of bloody nowhere. It's two buses, and a fifteen-minute walk at either end.'

Aoife felt bad for her uncharitable thoughts as she watched her sister pull on her coat and rush out the door. Mimi worked damn hard, and she was never less than professional – always punctual and prepared, fully committed to even the smallest, most insignificant role.

This morning she was heading out into the icy cold to spend half the day on public transport and standing at wind-blasted bus stops, and the rest of it shivering in a freezing field between takes, all for the sake of a couple of lines and a few minutes of film. But she threw herself into it cheerfully and wholeheartedly and never grumbled about the early mornings or the long days. She'd come home tonight after midnight, exhausted, frozen to the bone, starving, and completely blissed out about getting to do what she loved for another day.

Aoife couldn't grudge Sive her singing classes or tai chi workshops either. She worked hard all week, washing floors and scrubbing toilets, and she went for every acting job she was eligible for, even the most lowly extra work. She and Mimi always made dinner if they were home before Aoife, and they both contributed to the house and their life together in their own ways.

They deserved Halfpenny Lane – and the theatre deserved them. Aoife wanted it for them so badly it hurt. They'd dreamt of it for too long, worked too hard for it to be snatched away from them now. She just hoped she could find a way to save it for them.

12

'So, you got the valuation report?' Jonathan said when she met him in the foyer of the theatre on Saturday.

'Yes.' Aoife hung her head, reminded once again how futile this whole endeavour was before they'd even begun.

Jonathan raised his eyebrows. 'Why so glum?'

'It was worse than I'd thought. I mean, I had a pretty good idea what the valuation would be, but I was still hoping I was wrong.'

'I've never seen anyone look so unhappy about finding out they've inherited a small fortune. You'd have preferred if Detta had left you a worthless wreck?'

'Honestly, yes. Because then we'd have more hope of buying you out and keeping this place.'

Jonathan sighed. 'Sorry. I truly am, Aoife.' He met her eyes, and his were full of sincerity. 'But if this is my cue to tell you I'm going to sign my share over to you, that's not going to happen.'

'No, I know.' She struggled to look like she didn't mind. 'Of course not. I wouldn't expect that.'

'Good. At least we know where we stand. And you never know, maybe your fundraiser will be a rip-roaring success and you'll be able to buy me out twice over.'

'Yeah, fingers crossed.' Aoife smiled weakly, but she knew there was precious little chance of that.

'So,' he rubbed his hands briskly, his tone business-like, 'let's get started.'

They'd already done a tour of the building on the day of the will reading, but this time they had a specific goal in mind, and they listed the bare minimum that would need to be done to open to the public and put on a show. Aoife was grateful for Jonathan's pragmatism and objectivity as they walked around and made notes. She decided it was a good thing her sisters weren't available this morning. Jonathan had no sentimental attachment to the theatre and was completely focused on the task at hand. If Sive and Mimi were here, the three of them would inevitably start looking through the costumes and bits of memorabilia that were lying around, and then spend half the morning reminiscing about the old days.

When they'd done a quick walkabout, they sat on a couple of the less threadbare seats in the auditorium and went over their notes.

'I checked, and the public liability insurance is still in place,' Aoife said, pulling a notebook from her bag. 'Detta occasionally rented the theatre out for festival events and stuff, so she'd kept up the insurance. We'll need to apply for a new licence if we want to serve alcohol, though.'

'We should be able to get a temporary licence for a one-off event easily enough,' Jonathan said, making a note on his pad. 'I'll get one of my juniors to handle that.'

Aoife realised how useful Jonathan could be as an ally with his legal contacts, and was once again glad he was involved.

'At least we know it's structurally sound,' Jonathan said. 'The survey didn't throw up any major issues, so it's mainly cosmetic stuff apart from a few minor things that need fixing.'

'I've already ordered some skips for next week, so we can start clearing out the junk. Then the main thing is a lot of spit and polish.'

Jonathan nodded, glancing around. 'It looks daunting, but it probably won't take too much to get it looking decent. Especially if you keep the lighting low.'

Aoife laughed.

'All the better anyway if it doesn't look too perfect. You don't want people to think you don't really need the money when you've got the begging bowl out. If it looks a bit shabby and down on its luck, it'll remind them what they're here for.'

'A lot of this we can do ourselves,' Aoife said, running a finger down the list.

'Well, don't knock yourselves out. I'm happy to roll up my sleeves and get stuck in, but it might be more cost-efficient to get professionals in to do most of it. It wouldn't cost so much split four ways.'

'Well, realistically, it'd be split two ways. I'm the main breadwinner in our household.'

'What is it you do?'

'I'm an accounting technician.'

Jonathan looked startled. 'That's not what I was expecting. Why accounting?' he asked, putting his pen down and turning in his seat to give her his full attention. 'You couldn't find anything further removed from all this?' He waved a hand towards the stage.

Aoife smiled. 'Well, it wasn't my original intention. I'd planned to go to acting school like Mimi and Sive. But I like it.'

'What do you like about it?' His eyes were intent on her and it seemed like he genuinely wanted to know. No one else had ever asked her that question except in a mocking or teasing way, and she wasn't sure she'd ever really thought about it seriously. But the answer came readily enough.

'I like the certainty of numbers. It's right or wrong; there's no grey area, no room for wiggle—'

'Try telling that to some accountants I know,' Jonathan said dryly.

She laughed. 'I suppose I like putting order on things. It calms me.'

'You don't like chaos.'

'No, I guess not.'

'So maybe the real question is why acting? Were you just doing it to please your sisters? Or because it's what was expected of you?'

Aoife shook her head. 'No. It's just – I can't explain it. I feel so alive when I'm on a stage. It's like an out-of-body experience. I don't know how to describe it. It's as if I'm flying. It sounds crazy, but I've never been more myself than when I'm playing a part, pretending to be someone else.'

'And you've never had this out-of-body experience doing accounts?'

Aoife laughed. 'I can't say I have.'

'So what happened to acting school?'

'When our parents died, someone had to be the grown-up; get a sensible job.'

'And that had to be you?'

'I was the eldest. We needed the money. So I did an

arts degree instead of acting school, and then I trained as an accounting technician.'

'That must have been hard.'

'I told myself I was just deferring it for a couple of years, that I'd go later once Sive and Mimi had finished school. But then it never seemed like the right time. They worked part-time jobs while they were students, but it was never enough. Even when they started working as actors, they still weren't earning much. And I was making good money. I had a steady, reliable income. It seemed silly to give that up. It was easier to just keep working.'

'It doesn't sound like it was easy at all.'

He was looking at her intently, his eyes full of concern, and Aoife felt something happening to her face. It was crumbling and there was nothing she could do to stop it.

'Come here,' he said, and suddenly she realised there were tears spilling from her eyes and rolling down her cheeks. He reached across the seat and pulled her into his arms. She felt herself melt and collapse, all the hurt and anguish of those years suddenly bubbling up and pouring out of her, and all she could think was why now; why here; why him?

But he was right. It hadn't been easy. It had been difficult and stressful, and she'd felt unbearably lonely at times.

Jonathan didn't shush her or say anything. He just let her sob while he held her and stroked her hair.

'Sorry,' she said finally, brushing her eyes as she pulled away. 'I don't know what that was about.'

'You're grieving,' he said simply.

'Hardly.' She swiped roughly at her eyes and sniffed. 'You know Detta hadn't really been there for a while. I miss her, of course. But we'd already lost her. It was a relief more than anything when she died.'

'But what about your parents?'

She shook her head. 'That was a long time ago.'

'I get the feeling maybe you didn't grieve at the time.'

She frowned, considering. Perhaps he was right. 'Maybe I didn't,' she said. 'Not properly. There was no time.' There'd been no room for her to give in to her emotions and fall apart when she was trying to stay positive for Sive and Mimi, and keep them all moving forward. 'Someone had to hold things together.'

It had been an awful time, if she stopped to think about it – which she'd never let herself do really. It was too hard, too painful for her to dwell on. Sive had been inconsolable, and Aoife had focused all her energy on getting her to eat, trying to persuade her to leave her room, go to school, live her life. Mimi had been as much of a worry, going out of her way to make life difficult for Aoife, as if she was trying to punish her for taking the place of their parents.

They'd been dark, desolate days after their parents died. Even though she'd had her sisters, Aoife had felt so alone – abandoned and adrift, with no one to comfort or console her – and at the same time plagued by guilt for feeling that way. She knew their parents would never have left them if they'd had a choice. But she'd felt so weighed down by the responsibility of caring for her sisters and supporting them in their loss. There had hardly been time for her own grief.

She'd cry at night, alone in her room, but then she'd get up the next day and try to make things normal – making sure everyone ate, getting Sive and Mimi out to school on time with clean uniforms, packed lunches and the right books in their bags. She'd tried to make her sisters feel secure and that they had someone to rely on. But she'd had no one to lean on herself, and she'd wanted that so badly. She hated to admit it even to herself, but sometimes she'd resented Sive and Mimi's abandoned outpourings of grief, when she couldn't afford to let go and give in to her own.

'I think you've been holding onto that for quite a long time,' Jonathan said softly.

She shrugged. 'Someone had to keep the show on the road.'

'Ah! The show.'

She gave a little laugh. 'It must go on, you know.'

'Maybe sometimes it's okay to just let things slide. Try letting go now and then and see what happens.'

She narrowed her eyes at him. Was this what he'd been up to all along? Was he taking advantage of her meltdown, acting all kind and caring, and then using her moment of weakness against her to persuade her to give up on the theatre? Well, she was damned if that was going to happen.

'There are other people in the world, Aoife,' he said. When she looked up at him from under her lashes, his eyes were full of kindness and she knew she'd misjudged him. 'Your sisters are more capable than you think. They might surprise you if you let them. Maybe you had to take over back then – be the parent and hold everything together. But they're all grown up now. They can look after themselves.'

'You mean the world might not fall apart without me?' she said with a wry smile.

'No guarantees, but you never know.'

She dug a handkerchief out of her pocket and wiped her eyes. 'You might be right,' she said. She knew what he said made sense, but the thought of relinquishing control was scary.

'How about some lunch?' Jonathan asked.

She nodded. 'Lunch would be lovely. It turns out melt-downs make you quite hungry. Who knew?'

13

THEY WENT to a nearby Italian restaurant with a warm, cosy atmosphere, and Aoife luxuriated in letting someone else take care of her for a change. They both ordered pasta, and a bottle of wine to share. As a bowl of crab linguine was placed in front of her, Aoife felt a momentary twinge of guilt that she wasn't sharing this treat with her sisters. But then she dismissed it. It was okay for her to have something just for herself now and then.

'Sorry about the meltdown,' she said, winding linguine onto her fork.

'Don't apologise. I think you needed that. You've been under a lot of strain – not just recently, but since your parents died. You've been looking after your sisters, holding it all together, worrying about money ...'

Aoife nodded, grateful for his understanding, and took a large gulp of wine. She was afraid she'd start crying again if she tried to speak.

'Look, I'm not saying this to be mean, or because I want to take the money and run, but mightn't it be a relief to just ... let go?'

'Of the theatre?'

He held up a hand placatingly. 'It's just a suggestion. But have you given it any serious thought? I mean, *really* considered what it could mean for you?'

'Of course I have,' she said indignantly. It was a knee-jerk response. But had she? A fleeting thought had drifted across her mind from time to time, but she'd quickly dismissed it and shut it down. It felt disloyal and ungrateful, like she'd be cashing in on all Detta's years of hard work and dedication.

'You'd have money … freedom. You could do whatever you wanted – go to drama school, build your own theatre, travel …'

She wondered had Mimi and Sive ever thought about the advantages of selling Halfpenny Lane. She tried to imagine what it would be like to have that money – the freedom it would bring. But she had an immediate visceral reaction at the thought of giving up Halfpenny Lane, as if he was suggesting giving away her baby.

'It seems to me that place is putting a huge burden on you.'

She shook her head. 'I couldn't do it. Not if I have a choice.'

'Okay. I'm not trying to persuade you either way here. I just want you to properly think about it.'

'I could go to Moscow,' she said faintly. 'We could all go to Moscow.'

She didn't expect Jonathan to get the reference but he smiled and said '"To Moscow, and as quickly as possible." Detta was always quoting that line.'

Aoife felt oddly comforted that he understood what she'd meant – the shorthand she normally only shared with her sisters. It was like discovering they both spoke the same rare, almost extinct language. 'It was one of her catch-phrases.'

'That and "the show must go gangbusters"!'

Aoife laughed fondly.

'I hadn't seen Detta for a while – not before, you know …' Jonathan trailed off.

'While she was still herself, you mean?'

He nodded. 'I feel terrible about that now.'

'You were living abroad. And you always visited her when you were home, didn't you?'

'Usually, yes. I tried to. But I didn't get back as often as I should have.'

'She used to tell us when you'd been to see her and fill us in on what you were doing. I didn't know you'd moved back to Dublin, though.'

'It was about a year and a half ago, not long before Dad died. She did know – at least I told her. But she was quite confused at that stage. Sometimes she didn't even know who I was. And the last few times I saw her, she wasn't conscious.'

Aoife nodded. 'We used to visit every day. The three of us had a rota. We did it in shifts, so there was always someone there at least once a day. Mostly twice.'

'She was lucky to have you.'

'I don't know how much difference it made – if any. She never woke up again. She didn't know we were there. Some of the nurses said that if you talked to her, she'd hear you on some level. But I'm not sure I believe that.'

'But you did it anyway?'

'Yes. How did you know?'

'It just seems like something you'd do. If you thought there was any chance it might give her some comfort.'

'I spoke to her. We all did – just told her about our day or whatever. Nonsense really.' She smiled. 'I think I knew she couldn't hear me when she didn't rear up and tell me I was being boring. Or harangue me about becoming an accountant.'

Jonathan chuckled. 'Yep, that sounds like her.'

'So you didn't come back to Ireland often when you lived in London?'

'No, not that often. And when I did, I was catching up with friends and spending time with Dad and Sam—'

'Sam?'

'My brother.'

'Oh yes!' She'd forgotten he had a brother.

'But I should have made more of an effort to visit Detta whenever I was home.'

'Well, I don't think she was ever lonely, if it's any consolation.'

'No, she was always busy, living her life, wasn't she? Until she wasn't.'

'Yeah.' Aoife put down her fork and pushed her empty bowl away. 'So, what about you?' she asked, determinedly changing the subject. The afternoon was descending into melancholy, and she didn't want to risk another meltdown. 'Did you always want to be a lawyer?'

'Well, not always.' He smiled. 'I mean, it's not what kids dream of, is it?'

'No.' Aoife laughed. 'It's certainly not up there with fireman or superhero.'

'Architect,' he said, jerking a thumb at himself. 'That's what I wanted to be from the ages of six to about ten.'

Aoife raised her eyebrows. 'That sounds like a very sensible career choice for a six-year-old.'

'My head was turned by Minecraft.'

'Ah, right. That makes sense.'

'How about you? Did you always want to be an actress?'

'Pretty much. I mean, obviously accountancy was my dream when I was little—'

'Obviously,' he said with a smirk.

'But then I grew up and realised I'd have to get a proper job, so I decided to be an actress. It was what we all wanted to do. We were always putting on shows for our parents and Detta. How they must have suffered!'

'I'm sure they loved it.'

She smiled. 'They were very good at pretending they did at least. Though Dad was a bit worried about Detta's influence on us. He was afraid we'd follow her lead and end up broke and unemployable.'

'You could have done a lot worse. Detta was very happy.'

'She was. And hugely respected. But she didn't have much stability in her life.'

'Is that why you went into accountancy? To please your dad?'

'No, he wouldn't have wanted that. He'd come to terms with us all being penniless actresses if that's what we wanted.'

Jonathan was silent for a moment. 'I really want us to find a way you can keep the theatre,' he said finally.

'Oh?' Aoife reared back in her seat, surprised. 'That's a bit of a sudden change of heart?'

'I can see how much it means to you – all three of you. It doesn't seem fair for me to stop you.'

'It's perfectly fair. It's your inheritance too, and you have just as much right to decide what we do with it.'

'Not really. There's three of you and only one of me. So I'd be outnumbered on any democratic vote.'

'Well, that's not how wills work, as you know. We don't get to vote you off the island.' Aoife was no longer sure she wanted to, even if she could. Detta had wanted him to have this money. She must have had her reasons.

'Perhaps I have other motives for wanting to keep it.' He looked down at his fingers, toying with his glass.

'Such as?'

'I'd really like to see you in *Three Sisters*.'

Aoife cleared her throat, shifting in her seat. 'Well, you won't. No one will see that, no matter what happens. I'm doing the scene for the benefit concert, but that's it. Anyway, even if I wanted to, I don't think the grand reopening of Halfpenny Lane is going to happen. There's no way this benefit concert can raise enough money.'

'What if you had more time?'

'You mean … what? Are you changing your mind about selling?'

'No. I just mean we could hold off on putting the theatre on the market right away – give you some time to explore your options, maybe do a longer fundraising campaign. Clearly one benefit concert isn't going to raise enough, but you never know what else it might lead to.'

'I thought you were in more of a hurry for the money?'

'I can wait – just not for ever,' Jonathan said, looking uncomfortable.

'How much time are you talking about?'

'I could give it a month. I know it's not much, but we don't know how long it might take to sell.'

She nodded.

'If you can't come up with a way to buy me out by then, we put it on the market. What do you think?'

Aoife chewed this over. There was no way they could raise that kind of money in a year, let alone one month. But it would be a reprieve, a stay of execution for Halfpenny Lane. It would give them some breathing room … and who knew what might happen in the meantime? Maybe they could come up with some other ideas for financing it.

'Why?' She narrowed her eyes at him. 'Why would you do that? What's in it for you?'

'Nothing financially. But Detta loved that place, and I'm sure she would have wanted it to stay in the family. And I know how much it means to you and your sisters. I'd like you to have a fair shot at keeping it, if it's at all possible. I don't think it is, mind,' he added. 'But I'd be very happy for you to prove me wrong.'

'Not as happy as I'd be.'

'So, what do you say? Deal?' He lifted his glass.

'I'll have to discuss it with my sisters.' Aoife bit her lip. 'But I can't see them not agreeing. So, subject to their approval, yes,' she said, raising her glass and clinking it against his. 'You've got a deal.'

14

Of course Mimi and Sive were delighted when Aoife told them Jonathan had agreed to delay putting the theatre up for sale.

'I knew he was soft on you!' Sive crowed delightedly. 'This is great!'

'We'll still need money to keep it going and do all the work that's needed on the building,' Aoife said. 'That's on top of his share.'

'It gives us more time to come up with the funds,' Mimi said. 'And once we've bought Jonathan out, we can run the theatre on a shoestring and renovate it at our leisure.'

'Yeah.' Aoife sighed. 'So *all* we have to do is find a way to make half a million by June.'

'And we will!' Sive said. 'I have every faith in us.'

Aoife didn't share Sive's conviction, but now that there was a chance, however unlikely, that they could succeed in saving Halfpenny Lane, she threw herself into organising the fundraiser with renewed energy and enthusiasm. At least she didn't feel like a total fraud asking people to support a project that was doomed to fail from the start.

She took some leave from work to focus on getting the show ready. There was so much to do – organising cleaners and skips, getting the programme finalised and printed, ordering drinks and ice creams, recruiting volunteers to help front of house … the list was endless. She'd never been busier in her life. It was stressful and exhausting, and she loved every minute of it.

Sive had done a great job of canvassing local businesses and getting them to donate prizes for the raffle, and Jonathan had enlisted a couple of corporate sponsors to fund the show so that the expenses were covered and all the profits would go towards Halfpenny Lane.

'See? Even our arch nemesis wants to help!' Sive said when she heard.

'He's not our arch nemesis,' Aoife said.

Fortunately, all the actors were reprising performances of pieces they knew well, so there was very little rehearsal needed. It was more a matter of coordinating the various performances so that they flowed together, and working out sets, lighting and staging. Conor O'Neill's brother Lorcan had volunteered to direct – or been strong-armed into it, Aoife wasn't sure which. But he was a dream to work with – clever, talented and universally adored by all the actors – and the rehearsals couldn't have run more smoothly.

The only untried part of the show was their own scene from *Three Sisters*. Aoife was suffering from a severe case of imposter syndrome at the prospect of performing on the same stage as so many acclaimed actors. They were all professionals, apart from her, and even sharing a scene with her sisters was daunting enough. She spent her nights studying the play from back to front, running lines with Sive and Mimi and learning Olga's entire part from beginning to end, even though they were only playing one scene.

She wanted to understand the role inside out and inhabit the character as fully as possible. The three of them acted out scenes in the kitchen every evening after dinner, and Aoife was the happiest she'd ever been since their parents died.

She'd always loved acting, and she'd been one of the leading players of the drama society at college. When she started work, she'd joined an amateur dramatic society, but that hadn't lasted long. A lot of the members simply weren't very good, and she'd found it frustrating and disheartening working with a bunch of hobbyists who came unprepared, forgot their lines and missed their cues. She knew she was being unfair. They just wanted to have a bit of fun, and they probably found her equally annoying for taking it too seriously. So she'd quit, deciding she was happier not acting at all than not doing it properly.

Now, swishing around the living-room with her sisters in their make-believe gowns, dreaming of returning to a Moscow she'd never visited, she reconnected with a part of herself she'd lost touch with long ago.

But sometimes the parallels with their own lives were painfully on the nose – the three orphaned sisters living in penury together, eking out a meagre living while they watched their hopes fade and their dreams of returning to Moscow thwarted, none of them living the lives they really wanted. The sadness of it took her breath away at times and she could barely get through some of Olga's lines she was so overwhelmed by the poignancy. It was the sort of magical thinking she'd normally scoff at, but she was almost scared to speak the words aloud, as if she might manifest Olga's disappointment in her own life.

When they knew the script back to front, they started to have fun with it, experimenting with different ways of playing their roles, deliberately hamming it up before reining it in to make it subtle and life-sized. Aoife was in awe of her sisters' talents – how they could alter the meaning of a line with the subtlest change of inflection; how they conveyed emotion with the merest flicker of their eyes or turn of their heads; how easily they switched between different interpretations of a speech and made each one equally compelling and real. Mimi was a brilliant comic actress. At acting school, she'd excelled at cabaret and mime, and she'd done postgraduate courses in clowning and commedia dell'arte. She goofed around now, playing Masha as slapstick and making them all laugh.

'Are we weird, that this is our idea of a fun way to spend an evening?' Sive asked as they collapsed, laughing on the sofa.

'Probably,' Aoife said.

'But good weird,' Mimi said confidently, looking to them both for confirmation.

'Definitely,' Aoife said. There was nothing she'd rather be doing.

'The best kind of weird,' Sive agreed.

'Having said that, though,' Mimi said, pushing herself up to standing. 'Pub?'

'Pub.' Aoife nodded. 'If we want to walk among the normies without detection, we have to try to ape their ways now and then.'

15

A BONUS of having so much else on her plate organising the benefit gala was that Aoife hardly had the time or headspace to worry about her own performance. Rehearsals were just one more item on the schedule to be ticked off. Still, it did give her pause when she stepped onto the stage at the dress rehearsal and saw Margaret Brennan and Peter Bradshaw watching from the front row. But it was thrilling to be part of a company and to be treated like a professional when they gathered around after a rehearsal to take notes from Lorcan. She loved the creative collaboration and the opportunity to learn from such talented people.

Sive and Mimi were in their element. It was wonderful to see them so happy, doing what they loved, and it broke Aoife's heart that she couldn't do more to make this dream a reality for them. It was gutting to watch them throw themselves so wholeheartedly into an endeavour that had little hope of succeeding. But she tried to put those gloomy thoughts out of her mind. There would be time enough to worry about that another day. For now she should let herself enjoy this moment – the three of them on stage together playing *Three Sisters*, just as they'd always said they would.

The morning of the show, she went to the theatre early to have a final look over Halfpenny Lane. She let herself in through the main entrance and lingered in the foyer. It looked amazing. The brass rails shone, the polished wooden doors to the auditorium gleamed and the carpet, though still threadbare, was clean and fresh. Aoife and her sisters had done the initial clear-out themselves – only they knew what should be kept and what could be dumped. But they'd taken Jonathan's advice and hired professional cleaners, and it had paid off.

She pulled open the door to the auditorium and walked slowly down the aisle. It was beautiful. They couldn't afford to replace the seats, but they'd been cleaned and patched up, and it was no harm, as Jonathan had pointed out, that people be reminded how badly the funding was needed. Players and all the main theatres had been incredibly generous in lending them costumes and props for the show, but their own costumes for *Three Sisters* had been salvaged from Halfpenny Lane's own stock and painstakingly repaired by Sive. It was a labour of love, and gave their performance deeper meaning and resonance for them.

Her stomach fluttered at the thought of stepping out on stage in front of a full house, feeling the eyes of a packed audience on her, the weight of their expectation. The show had sold out quickly and this evening every seat would be filled. It was great news for the theatre, but daunting at the same time. It didn't help that the dress rehearsal had been disastrous, the cramped wings crammed with actors tripping over each other, elbowing through as they tried to get to the stage. They'd forgotten props, fluffed lines and missed cues. Aoife's mind had gone blank the first time the lights hit her face, and she completely forgot the lines she could recite in her sleep the day before. Sive's mic had been turned down low, so she'd started projecting loudly and was screeching her monologue at the top of her lungs when the volume suddenly increased. Meanwhile Sir Peter had stalked off-stage after his piece, not realising his mic was still on, and proceeded to share a salacious piece of gossip about a mutual friend with Margaret – and the entire company. But according to Mimi and Sive it was well known in theatre that a bad dress rehearsal meant a good show. She could only hope they were right.

Later that evening, it was time to find out. The benefit gala was starting at six, as they had so many acts to fit in, and there was a drinks reception afterwards in the foyer because the green room was too small to accommodate the entire audience.

Aoife and her sisters arrived early as they were performing first. Aoife hung around as long as she could with the front of house volunteers, going over everything again and again, making sure that drinks were ready for the interval, programmes were in place and glasses had been delivered from the local pub, until eventually Mimi and Sive dragged her away to get changed.

Backstage her first night jitters were almost crowded out by anxiety about the running of the show. If only she could be in two places at once – in the dressing room getting ready to perform and out front with a clipboard, making sure everything was running smoothly.

Her nerves jangled as it got closer to six and she knew people would be arriving out front. She longed to be there, greeting the audience, checking tickets, making sure everyone was shown to the right seats and got a programme. There were so many details to take care of. She'd had no idea what a headache it was putting on a show.

'I hope they remember to tell everyone to stay behind for the reception,' she said as she struggled into her corset.

'It's printed on the ticket,' Sive reminded her.

'Yes, but people don't always pay attention, do they?'

'It was in all the advertising too,' Mimi said, leaning into the mirror and brushing her eyebrows. 'And believe me, people sit up and take notice when there's a mention of free drink. It kind of leaps out at them.'

'True. I hope the extra glasses have arrived from the pub.'

'Calm down,' Sive said. 'Eileen is taking care of it. Everything's under control.' Most of the staff of Players had been roped in to help out for the night and Eileen was their front of house manager.

'She's right. We have other people to handle all that stuff so we don't have to. They're all perfectly competent. You don't need to breathe down their necks and oversee every little detail.'

Aoife gasped. 'I don't breathe down their necks, do I?' she asked in dismay.

'Well …' Mimi's mouth twisted meaningfully.

'I'm just trying to help.'

'We know you are,' Sive said in a soothing tone that did nothing to allay Aoife's worry that she'd been overbearing. Had her well-meaning efforts to assist the volunteers in doing their jobs come across as micromanaging and second-guessing?

'We're just saying you don't need to,' Sive continued. 'They're doing a great job. Everything will be fine.'

'Let's just concentrate on our own bit,' Mimi said, turning Aoife around so she could button up her dress. 'Let them do their job and we'll do ours.'

Mimi had dressed with impressive efficiency and had already arranged her curls in a complicated bun on top of her head when the hair and make-up team arrived. Aoife wasn't used to seeing her sisters at work, and she was constantly in awe of their professionalism and capability – their meticulous attention to every little detail, their instinctive understanding of what was required of them, the ease with which they incorporated Lorcan's notes into their performance, the facility with which they could adapt their interpretation of a character or their delivery of a line. She felt her lack of training more acutely each time they rehearsed together.

There was a knock on the door, and Aoife opened it to find Jonathan standing outside with a huge bunch of flowers, accompanied by a tall younger man.

'Hi!' Jonathan handed her the bouquet. 'I don't want to disturb you. I just wanted to come back and say … break a leg? Do you really say that?'

'We really do,' Mimi said, as she and Sive joined Aoife to meet their visitors.

'This is my brother, Sam.' Jonathan introduced them all to each other.

'Hello, lovely to meet you,' Sam said as he shook their hands. He had a friendly, open face and thick dark hair in a fashionable undercut with a heavy fringe falling over his forehead.

'How's it looking out there?' Aoife asked.

'Great!,' Jonathan said. 'There's a big crowd. Nervous?'

Aoife nodded. 'Yeah. A bit. Well, a lot.'

'Don't worry. You'll be great. It'll all be fine.'

'Anything we can do to help?' Sam asked.

'I don't think so. Just make sure to laugh in all the right places and applaud a lot.'

'Cheering and whooping would be a bonus,' Mimi added.

'Consider it done,' Sam said. 'Cheering and whooping is my speciality.'

'Well, we'd better take our seats,' Jonathan said. 'You'll be joining us later?' he asked Aoife.

'Yes, once our own bit is done and we've changed out of our costumes.' She was looking forward to having their own performance over and being able to relax and enjoy the rest of the show.

'Well, see you later, then.'

'Thanks for the support,' Aoife said smiling at him. 'And the flowers.'

'No problem. We'll see you out front later.'

'Break a leg, all of you!' Sam said and they turned to go.

'Ten minutes to curtain.' Sive glanced at the clock on the wall as she closed the door behind them.

The three of them stood in a circle and Mimi guided them in a quick breathing exercise. Aoife's eyes welled up as they finished and fell silent, clasping each other's hands.

'I can't believe this is happening,' she said. 'We're really doing this.'

'We really are.' Mimi said, squeezing her hand.

Aoife was almost sick with nerves as they took their places in the wings and she heard the low-level murmur and shifting of the audience drifting through from the auditorium. Her sisters appeared perfectly calm as they waited to go on, Mimi brushing down her skirt and Sive fiddling with her hair that had been twisted into soft, tumbling ringlets. But her heart was pounding and her hands were cold and clammy. What the hell had she been thinking letting them talk her into doing this? She wasn't an actress. She'd be shown up as the charlatan she was among all these consummate professionals – the one bum note in a perfectly pitched orchestra. She listened, her heart in her mouth, as one of the volunteers made the safety announcement and went through the drill about switching off mobile phones. Then the audience quietened down, Aoife and her sisters took their places on the stage, and after a breathless moment, the curtain pulled back.

To Aoife's surprise, the performance passed in a glorious blur and was over all too soon. She was grateful for all the weeks of practice, so she could do the mechanical part of the performance in her sleep and focus all her energy on giving life and nuance to her character. Once the scene started, she had that old feeling of flying where everything became easy and natural, and she didn't want it to end. And playing opposite her sisters was a dream. She'd seen the way they worked together before, so effortlessly in sync, and it was always a joy to watch. But it was thrilling to be a part of, and she wished it could go on for ever.

All too soon, they were taking their bows. Tears welled up in her eyes as she clasped her sisters' hands and they turned to each other, grinning as the audience rose to their feet, cheering and clapping. The sound was thunderous and echoed in Aoife's pounding heart.

'That went well,' Mimi said as they made their way back to their dressing room.

'It did, didn't it?' Sive said. 'The audience seemed to like it.'

Aoife couldn't believe how blasé they were about it, as if that sort of thing happened to them every day – but then, she realised, it did. It was all in a day's work for them. She'd never been so envious of them, getting to do that night after night.

In the dressing room, Aoife hugged them each in turn. 'You were amazing!' she said. 'I'm so proud of you both.' She wiped tears from her eyes.

'Just doing our job,' Mimi said matter-of-factly.

'I just hope I managed to hold up my end,' Aoife said.

'Aoife, you were incredible!' Sive squeezed her.

'You were,' Mimi agreed. 'You seemed to get over your nerves quickly enough?'

'Once I was out there, they just sort of … disappeared,' Aoife said wonderingly. 'I could have gone on all night. I just wish we could do the whole play.'

'We will,' Mimi said confidently. 'But right now, let's get changed and get into our seats, so we don't miss any more of the show than we have to.'

16

THE THREE OF them snuck into the auditorium between acts, exchanging nervous glances as they took their seats. But they needn't have worried. The show went brilliantly, and the moment Peter Bradshaw stepped out on stage, Aoife felt herself relax. He played a blinder, holding the audience rapt from the moment he opened his mouth.

There was such support in the auditorium for the project, Aoife could practically feel the audience willing the performers on, laughing a beat ahead of punchlines in their eagerness to enjoy themselves and show their appreciation. Margaret had them in stitches with a comic song she'd written herself specially for the occasion, and Tom and Shay went down a storm with their beloved Beckett, the audience roaring with laughter as the hapless tramps bungled their way through their pointless and interminable wait for Godot. There were moments when Aoife got so wrapped up in what was happening on stage, she even managed to stop feeling anxious and responsible, and just lost herself in enjoying the performance.

Nevertheless, she was relieved when the final curtain

fell and the audience rose to their feet, Conor O'Neill leading the standing ovation. She heard loud whooping and wolf whistling behind her, and turned to see Jonathan's brother Sam. She exchanged a smile with Jonathan as she stood and joined in the applause.

When the clapping died down and the audience resumed their seats, Tom and Shay, still in costume, wheeled on a lovely old tombola from the Players prop department and did the raffle in character, bringing the house down with lots of clowning and slapstick.

Finally, Aoife and her sisters took to the stage again to thank all the performers and everyone who'd helped with putting on the show. Then they took turns reading a short speech they'd prepared about the history of the theatre and their hopes for its future. There was enthusiastic applause when they finished and they took their bows to their second standing ovation of the night. Aoife's heart swelled with pride, touched that there was so much goodwill towards Detta and the theatre. It gave her a surge of confidence knowing that all these people were behind them, willing them to succeed.

The foyer was already buzzing by the time Aoife and her sisters joined the reception. Volunteer wait staff circulated with trays of drinks, and the performers milled about on a post-show high, throwing each other extravagant compliments and basking in praise from the punters as they mingled with the audience. Aoife, Mimi and Sive did the rounds, thanking everyone for their support. Her sisters were in their element, Aoife thought, as she watched them working the room, soaking up praise and adulation and doling it out in turn. This was their world, their natural habitat, and she felt a sting of envy that they belonged here in a way she didn't.

She spotted Jonathan and his brother chatting in a corner and she made her way over to them.

'Hi! Great turnout,' Jonathan said, looking around at the guests, the sounds of chatter and laughter rising into the air.

'Yes, it is. What did you think of the show?' she asked them anxiously. 'It went well, didn't it?'

'It was brilliant!' Jonathan said. 'You were … amazing.' The way he looked at her as he said it caused a fluttering in Aoife's stomach.

'It was fantastic,' Sam said. 'And it's great to finally meet you, Aoife. I've heard so much about you.'

'Oh, you have?'

'*So* much,' Sam said, rolling his eyes. His brother gave him a not very discreet whack. 'I never hear anything else – what you're doing here, how amazing you are, the way you can leap tall buildings in a single bound, et cetera, et cetera.'

'Oh!' Aoife looked at Jonathan in surprise.

'Don't listen to him,' he said with a smile. 'But it was all good things.'

'All these things you weren't saying about me?' Aoife teased.

'Yes, exactly.' Jonathan grinned at her. She tried to ignore the flush of pleasure she felt.

'I think it's great what you're doing here,' Sam said. 'It's a shame to lose these old theatres. I'd love if I could be involved in some way. I don't suppose you have any jobs going?'

'Do you have any theatre experience?'

'Not as such. Just am dram at college.'

'You're interested in acting?'

'Yeah, I loved it – and I was pretty good, if I say so myself. But I'd be happy to do anything.'

'Well, there'd be lots of jobs going, if we manage to keep the theatre and get it up and running – but that's a big if. Besides, I'm not sure … I mean, the sort of jobs you'd be qualified for … you might find them a bit beneath you.'

Sam shrugged. 'I'm not fussy – anything that'd keep me off the streets would be good for a start.'

'Well, we'd need an usher, a box office assistant, and some stage hands and things like that. I'm sure we could find a use for you, if you wouldn't mind mucking in with a bit of everything.'

'Sounds great! I'd love that!'

'If you were working here, we could let you go on in the odd part if you'd like – just walk-ons. "Butler carrying a tray" sort of thing. You might not have any lines.'

'That'd be amazing!'

'And if you were good, you could work your way up to trying out for bigger roles.'

'Brilliant!'

'It's probably immaterial anyway,' Aoife warned him sadly. 'It's unlikely we'll raise enough to be able to keep the theatre.'

'It doesn't look like it needs that much,' Sam said, looking around. 'You must have made a decent bit tonight.'

'Yes, but …' Aoife chewed her lip, glancing at Jonathan. Had he not told his brother about his inheritance?

'I know, the terms of Detta's will have to be honoured,' Sam said as if reciting from a script he'd heard many times. 'It's not fair. Why couldn't *I* have been the one with the fairy godmother? I think it'd be great fun to own a theatre.'

'We tried to tell him that,' Sive said, coming to join them.

'I'm sure it would,' Jonathan said tightly in an under-tone. 'Unfortunately, we can't all afford to fritter money away on *fun*.'

Sam's smile faded and he looked subdued. 'No. You're right. And in fairness, I wouldn't have been the fairy godson you were to Detta.'

Aoife wondered what he meant by that. Jonathan gave his brother a flinty look and something seemed to pass between them that she couldn't decipher.

'Jonathan's the sensible one,' Sam said, turning to her. He handles all my, um … finances, so it'd amount to the same thing, even if I had been the one to inherit this place.'

Interesting. Jonathan seemed cross, and Aoife wondered if he thought Sam had said too much. Was he afraid he'd been shown up as controlling and tight-fisted? Sam was a bit old to still have his brother telling him what to do with his money.

Sam turned to Sive. 'You were marvellous!' he said, his charming smile returning.

'Thanks.' She beamed at him.

'Seriously, you gave me goosebumps. Feel.' He held out his arm, pushing up his shirt sleeve.

Sive laughed and ran a finger lightly along his arm. 'You've still got them!'

'I may never recover.' He pushed his shirt sleeve down. 'Another drink might help.' He lifted his empty glass. 'Let's go and get one.'

Someone called to Jonathan from across the foyer – a friend from work, he told Aoife and he excused himself to go and talk to them.

'Do we need to remind Sive that she has a boyfriend?' Mimi murmured in Aoife's ear as she appeared beside her.

Aoife followed her gaze to Sive and Sam, smiling at

each other as they chatted at the bar. They did look very flirty. 'I'm sure not.' She couldn't imagine Sive ever cheating on Ben. 'But maybe someone should warn Sam off.'

Jonathan returned just as Mimi drifted away to join another group.

'I hope you don't mind me saying Sam could work here,' Aoife said to him. 'He probably needs to do something more … sensible.' She worried that his comment about frittering money away on fun had been aimed at her and her sisters.

'No, I'd love if he found something he could be passionate about – something other than pissing money up the wall, that is.'

'What does he do now?'

'He's just doing casual jobs at the moment – waiting tables, doing takeaway delivery, stuff like that. He's been a bit lost, to be honest. He fancied himself as an entrepreneur for a while and was involved in a couple of start-ups that … didn't. Then a friend got him into day trading, persuaded him that'd be how he'd make his fortune. That was a disaster. Basically, he's always looking for some get-rich-quick scheme.'

Aoife laughed. 'Then he definitely shouldn't go into the theatre.'

'But maybe if he was doing something he loved, he'd be more content and settled, and not get distracted by every shiny new money-making racket.'

'Well, he may not earn much here, but at least he wouldn't be actually losing money.'

'It'd be great to see him getting his teeth into something.' Jonathan said. 'If acting's what he wants to do, then I'd love him to make a go of it.'

Then why not put your money where your mouth is and let us keep the theatre? 'Well, it's unlikely we'll be able to help him with that anyway. I can't see us still being here beyond the end of the month.' She tried not to sound bitter. After all, Sam was an adult and there were plenty of other theatres in Dublin if he was intent on acting. It wasn't up to Jonathan to prop up the theatre just to give his brother a career.

But she didn't think she quite succeeded in hiding her resentment. It was too frustrating, and not just because of the theatre. If only Jonathan wasn't the reason they were going to lose Halfpenny Lane, she could give in to this attraction between them. She'd already sensed it was mutual, and what Sam had said tonight seemed to confirm it. But as things stood, she couldn't go there. Because how could she be with the person responsible for crushing her dreams and breaking her sisters' hearts?

17

AOIFE WAS VERY glad she'd taken the day after the benefit gala off work. She didn't think a bomb could have got her out of bed the following morning. She felt bone-weary, but in a deliciously satisfying way. She was not only crashing after all the stress and hard work of the weeks leading up to the show; she was also experiencing the comedown from the post-show high that she'd witnessed her sisters going through after a successful opening night. So when her alarm went off at seven – because she'd forgotten to unset it – she switched it off and snuggled deeper into her warm bed, hugging the feeling to herself as her head spun with flashbacks of the night before.

It had all gone so well, and she'd loved every minute of it. She replayed again and again the moment she'd stepped onto the stage with her sisters, the thrill of feeling all those eyes out in the auditorium watching them, the audience's held breath – and then the moment of hush at the end before the silence was broken with a thunder-clap of applause. She'd never experienced anything like the rush of that moment. She wished she could have bottled it to relive over and over.

Even though she stayed in bed until almost nine, she was still the first up. Her sisters were more practised day-sleepers than she was. Marlowe stalked out of Mimi's room and followed her downstairs, yowling for food, not used to having to wait so long for his breakfast. When she'd fed him, she made herself tea and toast, but found she couldn't sit still, twitching as she sat at the table and ate. She had an irresistible urge to be back at the theatre. They'd need to go there at some stage today anyway, to clear up after last night. It would probably be hours still before Sive and Mimi crawled out of bed. So she finished her breakfast quickly, pulled on her coat and went out.

She could have got a bus or a tram, but she decided to walk to Halfpenny Lane. It was a lovely May morning, the promise of summer hovering on the horizon, and besides, she needed the exercise to work off some of her nervous energy. She knew this feeling reminded her of something, and it came to her now – it was like falling in love, the rush of those first days when all you could think about was the other person, when whatever else you were doing, they were always there under your skin making your nerves tingle and your heart race.

When she got to Temple Bar, there was an uncharacteristic hush on the winding cobbled streets. Most of the shops were still shuttered, but several small cafes were open and serving breakfast, delicious smells of coffee and freshly baked bread wafting from their half-open doors. The Halfpenny Place, the little cafe and bakery at the top of Halfpenny Lane was setting up for the day as she passed.

She unlocked the main door of the theatre and stepped into the foyer. It was so silent and still after the buzz of the concert, and it felt sad and ominous to find it empty, forsaken by all the friends who'd rallied to its support last night, the enthusiastic throng who'd crowded to fill its seats.

Aoife felt like she was letting it down already. Sive was right – a theatre needed life. It needed players and audiences, lights and applause, and Aoife didn't think they could give Halfpenny Lane that. Last night had been an amazing success, better than they'd dreamed. But it wasn't enough. She knew it would never be enough, and she could feel the dream slipping away already.

They'd counted on this for so long – not that they'd been waiting for Detta to die, but Halfpenny Lane had always been out there – a bright, glistening future that belonged to them, ready for them to step into whenever the time came. Now she saw how unrealistic they'd been about it. They hadn't thought about maintenance and public liability insurance and electricity bills. They'd just talked endlessly about the plays they'd put on, the actors and directors they'd get to collaborate with; how hard they'd work and what fun they'd have. Their daydreams had been filled with applause and adulation, and dressing rooms filled with flowers on opening night. They'd imagined rehearsals and after-show suppers, festivals and glowing newspaper reviews; sets and costumes, lights and make-up – everything but where the money would come from to pay for it all.

Inheriting the theatre had been the beginning and end of the dream. But the theatre wasn't enough. She saw now that it was exactly what Jonathan had called it – a seemingly bottomless money pit. Last night had been a brilliant success – and an abysmal failure.

She moved into the auditorium, picking up stray programmes from the seats as she went. The theatre had looked so glittering and alive last night, but now in the broad light of day it was shabby and forlorn again, and she was weighed down by the enormity of the task of reviving it.

Maybe Jonathan was right and they'd be better off selling. She felt traitorous entertaining the thought even for a moment – as if she was betraying not only Detta and her sisters, but the theatre itself. But they'd invested too much in this place, expected too much from it. It couldn't deliver their dreams. The money would allow them to fund their careers in other ways. She could afford to give up work and go to drama school. Sive could take as many classes and workshops as she liked. None of them would have to do casual low-paid jobs in between acting gigs to make ends meet. Moreover, it would give them the freedom to travel. There were so many places Aoife longed to go that she'd never been. They could see all the big shows in the West End and on Broadway.

Back in the foyer, the trestle tables teemed with glasses stained with red wine and lipstick, some still half-full. She got a cooler and some boxes that they'd stashed in the box office. Then she rolled up her sleeves and started packing the glasses into cardboard boxes ready to return to the pub, throwing the dregs into the wine cooler as she went. They'd have cleaners come in later, but at least it was a start and she needed the activity.

When she'd done all she could, she pulled on her jacket, locked up the theatre again and set off for home. It was busier now as she wended her way back along the lane, the shops pulling up their shutters. Delicious smells of freshly cooked bread wafted from The Halfpenny Place, and on an impulse she went in to get bagels and croissants to bring home, deciding they deserved a celebration breakfast.

It was a small shop with just a couple of tables for

customers to sit at. A fresh-faced young girl with blue hair stood behind the counter. 'You're one of Sive's sisters, right?' she asked as Aoife approached.

'Yes. Aoife.'

'Hi! I'm Chloe.'

'Oh, of course! You donated the basket of muffins for our raffle. They looked amazing!'

'Thanks. It wasn't much,' she said. 'How did last night go?'

'It went brilliantly.'

'It'd be great to see the theatre open again – bringing a bit more life into the lane.'

Aoife felt even more guilty about contemplating selling, faced with this stranger's interest.

'So, what can I get you?'

Aoife contemplated the baked goods spread out under the glass counter. Everything looked so tempting, it was difficult to choose, but she ordered a selection of sesame and poppy seed bagels, plain croissants and pain au chocolat.

'Enjoy,' Chloe said as she handed them over, still warm from the oven in their paper bag.

Somewhere in the back of the cafe there was a ping. 'Hang on a minute,' Chloe said, turning away and disappearing from view. She came back moments later, bearing a tray of freshly baked baklava and slid it onto the counter in front of her. The smell was mouth-watering.

'This is a new recipe I've been experimenting with.' She picked up three pieces and slid them into a paper bag. 'Pistachio, cardamom and rosewater. On the house,' she said, holding the bag out to Aoife. 'As a welcome to the lane.'

'Oh, thank you. That's so kind.'

'Let me know what you think.'

'I will, and thanks again for the muffins.'

Sive and Mimi were up when Aoife got home. They seemed to be just out of bed, both still dressed in pyjamas and dressing-gowns, and looking dishevelled and bleary-eyed, their hair tousled. Mimi still had crease marks on her face from the sheets.

'I got breakfast,' she called as she sailed into the kitchen, holding the paper bag aloft.

'Yay!' Sive clapped her hands. 'You went to Chloe's?'

'Yes.' Aoife removed her coat and hung it on the back of a chair, then unloaded the bag onto a big plate. 'She seems lovely. She gave me freebies too.'

'That's great. We'd only got as far as coffee,' Mimi said, lifting the mug in her hand.

'I'll make more.' Aoife switched on the kettle and the coffee machine. As she made tea and put jam into dishes, she thought about broaching the subject of selling with her sisters. But maybe now wasn't the time. Perhaps she should let them all have a moment to celebrate and enjoy last night's triumph. She could bring their dreams crashing down to earth tomorrow.

When they were all sitting at the table, enjoying Chloe's delicious bagels, they chattered happily about the gala, going over the highlights of the night again and again. Now definitely wasn't the time to discuss selling, Aoife decided, watching her sisters' faces glowing with happiness. It wasn't fair. For the umpteenth time, she wondered what Detta had been thinking leaving Jonathan a share in Half-penny Lane when the theatre so clearly meant nothing to him. Whereas her sisters …

As they moved on to croissants and a second round of

coffee, Aoife pulled out her notebook where she'd recorded the takings from last night.

'How much did we make from the tombola?' Sive asked, peering across the table at the notebook.

'Just over four thousand euro.' Aoife tapped her pen on the page.

'Take that, Jonathan Hunt!' Sive crowed. 'And he tried to tell us we'd have no option but to sell.'

'Well, it's great,' Aoife said, 'but it's nowhere near what we need.' She felt she should introduce a note of caution. She could see Sive getting carried away by the success of the gala, and she didn't want her disappointment to be any more acute than it had to be. But just as she was about to say something, Sive spoke first.

'I know that. But it's a good start. And we'll think of something. If we all put our heads together, I'm sure we can find a way.'

Mimi glanced at Aoife from under her brows as she tore apart a croissant. She didn't look any more convinced than Aoife, but neither of them said anything to burst Sive's bubble. Today was a good day. They'd done what they set out to do, and pulling off the gala was a huge achievement in itself. They deserved to take time to celebrate that.

18

'I've GOT IT!' Sive announced as she breezed into the kitchen the following evening. Aoife and Mimi were sitting at the table peeling vegetables for dinner.

'The clap?' Mimi glanced up at her with a cheeky grin.

'No, silly.' Sive took off her hat and flopped into a chair beside Aoife. 'I've had an idea for how we can save the theatre!' She was practically bouncing in her chair with excitement. 'And it's a brilliant one, if I say so myself. I couldn't wait to get home to tell you.'

'Okay.' Aoife turned to her. 'We're listening.'

Sive looked from one to the other of them in turn before speaking, master of the dramatic pause.

'Come on, spit it out,' Mimi snapped.

'Crowdfunding!' Sive beamed at them both and sat back in her chair, folding her arms in a way that said she was waiting for their applause.

'You think we should set up a crowdfunder for the theatre?' Aoife asked. 'Aren't they more suitable for new inventions and tangible products?'

Sive shook her head. 'You can use them to get charitable donations too.'

'But shouldn't they be for, like, a good cause?'

'This *is* a good cause,' Mimi said, clearly already taken with the idea. 'You heard what everyone was saying last night about how much the theatre meant to them, how it was such a vital part of Dublin life. I'm sure there are loads of people who'd be happy to support it – and it wouldn't just be limited to Dublin.'

'That's the beauty of it.' Sive nodded. 'Think of all the famous actors who knew Detta and who started out at Halfpenny Lane. I'm sure there are people from all parts of the country – all over the world even – who'd want to help.'

'Besides, you can do a crowdfunder for anything you like,' Mimi said. 'My friend Susie did one for a holiday in Ibiza when she was broke and desperate to get away.'

'Was she in an abusive relationship?' Sive asked.

'What?' Mimi frowned. 'No. She was single at the time, in fact.'

'What was she trying to get away from, then?'

'Just work. And the rain. Plus I think she fancied a holiday fling.'

'Surely no one gave her money for that?' Aoife said.

'No, they did. She put up some sob story about how she was skint and knackered, slaving away twenty-four-seven to support her family, living on tinned beans—'

'Hang on, what family?' Aoife interrupted. 'She doesn't have any kids.'

'She had that hamster. It's dead now, but she *was* supporting it at the time. Anyway, it worked! People actually paid for her to go to Ibiza, get shit-faced for two weeks and shag a local named Enrico.'

'Wow! People are so kind,' Sive said.

People are suckers, Aoife thought.

'But our crowdfunder wouldn't be like that,' Sive said quickly, obviously picking up on Aoife's scepticism and wanting to disassociate their project from any dodgy vibes. 'Halfpenny Lane is a genuine cause. We'd be doing something truly noble with the money – restoring one of Dublin's most important theatres and maintaining part of the city's cultural heritage.'

'Maintaining *our* heritage,' Aoife said.

'That would just be a by-product.' Sive waved away her concerns. 'We wouldn't just be doing it for ourselves. We'd be giving back to the city, providing an important cultural amenity.'

'Besides, I think we've established that running a theatre is never going to cut it as a finance scam,' Mimi pointed out. 'Even if we got it back on its feet, we'd never exactly make a killing from it – you said so yourself.'

'And we're not trying to trick anyone,' Sive said. 'We'll be using the money for exactly what we say we're going to – reopening the theatre. It's totally up to people then if they want to donate to that or not.'

'Okay.' Aoife nodded. This was definitely interesting. It might actually work. 'You could be onto something.'

'I think it's a brilliant idea!' Mimi said. 'Why didn't we think of it before?'

Aoife nodded slowly. 'I agree.'

'So we're doing it?' Sive asked.

'We'll have to discuss it with Jonathan, of course,' Aoife said.

'But there's no reason for him not to agree, is there?' Mimi said. 'He'll be getting his money either way.'

'True.'

'It's our best shot at getting the money for his share so

we don't have to sell,' Mimi said. 'And then, once we buy him out, we'll never have to deal with him again.'

Aoife wasn't as happy at the thought of that as she ought to be. She'd no longer have a reason to see Jonathan, and she'd miss spending time with him. But that was silly. She'd developed a bit of a stupid crush on him, but they were totally incompatible. He'd never like her that way anyway. It wasn't that he was out of her league exactly. It was that he played in a totally different league. Besides, even if he did like her that way, she could hardly act on it. How could she go out with someone who her sisters saw as their adversary? Even Sive had called him their arch-nemesis, and Sive didn't do enemies. No, it would be all the better for her if he was out of their lives for good and she could forget all about him and his green eyes.

'We should do some research first and make a plan,' she said. 'Then we'll have a solid proposal to bring him when we tell him the idea.'

When they'd finished dinner, they cleared the kitchen table, got out their laptops and spent the rest of the evening researching crowdfunding.

'So, how much do we ask for?' Aoife asked, pen poised over her notepad.

'Enough to buy Jonathan out, first and foremost,' Mimi said. 'If we raise enough to get the repair work done, so much the better. But if not, we can do that gradually as and when we can afford it.'

'The first priority is to get one hundred percent owner-ship of the theatre,' Sive agreed.

'It's an awful lot of money,' Aoife said as she wrote the figure for Jonathan's share of the theatre at the top of the page. It seemed even more daunting seeing it written down.

'But I think it's achievable,' Mimi said. 'It's a great

cause. And if Susie can make enough for a holiday in Ibiza – and at a very nice hotel too, might I add …'

'And look at this campaign,' Sive said, peering at her laptop screen. 'They made over five hundred thousand dollars in thirty days. And there's another one here that made five hundred grand in sixty days. That could be us!'

As they researched and read success story after success story, Aoife felt the first real stirrings of hope she'd had since the will reading. 'Okay, this is looking feasible. I think we can bring this to Jonathan. We need to get him to give us a bit more time, but it's a realistic idea, isn't it?'

Mimi nodded. 'It is.'

'We should go see him to discuss it as soon as possible. I'll see if he's free some time tomorrow.'

'I can't do any day this week,' Mimi said. 'I'm recording that audiobook.'

'And I'm on call for an extra job,' Sive said. 'But there's no need for us all to go, is there?'

'No.' Aoife said. 'I can do it.' The truth was she didn't mind at all. She was actually worryingly happy to have a reason to see Jonathan on her own. 'I think the sooner we get going on this, the better.'

She felt a tingle of excitement. This could work. It was a solid idea, not just a pipe dream. If they hit their target, they'd at least be able to buy Jonathan out. If it went really well and they exceeded their goal, they might even be able to carry out the renovations that the theatre needed.

She went to bed that night feeling optimistic for the first time in ages – not just hopeful, but exhilarated, her mind spinning with ideas about social media campaigns and rewards for investors. Maybe their dreams of glitter and stardust weren't so out of reach after all.

19

SHE RANG Jonathan the next day when she got to work, and he was free to see her that afternoon at his office.

'So, what did you want to see me about?' he asked, when she was seated in front of his desk.

She dug her notepad out of her satchel. 'I – we – my sisters and I have a proposition for you.'

'I'm all ears.' He nodded for her to continue.

'As you know, we want to buy you out of the theatre, but—'

'You don't have the money.'

'No, but we think we've come up with a way we can get it. We just need time.'

'How much time?'

'Three months.' Most successful crowdfunding campaigns seemed to run for sixty days maximum, but they'd need time to prepare and set it up.

He narrowed his eyes at her. 'How do you propose to come up with that kind of money in three months?'

'That's not your problem,' she said, goaded by his attitude. She knew she was being ridiculous – after all, she'd come here precisely to tell him about the crowdfunder. But his questioning got her back up – it was as if he didn't trust her, and thought they were trying to get one over on him.

'I'd argue it is. That's not a lot of time to raise half a million. If this is just a stalling tactic, or some harebrained money-making racket—'

'It's not! If you'd just give me a chance, I'll tell you. Sorry, I don't know why I said it's not your concern. Of course it is, which is why I've come to discuss it with you and see what you think.' She took a deep breath. 'We're going to set up a crowdfunder.'

He jolted upright in his seat. 'A crowdfunder! I see.' He steepled his hands, resting his chin on them.

'I know you probably think it's completely unrealistic, but—'

'No, I think it's a good idea.'

'You do?'

'Yes – a very good idea.'

'We don't know if it'll work, of course. But we've done a bit of research and we're optimistic. All we ask is that you give us three months to get the money to buy you out. If we don't have it by then, we'll put the place on the market.'

He was quiet for a moment, considering. Then he nodded. 'I think I can live with that.'

'In the meantime we can get it cleared out and ready for sale, so we won't lose any more time if this doesn't work. And three months isn't long in the grand scheme of things – not when it comes to selling property.'

'Aoife, I said yes. You don't have to convince me.'

'Oh. Yeah. Okay.' She'd expected him to take some persuading, and she'd rehearsed all her arguments. His agreeing so readily had knocked her off balance. 'I thought you just wanted to sell to the highest bidder, let someone turn the place into a trendy bar or whatever.'

'No. I'm glad you've come up with an alternative solution – and a really smart one.'

'Well, I can't take credit for that. It was actually Sive's idea.'

'I'd love you girls to keep Halfpenny Lane, carry on Detta's legacy. If I could afford to just sign my share over to you, I would, in a heartbeat. But despite what you seem to think, I'm not made of money.'

'Right.'

'Why do I get the feeling you don't believe me?'

'Well, I suppose it's all relative, isn't it?' Aoife said tightly. Even as she said it, she winced at how pricklish she was being, but she couldn't seem to help herself.

He frowned irritably. 'Meaning?'

'I'm sure you believe that you can't afford it. But I suspect what you mean by that is different to what I mean when I say I can't afford something.'

'Really? And what do you mean when you say that? Enlighten me.'

'I mean I literally don't have the money.'

'Whereas I mean …?'

She shrugged. 'I don't know. Something about cash flow or liquidity? Like maybe your money is all tied up in property or stocks and bonds or something.'

'I see. I sound like quite the mogul.'

'Well, I don't know,' Aoife said peevishly. 'I have no idea what rich people mean when they say they can't afford something. Maybe you'd lose interest, or you'd have to sell shares and miss out on the dividends.' She thought of some of O'Brien Sweeney's rich clients and their so-called money 'problems', which mainly involved moving it around between different investment funds, and finding new and creative ways to avoid tax. 'Whereas for someone else, it means working longer hours or getting another job or selling their home—'

'Do you seriously think I'd let you sell your home for the sake of freeing up some cash or losing out on interest?'

Aoife looked down at her hands. She'd obviously hurt his feelings. 'No. I suppose not.'

'To be clear, I wouldn't.'

'We don't expect you to just hand it over to us anyway,' she said. 'We were never saying that. You're entitled to do whatever you want with your share of the theatre.'

'Even if that means selling it to a soulless restaurant chain?'

'Even then.'

'Well, I don't want to do that if it can be avoided. I really hope this crowdfunding idea works. And of course I'll do whatever I can to help.'

'I think we can manage, thanks,' she said stiffly.

He raised his eyebrows, leaning back in his chair. 'As you pointed out, I'm a part owner, so it's as much my responsibility as it is yours. If I'm sharing in the profits, it's only right I should share the workload too.'

Aoife nodded. 'Thanks.' She really should climb down off her high horse. It would be good to have him on board. They needed all the help they could get.

'You don't have to thank me. It's in my interests just as much as yours.'

'Not quite. If this doesn't work, we'll be forced to sell. You'll get your money either way.'

'All the more reason I need this to work,' he said with a crooked smile.

Aoife frowned. 'I don't see how.'

'Because if you have to sell Halfpenny Lane, you'll end up hating me. And I can't stand the thought of you hating me.'

She blushed and looked away, unable to hold his gaze. 'I wouldn't hate you.'

'Maybe not. But you'd never be able to forgive me,' he said sadly.

It was her cue to protest, but Aoife couldn't bring herself to say it. She suspected if she did, it would be a lie. She may *want* to forgive him, but in her heart she'd probably always harbour some resentment towards him.

'So,' he said briskly, 'let me know whatever you need me to do.'

'Great! We should get together and start setting it up as soon as possible – I mean, if you want to be involved, that is. Otherwise I could just send you the link once it's live–'

'No, I'm all in. Involve me.'

'Okay. Why don't you come over to our place? How's Sunday morning? Around eleven?'

'Perfect.' He picked up his phone from the desk and tapped it into his calendar. 'I'll be there.'

20

JONATHAN ARRIVED PROMPTLY on Sunday morning and they gathered around the large table in the dining room, armed with coffee, notebooks and laptops. As they were getting settled, Marlowe came to check out their visitor, weaving between Jonathan's legs and giving him a thorough sniffing.

'This is Kit Marlowe,' Aoife said as Jonathan bent to pet the ball of ginger fur at his feet.

'Great name. Is he yours?'

'He's Mimi's originally. But he kind of belongs to all of us now.'

'Insofar as he belongs to anyone,' Mimi said as Marlowe stretched his neck, nudging Jonathan's hand. 'He's very much his own cat.'

When they'd taken their seats at the table, Marlowe leapt onto the chair beside Mimi, eyeballing Jonathan and blinking at him slowly.

'That means he likes you,' Sive said.

'I guess he's staying for the meeting, then,' Jonathan said.

'Oh, Marlowe's very invested in this,' Sive told him. 'He wants to be a theatre cat.'

'He just wants attention.' Mimi smiled indulgently at him, nuzzling his head.

'So, first things first,' Jonathan said, opening his laptop. 'What's the target for the crowdfunder going to be?'

'Obviously, we need a minimum of five hundred thousand to buy you out.' Aoife felt breathless just saying that figure out loud. 'But we can't leave it at that. If people are paying to finance the restoration of the theatre, they'll expect to see some results. We can't just take the money and say thanks very much, but we won't be carrying out the work any time soon.'

'Right. So we should get an estimate for whatever work needs to be done. It doesn't have to be an extravagant renovation job – just enough to be able to reopen.'

'What happens if we don't hit the target?' Sive asked.

'There are two main ways it can be set up,' Aoife said, having researched the various crowdfunding platforms. 'We can make it so that if we don't hit the target, we don't get any money and everyone keeps their donations.'

'I don't like the sound of that.' Sive wrinkled her nose.

'Or we can keep whatever money's been raised at the end of the campaign.'

'Well, that sounds like the obvious way to go, doesn't it?' Mimi said. 'We might be able to pay for some of the renovation works, even if we didn't make the target – enough to reopen the theatre, at least.'

'But what if we don't even get enough to buy Jonathan out?' Aoife asked. 'We'd have to sell then anyway, and it would be like we were taking the money under false pretences.'

'But we're not,' Sive said. 'We're acting in good faith.'

'Maybe we could start doing some of the smaller stuff

with the money from the gala,' Jonathan said, earning a surprised look of grudging admiration from Mimi. 'It would help build confidence in the whole project if we had some concrete progress to show people along the way.'

'How about if we use the gala money to do *Three Sisters* and make the production part of the goal?' Mimi said, eyes sparkling with enthusiasm. 'We can hire cast and crew, and start rehearsals, and then even if we don't make the money, we could still put on the show.'

'We could do it in Halfpenny Lane, like the gala concert,' Sive said. 'One last show before it's put up for sale.'

'A grand reopening and a closing night all rolled into one,' Mimi said wryly.

'That's a great idea,' Jonathan said with a nod to Mimi. 'I think the crowdfunder is much more likely to be a success if people have something tangible to get behind.'

'We could build the show in as a reward,' Aoife said. 'But I definitely think we should go with the all-or-nothing model for the crowdfunder, and use the money we raised from the gala to do small works and pay for rewards. If we can't make half a million plus, we'll have to sell anyway.'

Mimi sighed, slumping in her seat. 'You're right.'

Sive nodded in agreement.

'We'd only need to get the most essential works done on the building,' Jonathan said. 'There's no point in doing too much to it anyway if we might end up selling it. Whoever bought it would just gut it first thing.'

Aoife struggled not to flinch at the thought of Halfpenny Lane being 'gutted', imagining it as an empty shell, its heart ripped out.

'So we just have to make sure this crowdfunding campaign kicks ass!' Sive said.

'It shouldn't take too much,' Mimi said. 'We just need

it to function as a theatre, and we were able to put on the gala concert already.'

Jonathan nodded. 'So we'll get a quote for the essential work, and we can get an estimate for the full restoration at the same time, so we can decide how to pitch the crowd-funder. Then we can start doing the smaller jobs so we have some progress to show donors.'

'Good idea,' Aoife said.

'We should meet up with an architect as soon as possible. I know someone we could use. He'll do the quote for free, but, if we ended up using him, I could get mates' rates.' Jonathan pulled his phone from a pocket. 'I'll see if I can schedule a meeting with him next week. When would be convenient for you?' He looked questioningly at the three of them. Aoife noticed he'd phrased it in a way that didn't make a refusal easy. She wondered if that was some sort of business tactic he'd learned.

'I can't do any day next week,' Sive said quickly.

'Me either,' Mimi said. 'I'm filming an episode of Kelly's Law. But I could do the following week.'

'We don't all need to be there, do we?' Sive asked.

'No. But since you three know more about what a theatre needs than I do, I think at least one of you should be there.'

'I nominate Aoife, then.'

'Seconded,' Mimi murmured.

Jonathan looked at Aoife questioningly.

'Any day is fine for me, apart from tomorrow. I can take some flexi-time.'

He thumbed through the calendar on his phone. 'Wednesday's best for me?'

'Wednesday's fine.'

'If he's available then, I'll set it up and get back to you.'

21

ON WEDNESDAY, Aoife met up with Jonathan and the architect, who he introduced as Gordon, in the lobby of Halfpenny Lane. Gordon was a gangly russet-haired man with an open, friendly face and looked about the same age as Jonathan.

'This is Aoife, one of my partners,' Jonathan said as he introduced them. So they were partners now, she thought, as she shook Gordon's hand. Her teen self would have been thrilled with this development and the opportunity it presented to spend time with him. She wasn't sure yet what her twenties self made of it.

Gordon was brisk and business-like, displaying a depth of knowledge and an appreciation of the old theatre that immediately made Aoife warm to him and wish they could hire him on the spot. He was aware of the specific needs of a performance space, and sensitive to the age and character of the building.

'They really knew how to do things in those days, didn't they?' he said, looking up at the high beamed ceiling as they stood in the auditorium.

Aoife smiled, reassured that Halfpenny Lane would be in safe hands with Gordon if they ever got to do the renovation. As they walked around, he enthused about the many period features, the quality of the materials used and the robust construction. But she felt increasingly nervous as they listed everything they'd like to get done and Gordon explained the limitations imposed by the listing and the special materials they'd have to use, even down to a particular (and of course more expensive) type of plaster. She dreaded hearing what it would all cost.

She tried to channel a little of Sive's optimism as the list grew ever longer and more daunting. She shouldn't be so defeatist. After all, they hadn't even set the crowdfunder up yet. There was always a chance it would be a massive success.

'I'll draw up a plan when I get back to the office and give you an estimate as soon as possible. It'll probably be tomorrow or the next day before I get back to you.'

'Could you give us a rough ballpark now?' Aoife asked, not sure she could wait that long.

'I'd say you're looking at around five hundred grand to do everything here,' he said, tapping his clipboard. 'But that's just a very rough idea.'

Aoife gulped, nodding. 'Thanks.'

Gordon smiled. 'Don't look so worried. We can always make some adjustments, adapt the plans to fit your budget. I'll give you an estimate for everything we've talked about, and then show you where we can make cuts.' Aoife must have looked alarmed, because he quickly added, 'I'm not talking about cutting corners or doing anything half-assed. But there'll be places where we can make savings while still maintaining the integrity of the overall vision.'

'And not much of this is essential, right?' Jonathan asked.

'No. I'll let you have a separate quote for the absolute minimum you'd need to get done. But the building is structurally sound, and you're lucky that it was in use until relatively recently.'

'And there's plenty of smaller, superficial stuff here that we can be getting on with,' Jonathan said to Aoife, nodding to Gordon's clipboard.

The next day, Jonathan called Aoife and told her the estimate was in.

'I'll email it to you, and then maybe we could meet up to discuss it? Then we can decide what to set the crowdfunder target at.'

The email arrived a few minutes after they'd hung up, and Aoife had to brace herself before opening it. She skimmed over the details and went straight to the bottom line. Thankfully, she'd been prepared for the worst, and it was close to the rough estimate Gordon had given them, so it didn't come as a shock. It was still daunting seeing it in black and white, but instead of being despondent, she was excited as she read through the plans in more detail. If the crowdfunder was a success, there was a chance they could keep Halfpenny Lane and do all of this. She was pleased to see the quote for essential work was reassuringly modest, and could largely be covered by the funds they'd raised from the concert. When she'd absorbed it, she rang Jonathan back and he arranged to come to their house that evening to discuss it with the three of them and start planning the crowdfunder.

Jonathan was working late, so Aoife had a chance to discuss the estimate with her sisters over dinner. Their eyes shone as they pored over the architect's plans.

'Wow, if we could do all this ...' Mimi said longingly.

'It'd be amazing!' Sive breathed.

Jonathan arrived just after eight, looking tired.

'Have you eaten?' Aoife asked him as she led him into the dining room. Mimi and Sive were sitting at the table, still poring over the architect's plans. 'Would you like something?'

'Thanks, but I'm fine. I had lunch with a client and grabbed a sandwich at my desk later.'

'Something to drink, then? Tea? Coffee? Wine?'

'Tea would be great, thanks.'

When Aoife had brought him a mug of tea, they sat down around the table and began planning the crowdfunder.

'Our goal should be realistic, but as achievable as possible,' Aoife said. 'We don't need to do all this.' She tapped the architect's plans. 'If we can make enough to buy Jonathan out, fulfil whatever rewards we're offering and do the most basic renovations, we'll be able to save the theatre.'

'And there's always the chance that we'll exceed the goal,' Sive said cheerfully. 'I read about loads of campaigns that hit their targets in a couple of days and made double what they'd asked for. We could do that!'

'We have the money we raised at the concert to use for expenses and do some of the smaller stuff,' Mimi said. 'So say we add another fifty grand? That should be enough, shouldn't it?'

They all agreed it would be.

'We have to set a timeframe for the campaign too,' Aoife said, tapping her pen on her notepad. 'They're usually thirty to ninety days.'

'How about sixty days?' Mimi said. 'Split the difference.'

Jonathan nodded. 'We don't want it to drag on. And

we should get it set up as soon as possible – keep up the impetus from the benefit concert.'

'Okay, sixty days it is. And an all-or-nothing campaign.' Aoife jotted this in her notepad, relieved they'd all agreed to go for that model.

'So, rewards,' Mimi said. 'What are we going to do for those?'

'They have to be things we can deliver even if we don't reach our goal.'

Mimi's mouth twisted. 'Names on the backs of seats is out, then?'

'I'm afraid so. It's a good idea, but if we end up with no theatre …'

'We can always add new reward tiers along the way,' Jonathan pointed out. 'If we're exceeding our goal, we could add names on seats later.'

Aoife nodded. 'Okay, we'll keep that in reserve. What about lower-level perks – things we could definitely deliver that don't cost too much?'

'We could do swag,' Mimi said. 'T-shirts, mugs, all sorts of branded Halfpenny Lane stuff. We'd need to get some artwork done for a logo.'

'Great!' Aoife jotted the ideas down. 'We'll get some prices and then decide what we can offer for different levels of funding.'

'How about getting a really nice photograph or drawing of the theatre,' Jonathan said, 'and offering prints of that?'

'Oh, I love that idea!' Aoife said, writing it down. 'We could commission a local artist or photographer to do it.'

'And we could make it a limited edition,' Sive said. 'And offer it framed or unframed for different tiers.'

'Brilliant! What else?'

'We're doing the show,' Mimi said. 'That's one thing

we know we can deliver. So we could offer tickets for that … and maybe a special opening night for a higher tier?'

'How many nights are we going to do?' Sive asked.

'We can decide that later.' Aoife said. 'I thought two or three weeks? We'll need to make a schedule and budget, but let's concentrate on the crowdfunder for now.' Planning the show would be a headache for another day. It was too overwhelming to think about everything at once.

'The theatre seats, what – two hundred?' Jonathan asked, scribbling on his pad.

'A hundred and thirty-eight,' the sisters chorused in unison.

'We can only offer a very limited quantity of tickets, then. You could make opening night a top tier reward, and include some kind of reception.'

'We could have an exclusive package for a small number of larger investors – a stay in one of the nearby hotels, say, and dinner in a local restaurant as well as tickets to the show.'

'And we could invite them to an exclusive drinks reception with the cast and crew,' Sive added.

'That's a great idea,' Jonathan said, 'especially if we could get some local businesses on board as sponsors.'

'We can call it the Halfpenny Lane experience,' Sive said, smiling.

'We could offer advertising in the programme for some big investors,' Mimi put in.

'What about backstage tours?'

'Season tickets?'

'We could set up a Friends of Halfpenny Lane where they get discounts and advance booking, and we could give membership as one of the rewards.'

'That would have to be further down the line, though, once we're sure we're not selling.'

Aoife noticed that Jonathan looked decidedly uncomfortable whenever selling the theatre was mentioned, and she couldn't help but wonder once again why he wouldn't agree to co-own it with them.

'The show is definitely your most compelling asset,' he said. 'I think we should focus on that as the main offer.'

'It's such a small theatre, though,' Mimi said. 'And we might only have a short run. So even if we made it a top tier reward, it's limited what we can make from it.'

'Besides,' Aoife said, 'we don't want the audience to be limited to top investors only.'

'It's not ideal,' Sive agreed. 'But like Jonathan said, it's the best thing we have to offer. Maybe we should make the most we can of it. If the crowdfunder is a success, we could always extend the run, or revive the show later on.'

'But if it's not a success …' Aoife hated always being the naysayer, but she suspected there'd be no second run of the show. 'If only there was a way we could get more people to see it.'

'We could put it on somewhere else?' Sive suggested. 'Conor O'Neill would probably let us use Players again.'

'No, putting it on in Halfpenny Lane is the whole point,' Aoife said.

'I know!' Mimi exclaimed, shooting up straight in her seat. 'We can film one of the performances and live stream it!'

'Oh yes! Of course!' Aoife slapped a hand to her forehead. 'Why didn't I think of that?'

Mimi gave her a cross look. 'You don't have to think of everything. Sometimes other people are capable of coming up with ideas. Shocker!'

'Sorry, I didn't mean … It's a brilliant idea.'

'I know.'

'Fantastic!' Sive beamed. 'Then as many people as want to can watch the show and we can charge a regular ticket price for the live stream.'

Aoife felt her heart racing as her pen flew across the page, struggling to keep up with the flow of ideas her sisters were pouring forth. The crowdfunder was starting to sound very exciting – perhaps even achievable.

'For the absolute minimum donation – say five euro – we could just offer an acknowledgement,' Jonathan said. 'We can print the names in the programme for *Three Sisters*, or put them on the website.'

'First we need to make a website!'

'That's the next item on the agenda,' Aoife said, pointing to the list they'd made earlier.

Mimi groaned. 'I'm hopeless at anything like that.'

'Me too,' Sive said.

'I'm not great at it either,' Aoife said. 'I can do a bit, but it'd take me forever – and it probably still wouldn't be right. I suppose we could hire someone. Unless you …' She looked at Jonathan hopefully.

He shook his head. 'I'm clueless on that score, I'm afraid. But Sam's pretty good at that stuff. I could get him to do it for us.'

'Great!'

'Okay, marketing,' Sive said, scrolling through the to-do list on her tablet. 'We need to set up social media for Halfpenny Lane, separate from our personal accounts.'

'A Facebook page, Twitter, Instagram …' Aoife jotted down a list, trying not to panic at how much there was to do.

'We should set up some PR in the media too – try to get some features in papers and magazines, maybe even some TV and radio interviews,' Sive said.

'And we need to make a campaign video,' Mimi said. All their crowdfunding research had suggested that a video was important. 'I'll write something, and the three of us can be in it. I can get some of my film school mates to shoot it for us.'

'I'll get Sam to start setting up the website,' Jonathan said, 'and you can work on the video and whatever other content you want to have on it.'

'We should make a budget for all this before we start,' Aoife said. 'Get prices for swag and cost the marketing. Then, once we have the video and social media set up and the website's live, we can set up the crowdfunder.'

When they'd agreed what they were all doing and shared out jobs, Mimi excused herself to read a script and Sive went to her room to call Ben.

'Would you like more tea?' Aoife asked Jonathan when they'd gone.

'No thanks. I'd better be off,' he said, standing. 'I've got a breakfast meeting at eight tomorrow.'

Aoife tried to brush off the pang of disappointment she felt.

'I really hope this thing works,' he said, stopping in the doorway as she saw him out.

'Me too.' As she met his gaze, a look passed between them, and suddenly Aoife felt the stakes had been raised. This crowdfunder had better deliver because there was a lot more riding on it than the future of Halfpenny Lane.

22

AOIFE and her sisters spent all their free time the following week working on the crowdfunder. Aoife researched and priced swag, while Mimi and Sive planned the website and wrote content, including a very moving piece by Mimi about Detta's theatrical legacy and the history of the building. Mimi liked writing and had also scripted a short video, which they shot at the theatre with the help of some of Mimi's film school friends. They'd set up social media accounts on Facebook, Twitter and Instagram and started posting content, sharing photos from the benefit concert and snippets about the theatre and its history. They got all their friends to help spread the word, and they were already getting some traction on social media.

Jonathan's brother Sam had set up the website and was ready to upload content, and Aoife and her sisters had drawn up a budget for the production of *Three Sisters*. Everything was progressing nicely, and they were almost ready to make the crowdfunding campaign live by the weekend. When she spoke to Jonathan on Friday for a progress report, they arranged for him to come over on

Wednesday evening to make a campaign budget and set up the crowdfunding page. But when she told Sive and Mimi at dinner that evening, they both had plans for Wednesday night.

'I wish you'd asked first,' Mimi said, looking put out. 'I've got a date.'

'And I've got night shoots all next week.' Sive had got a small part in a big-budget movie that was filming on location in Dublin.

'Should I put him off until the weekend, then?' Now that all the background work was done, Aoife was impatient to get the crowdfunder started. But she supposed a few days' delay wouldn't make much difference.

'It'd be best to get it set up as soon as we can,' Mimi said, echoing her sentiments. 'I could cancel my date.'

'No, don't do that.' Aoife figured Mimi would be only too glad of an excuse to drop her date. But it was good that she was pushing herself to get out there and make the effort to meet someone new and move on. 'I can meet him on my own.'

'Okay, if you're sure,' Mimi said. 'I honestly don't mind ditching my date.'

'No, it's fine.'

'You speak for all of us,' Sive said.

She rang Jonathan the following day and told him her sisters couldn't make it on Wednesday. 'So it's just the two of us. Unless you'd rather leave it until another time when we can all be there.'

'No, there's no need for that. I'll come straight from work, if that suits you?'

'That's fine. I'll make dinner, then. Is there anything you don't eat?'

'Don't worry about that. I'll bring pizza.'

An automatic refusal was on the tip of her tongue, but then she thought better of it. 'Thanks. That'd be great.' She knew she was bad at accepting help and she needed to work on that. Maybe she should test out Jonathan's theory that the world wouldn't fall apart if she let go once in a while and stopped trying to do everything herself. She decided to practise being grateful and accepting graciously when someone offered to do something for her.

'Great,' Jonathan was saying in her ear. 'I'll see you then.'

'You look nice,' Mimi said as she was on her way out on Wednesday evening.

'Oh, thanks.' Aoife felt her cheeks warm. She'd showered and changed when she got home from work. Instead of the tatty joggers and T-shirts she habitually slobbed around in for the evening, she was wearing a long pinafore dress in a summery pink and purple print that she knew contrasted flatteringly with her dark colouring, with a white T-shirt underneath. She'd even put on a little make-up. 'I just felt a bit grungy after work,' she said, feeling the need to explain herself. 'You look great. Enjoy your date.'

'You too,' Mimi said with a sly smile.

'It's not—' But Mimi was gone before she could protest.

Jonathan appeared at the door just after seven, carrying a vast pizza box wafting mouth-watering aromas of garlic, herbs and freshly baked dough. 'I collected it on the way here,' he said, nodding to the pizza, 'so it's hot.'

He followed her down the hall to the kitchen. She'd heated plates and opened a bottle of red wine that sat breathing on the table along with glasses and napkins.

'Thanks for this,' Aoife said, as they decanted the pizza onto two plates. 'I'm starving. Wine?' She lifted the bottle.

Jonathan grimaced regretfully. 'I'd better not. I'm driving.' He loosened his tie as they sat at the table. He was looking very handsome in a dark suit and crisp white shirt, and the kitchen suddenly seemed very small with just the two of them in it.

'Oh, pity. You could always leave your car here and come back for it tomorrow?'

Jonathan considered for only a second. 'Good idea.' He nodded to his glass and Aoife poured. 'I'll get a cab home tonight.'

It was a good thing this *wasn't* a date, Aoife thought as she bit into a slice of pizza and the oily sauce trickled down her chin. She swiped it away with a napkin. This was not a good look, but there was no way to eat such deliciously oozy pizza elegantly. She sighed happily as she swallowed. 'I've had the day from hell, so this is a real treat.'

'Shall we eat first or dive straight in?' Jonathan asked, nodding to the laptop and paperwork Aoife had piled up on the table.

'Let's just eat first. This pizza deserves our full attention.'

Jonathan smiled and nodded. 'Agreed.'

They made small talk as they ate, talking about their respective work days and the research they'd done for the crowdfunder. When they'd finished eating, Aoife cleared a space on the table for the laptop and Jonathan moved to the chair beside her. She was very aware of him sitting so close their legs were almost touching, and she breathed in the citrussy tang of his aftershave.

'Right, let's get to it,' Jonathan said, rubbing his hands. Aoife opened an Excel spreadsheet and they began making a budget, itemising all the marketing costs and materials for the crowdfunder as well as the cost of putting on *Three Sisters*.

'We should put in an amount for contingencies,' Jonathan said, when they'd totalled everything up.

Aoife nodded, grateful that they were of the same mind and Sive and Mimi weren't here to pooh-pooh the idea of contingencies. 'Five per cent?'

'Sounds good.'

'Okay,' Aoife said, pulling up the crowdfunding website. 'Let's do this.' They set up their page with the goal, uploaded their video pitch and entered the text for the appeal that Aoife and her sisters had already written. Then they added all the rewards for the various tiers of investors. Aoife tried not to feel hopeless at seeing the goal there on the screen. It seemed impossible.

'It's an awful lot to ask for,' she said, looking at the figure with dismay. 'Do you think we've any hope of reaching it?'

'Honestly, I have no idea,' Jonathan said. 'But if you don't ask, you don't get.'

When they'd finished setting the campaign up, they made a list of final steps for the launch.

'So, we're going live with it on Monday?' Jonathan asked.

Aoife nodded. 'Monday.' She just wished it didn't feel like the beginning of the end. While they were in the planning stage, it had seemed like a tantalising possibility for some vague time in the future. Once they went live, the clock would start ticking, and they'd be on a countdown to a deadline that would mean life or death for Halfpenny Lane.

. . .

Aoife was reading in bed when Mimi came home later that night, Marlowe curled up asleep at her feet.

'How was your date?' she called through her half-open bedroom door when she heard Mimi on the landing.

She appeared in the doorway. 'It was … okay.' Mimi frowned.

She was unusually subdued, and Aoife thought she seemed upset. 'What happened?'

'Nothing. It was fine. We had a good time … I thought. We went to Troc. I had fish. He had steak. He seemed nice.'

'Sounds good.'

Mimi pushed away from the door and moved into the room. She sat on the side of Aoife's bed. 'But then we went back to his place and he wanted to do this weird thing …'

Aoife sat up straighter. 'What? A weird sex thing?'

'No!' Mimi frowned. 'At least I don't think it was a sex thing.' She laughed. 'God, I hope not!'

'So what was it?'

'He wanted us to, um … wash his cat together.'

Aoife gave a hoot of laughter. 'Wait, is that a euphemism?'

'Nope. It was an actual cat.'

'Well, on the plus side, at least he has a cat. He can't be all bad.'

'I guess. Nice cat too − a Maine Coon. He was no Kit Marlowe, though.' She looked down at him fondly.

'Well, Kit sets the bar very high.'

'True.' Mimi played with a thread on Aoife's bedspread.

'And was that it? Did the cat-washing foreplay lead to anything?'

'Just a few scratches.' Mimi held up her hand, which

bore several angry-looking red claw marks and rolled her eyes. 'Turns out cats don't like baths. Who knew?'

'Doesn't he know cats are self-cleaning?'

'I tried to tell him, but he wouldn't listen. Anyway, I got more action from Fluffy – that's his cat's name – than I did from him.'

'Fluffy! So imaginative.'

Mimi smiled crookedly. 'I know.' She sighed. 'The thing is, I was relieved it didn't go anywhere. Even when we were at the restaurant and he seemed like a perfectly nice, good-looking, sane individual, I still didn't want anything to happen. I felt so disengaged and bored and … out of it. I was just going through the motions until I could escape and come home. This was before I knew he was a nutter with a possible cat-washing fetish. What's wrong with me?'

'There's nothing wrong with you,' Aoife said. But there *was* something wrong with Mimi's date, and she knew exactly what it was – the same thing that had been wrong with every guy she'd dated in the last couple of years. He wasn't Rocco.

'This is the only guy I want in my life right now,' Mimi said, leaning down and burying her face in Marlowe's fur. He opened his eyes and blinked at her briefly, then went back to sleep.

'How did it go with Jonathan?' she asked, lifting her head. 'Did you have a nice time?'

'Yes, it was … good. He brought pizza. We've got the crowdfunder all set up ready to go.'

Mimi looked at her consideringly. 'It's okay if you like him, you know.'

'What?'

'Jonathan. If you want to like him, you can.'

'You're giving me permission?'

'I am.' Mimi's mouth widened in a grin. 'Just go right ahead and like him if that's how you feel. We won't mind – Sive and I. I just thought you might need to know that.'

'Well, thanks for the offer. That's very decent of you. But I don't think I'll be taking you up on it. You may not disapprove, but I think I'd be disappointed in myself.'

'Well, suit yourself. But don't let us stop you.' She stood to go.

'So you won't be seeing Fluffy's dad again, then?' Aoife asked, looking up at her.

'Certainly not,' she said indignantly. 'Unless I decide to report him to the ISPCC for inappropriate cat-washing. I high-tailed it out of there as fast as my legs would carry me.' She smirked. 'Which wasn't very fast, actually. I really need to get back to jogging.'

23

'Aoife, could you come in here a moment?' Aoife looked up from her computer to see her boss Aidan sticking his head around the door of his office.

'Sure.' She jumped up and followed him inside, and he waved her to a seat on the opposite side of his desk.

'So,' he said, leaning forward, his hands clasped in front of him. 'I don't know if you heard, but Fran isn't coming back.' Fran was the woman whose job she was covering.

'Oh! No, I didn't know.'

'So we'll need to take on someone to replace her. I don't know if you're looking for something more permanent, but we'd like to offer you the job first.'

'Oh! Gosh.'

'We're very happy with your work here, Aoife.'

'Right. Thank you.'

'I know I'm springing this on you suddenly,' he continued as Aoife floundered for words. 'But we didn't get much notice from Fran. You can take some time to think about it. Let us know next week?'

'Okay, thanks. So it'd be full time?'

'Yes, nine to five, full time and permanent. The salary would be a little more than you're on now, pro rata. We'd be saving on the agency fees, so we could give you a bit of a raise. Are you interested in permanent work?'

'I'm not sure. I hadn't considered it.'

'Right. Well, think about it over the weekend.' Aidan pushed away from his desk and stood, signalling that the meeting was over.

Aoife returned to her desk in a daze, not sure how she felt about the offer. Her overriding feeling was annoyance with Aidan for giving her another decision to make. She had enough on her plate right now. This was a headache that she could do without. She didn't have the bandwidth for making big life decisions on top of everything else.

She'd been perfectly content five minutes ago, before Aidan sprang this on her. Damn Aidan! Why couldn't he have just left things as they were? And what if she refused? Would they still want her to temp here?

'What was that about?' her colleague Liz hissed at her when she sat down again.

'I … Did you know Fran's not coming back?' She didn't know if it was supposed to be a secret, but it would be common knowledge soon enough anyway.

Liz nodded, flicking her eyes to Aidan's closed door. She scooched her wheelie chair across to Aoife's desk so she was close enough to whisper, and leaned in. 'She told me before she left that she wasn't coming back. But she wanted to max out on her maternity pay and sick benefit.'

'Oh!' Aoife tried not to look too disapproving of this behaviour. If she took the job here, she'd have to be in cahoots with Liz about stuff like this. It was a depressing thought.

'Did they offer you her job?' Liz asked.

'Yes, they did.'

'That's great! You're practically part of the furniture already. And it's nice for me – means I won't be lumbered with showing some newbie the ropes – or even worse, another temp! No offence, but they're not all like you,~you know. Most of the ones they send us are completely clueless.'

'Well, I haven't decided to take it yet,' Aoife said, almost tempted to refuse it just so that Liz would have to do a bit of work. She spent most of her time on the internet, playing computer games, getting into arguments on social media and reading celebrity gossip.

'But you'll say yes – why wouldn't you?'

'I don't know. I have to think about it.'

'Aidan's a decent boss for all his faults. And they're good to work for. You get your Christmas bonus, and you have your seven paid sick days on top of your holidays.'

Liz always made sure to take her full quota of sick leave, regardless of whether she was ill or not.

'And you're well able for the work,' Liz continued encouragingly. 'You could do it in your sleep. What more could you ask?'

What more indeed? It was true O'Brien Sweeney were excellent employers, Aidan was a good boss and she enjoyed the work. But something in her instinctively recoiled at the thought of committing to it on a more permanent basis – and it wasn't just the thought of joining Liz, sleepwalking through her days and phoning it in. It would be like finally giving up on her dreams, closing the door on that other life she always thought she'd have some-time in the future. As long as she was temping, she could hedge her bets and keep a foot in both camps. Even though she'd got comfortable here on a long-term contract, she could still tell herself it was just a stop-gap and she hadn't settled. She could drop it tomorrow if she chose and pursue an acting career. There was no stability to lose, no perks to forego. Now she had to decide whether to slam that door shut for good. Damn Aidan!

'I got offered a job at O'Brien Sweeney today,' she told her sisters that evening at dinner.

'What?' Sive frowned. 'But you already work there. Is it a different job?'

'No. Same job, but it'd be permanent.'

'Permanent?' Mimi screwed up her face in disgust. Her reaction was so comical, Aoife wanted to laugh. 'You're not going to take it?'

'I haven't decided yet. The money would be good – and the security.'

'Aoife, you sound like a blasted pensioner. You don't want security at our age.'

'I don't know. Maybe I do. Security is a nice thing.'

'No, it's not – at least not when it comes to jobs. It's boring and stifling. It's basically death.'

Aoife laughed. 'It's not death! You're being melo-dramatic.'

'But it's no fun,' Sive said, reaching across the table to clutch her hand. 'And if you take this, it'll be the end of your acting career.'

'What acting career? I don't have an acting career.'

'That's just because you haven't got around to it yet. But you will have – as long as you don't take this accounting job.'

'Sive's right. You're just about to get started – finally! You can't give up now.'

'I know it can be scary at first. We all felt a bit wobbly at the start, didn't we?' Sive looked to Mimi for back-up. 'But you'll get over that.'

'It's defeatist,' Mimi said. 'You'd be like Olga taking the headmistress job when she doesn't even want it. There'd be no chance of Moscow.'

'Exactly! No chance of Moscow – imagine that!' Sive's eyes were wide with horror.

'There's precious little chance of Moscow anyway,' Aoife said.

'Don't be so negative.'

'You're just feeling a bit shaky because of losing Detta and now the whole thing with Halfpenny Lane.' Sive gave her a sympathetic look. 'Of course you're tempted to cling to the security. But that's all the more reason it's not a good time to be making big decisions.'

'But what about the money? One of us needs to earn a decent living.'

'We have enough to get by. We can manage,' Mimi said briskly.

'You're the most talented of all of us,' Sive said. 'It'd be criminal to throw that away.'

'She's right.' Mimi nodded. 'It's so unfair – you don't even have to work at it, you're just naturally gifted. The least you can do is play the winning hand you've been dealt.'

Aoife would never understand how severely Mimi and Sive underestimated their own talents. She was constantly in awe of them.

'I'm good at my accounting job too,' she said meekly. 'And it was really nice of them to offer it to me.'

'I think it was a horrible thing to do, trying to tempt you into a life of … office drudgery,' Mimi said crossly. 'You're not seriously considering it?'

'I am. I said I'd think about it, and I will.'

But as she tossed and turned in bed that night, she couldn't help thinking that perhaps Mimi was right. She knew the sensible decision would be to take the job and the steady income. But she couldn't shake off the sense of claustrophobia whenever she thought about becoming a permanent employee, as if the walls of O'Brien Sweeney were closing in on her. The idea of turning down the offer was scary, but it was an exhilarating kind of scary, like tobogganing down a steep snow-covered hill, and it gave her a feeling of lightness and freedom.

On the other hand, it was no fun worrying about money, and it wasn't as if she was unhappy at O'Brien Sweeney. She wouldn't have to be like Liz, doing the bare minimum and taking the piss. She'd be conscientious and do a good job. There'd be satisfaction in that. Besides, had she dragged them all through the hardest times and the leanest years only to throw them back into precarious impecunity just when she had the opportunity to improve their lot?

She still didn't have an answer by Friday, when she met Jonathan for lunch. He had some forms for her to sign in relation to Detta's will, and they met at a little Mexican cafe near Baggot Street Bridge, halfway between O'Brien Sweeney and his offices. It was a popular place, bustling with the lunchtime crowd.

'I got offered a permanent job at O'Brien Sweeney,' she told him as they squeezed onto metal chairs at a little table in the corner. She decided it would be good to get his opinion. He was a sensible grown-up in a responsible job –

a 'proper man' as Detta would have said. He'd have a more realistic and objective take on the matter, and she was confident that talking it over with him would reassure her that accepting the offer was the right thing to do.

'The accountancy firm?'

'Yes.'

'And?'

'It's a good offer. I should probably take it. Don't you think?'

'That's called leading the witness,' he said with a smile.

'Okay, let me rephrase my question. Do you think I should take it?'

'Is it what you want?' He frowned.

Aoife shrugged. 'It's the sensible thing to do – the responsible thing.'

'Evading the question. That's not what I asked.'

'The work is fine, and the pay and conditions are good. It'd be permanent. And the people there are nice – mostly,' she added, thinking of Liz, who really wasn't very nice at all. 'It's not as if I hate it.'

'It's not as if you love it either, is it?'

'No, but how many people actually love their work?'

'Your sisters? To name two.'

'Okay, granted. But everyone can't follow their heart, can they? We're always told we should do something we love as work, but that's not realistic, is it? We can't all be artists or musicians or whatever. Some people have to collect the bins and do the books and ... stand up for people in court. Do you love your job?'

He smiled. 'Love is putting it a bit strongly. I've never felt like I was flying when I was working on a case. But I enjoy it, yes. And I'm good at it, which is satisfying.'

Aoife huffed. That wasn't the answer she'd been

expecting. 'It's all very well telling people to follow their dreams, but if your dreams also stretch to living somewhere nice and eating good food on a regular basis, maybe even going on the occasional holiday, and not waking up in a cold sweat every night worrying about how you're going to pay the bills—'

'Your dream quickly becomes a nightmare.'

'Exactly.'

Jonathan was looking at her intently. 'If you're asking for my advice, I think you should follow your heart for once. It seems to me you've always done the sensible thing, whether it's what you want or not. You've sacrificed yourself for your sisters. But they don't need you to do that anymore – and I strongly suspect they don't want you to either. It's your turn. You deserve it.'

'This doesn't sound like you.'

'Doesn't it?' He seemed mildly annoyed. But he was right, she thought – she didn't really know him. Maybe this did sound like him.

'You're a smart person, you're obviously good at what you do. You can always get another accounting job. But you may not get another shot at this acting thing. If you don't give it a try, I think you might regret it.'

Aoife picked up the menu card from the table as Jonathan caught the eye of a waitress and she indicated that she'd be over in a moment.

'So, have you decided what you're having?' he asked, nodding to the menu in her hand.

'Hmm. I suppose the sensible choice would be the veggie burrito bowl.'

'Very sensible.' He kept his eyes lowered, but his mouth curved in a smile. 'It's the permanent pensionable job of Mexican cuisine.'

'So I'll have the loaded nachos,' she said, putting the card back on the table. She relaxed back in her chair, feeling the rightness of the decision in her body – in the loosening of her muscles and the expansion of her chest.

'Excellent choice.' He looked up and beamed at her. 'It's what Detta would have wanted for you.'

24

A WEEK LATER, Aoife and her sisters sat around the table after dinner updating the crowdfunding page. She felt a surge of pride as she watched Mimi and Sive, heads bent over their laptops. Jonathan was right. She didn't give them enough credit. After all, Sive had come up with this idea all on her own, and it was a good one. And no one could accuse either of them of slacking. They were both working incredibly hard to spread the word and bring in donations, as well as maintaining their mailing list and keeping investors updated on progress.

Sive had set up a newsletter with an email service provider so they could keep in contact with investors. Mimi took photographs and wrote posts for social media, and Jonathan had been as good as his word, using his business contacts to land some big corporate investors.

The crowdfunding page had been live for a week and already money was … not flooding in, but it was definitely more than a trickle. Aoife was pleasantly surprised how much it had increased when she logged onto the site every morning. She was confident that they'd reach their halfway goal by the end of the month. But she still tried to manage her expectations. She mustn't get carried away by their initial success and assume it meant they'd hit their target. Realistically, she knew that their most enthusiastic backers would pledge their support at the beginning of the campaign, and donations were likely to dwindle as time went on. They needed to work hard to keep broadening their reach and bringing in new investors.

They'd had lots of uptake already for the lower tier rewards items, and Aoife could see they were going to have to reorder the mugs, T-shirts and tote bags soon. They'd commissioned a local artist to do a sketch of Halfpenny Lane Theatre to put on swag, and limited edition prints of that were also proving very popular. They were gaining traction on social media, and they had several features lined up in newspapers and magazines, as well as a couple of radio slots. Mimi was even booked to go on a morning TV show to talk about the campaign.

They'd chosen some small period features and interesting memorabilia to work on so they had concrete signs of progress to show in their socials and newsletter. Old photographs of performances had been cleaned and reframed, antique lamps in the foyer had been repaired, and Sive had done excellent work mending several of the most opulent costumes, restoring them to their former glory.

It was all going promisingly so far. But having turned down the permanent job at O'Brien Sweeney, Aoife was more jittery than ever about the crowdfunder succeeding. She'd had the double blow of Aidan telling her that they could no longer keep her on as a temp and would be interviewing soon for someone permanent to replace Fran. Aidan had been disappointed when she turned the offer down, but he'd been very nice about it, and she totally understood it from his point of view. He told her they'd only kept renewing her temp contract for as long as they did because they'd hoped to offer her a permanent job somewhere down the line and keep her on. Her refusal obviously changed things.

Aoife had briefly considered offering to temp for them on a freelance basis, but she decided against it. If she was going to give acting a proper go, she should commit to it fully and embrace that life in all its precariousness – no safety nets, no Plan Bs. If she couldn't handle the uncertainty of it, it was best she find out once and for all. She'd agreed to stay on until they found a replacement, but they were interviewing already and she didn't think it would take long. Then she'd go back to temping from week to week, with the flexibility to take breaks whenever she needed to in between short assignments.

She'd be sorry to leave in ways – she'd miss having somewhere to go every morning, knowing what the day would hold. But the excitement of starting something new overrode that, and as planning for *Three Sisters* got underway, she realised it wouldn't be feasible to do both anyway. The crowdfunder was already taking up all her free time and there was so much to do, she was stretched to breaking point. By the time her last day at O'Brien Sweeney rolled around, she was impatient to go. She had enough savings to live on for the next few months, so she could afford to take a break from temping and concentrate on the theatre.

The next step was to get *Three Sisters* cast and into rehearsals. They'd hired Lorcan O'Neill to direct, someone whose work they all greatly admired. They'd approached him tentatively, not expecting him to accept. But he was first on the list of their dream cast and crew, so they asked him anyway, and were amazed at how enthusiastically he'd said yes – even with the proviso that casting Aoife, Mimi and Sive as the three leads was non-negotiable.

But just as she was about to embark on her new life, disaster struck. Her first Monday after quitting work, she woke with a pounding headache, weak limbs and pains all over her body. She was alternately shivering and sweating, and she could barely lift her head from the pillow. Her head spun as she sat up and threw off the covers. She made it to the bathroom and took the thermometer from the cabinet over the sink, then went back to bed to take her temperature. She already knew she had a fever, but she was alarmed at how high her temperature was. She groaned and lay back down. How could this happen – and today of all days? It was an inauspicious start to her new life, and it almost felt like an omen – as if the universe was telling her she'd made the wrong decision and she'd regret giving up her sensible well-paid job. She could be getting paid to stay in bed today.

Auditions were due to start this morning. They couldn't ask Lorcan to postpone. His time was precious, and he was already doing them an enormous favour directing the play in the first place and taking a reduced fee. Besides, they needed to get on with it if they wanted to get the show up and running in time for the theatre festival. There was also publicity for the crowdfunder to organise and admin to be done, and a photocall to arrange once the play was cast. And who'd co-ordinate the auditions and make sure they ran on schedule, while keeping everyone calm and happy?

She felt like her head might explode when she thought of all there was to do. She'd just have to pull herself together and get through the week somehow. After all, that was what theatre folk did, wasn't it? They were troopers, and she was one of them now. It was time to nail her colours to the mast. The show must go on!

But even as she thought it, she didn't budge. She knew it wasn't going to happen, and tears of frustration welled in her eyes. So much for her new life – she was failing at the very first hurdle. She lay back down and closed her eyes. Maybe if she just had another hour or two in bed, she could sleep it off. Or better yet, she'd wake up and discover this was just a nightmare …

'Oh my god!' Mimi's eyes widened with alarm when Aoife shuffled into the kitchen a couple of hours later. 'You look awful!'

'Don't worry, I feel worse than I look.' She'd woken again a few minutes ago and managed to haul herself out of bed and into her dressing gown. But even walking down the stairs had been a struggle. Her legs felt like jelly, barely able to hold her up. 'I think I've got flu.'

'Oh, you poor thing!' Sive gave her a sympathetic look.

Aoife flicked on the kettle and got a mug out of the cupboard. 'I'll be fine once I've had some tea – or maybe I should have coffee?' Her eyes were drifting closed as she spoke. New plan: she'd make it through the day on caffeine and crash out later when she was home.

'You will not!' Mimi stood and joined her at the counter, putting a hand on her forehead. 'You're burning up. You should go back to bed immediately. Why did you even get up?'

'Because … I've got all these auditions to coordinate and the publicity photoshoot to organise, and—'

'I think you mean *we*,' Mimi said, her tone brittle. '*We* have all this stuff to do. You need to stay home and rest.'

'But what about the photocall?'

'Sive and I can take care of that.'

Sive nodded. 'And you don't need to be there for the auditions. We're already cast.'

'Exactly,' Mimi chimed in. 'We need you well for when rehearsals start. Anyone can do the organisational stuff. Only you can play Olga.'

Aoife groaned inwardly. They didn't understand. She may not need to audition, but she still needed to be there to corral the actors and make sure the auditions ran on schedule. Theatrical folk weren't renowned for their discipline and rigorous time-keeping, and she had nightmares about Lorcan going over the allotted time with each actor and leaving some of the oldest and most distinguished stars of Irish theatre waiting like wannabes. She had visions of Margaret sitting out in the corridor kicking her heels as she waited her turn. If she wasn't there, who would keep everyone in line, make sure things ran smoothly …

'Besides, we don't want you giving it to the rest of the cast,' Mimi said.

Aoife knew when she was defeated. 'You're right. You probably shouldn't even be standing so close to me.'

Mimi waved away her concern with a flap of her hand. 'I'm holding my breath. You go back to bed and I'll bring your tea up.'

Aoife bowed to the inevitable and agreed to stay home. She knew it was the sensible thing to do. It was what she'd have told either of her sisters if they'd been the ones to get sick. She thought of what Jonathan had said about her helicopter sistering, and tried to reassure herself that she was fussing unnecessarily. Sive and Mimi were grown women who successfully managed their own careers in a tricky field. They weren't going to fall apart just because she wasn't there to supervise them. They could handle things perfectly well without her … couldn't they?

She'd just have to trust that they could cope, she

thought as she got back into bed and pulled the covers over herself. Because all the coffee in the world wasn't going to save her now.

Nevertheless, when she woke again a couple of hours later, she couldn't help worrying about what was going on at the theatre. She looked at the clock on her nightstand. It was after eleven, and the auditions would have started … unless something had gone wrong. Would Mimi and Sive be able to keep discipline, or would it all descend into chaos? Would they keep the schedule running on time? But worrying as it all was, she found she didn't have the energy to get too wound up about it. She took some pills for her pounding head and washed them down with water from the bottle Mimi had left beside her bed before she fell back asleep.

When she woke again, it was to a light knocking on the door.

'Come in,' she croaked, surprised either of her sisters would bother knocking. Usually they just barged in. 'Oh! What are you doing here?'

Inexplicably, Jonathan was standing in the doorway, and she struggled to sit up, looking down at herself in a panic to make sure she was decent. Thankfully, the T-shirt she'd slept in wasn't remotely revealing.

'I brought you some soup.' He lifted a large paper bag in his hand, and Aoife noted it was from the neighbourhood Thai restaurant.

'Oh!' She flushed, realising how rude she'd sounded. 'Sorry, I thought it was going to be Mimi or Sive.'

'Sorry to disappoint.'

'You're not disappointing. Especially if that's tom yam.'

'It is.'

But as he made to step inside, she held a hand up to stop him. 'You shouldn't come in, though. I'm contagious. You don't want to get this. But thanks for the soup. You could leave it at the door?'

He shook his head. 'I'll take my chances,' he said, striding over to the bed. He took a large takeaway tub from the bag and put it on the nightstand. 'Anyway, I have the constitution of an ox.' He took the lid off the soup and handed it to her with a spoon. 'Eat up. It'll do you good.'

Aoife inhaled the fragrant spicy aroma before taking a spoonful of the soup. The fierce chilli hit was at once soothing and restorative. 'Thanks for this. It's delicious.'

To her surprise, he sat in the window seat and took another identical container from the bag. She glanced at the clock as he lifted the lid and began to eat. It was just after one. He must have come here on his lunch break. That was nice of him.

'How did you even get in?' she asked, realising he hadn't rung the doorbell.

'Mimi gave me her key, so I wouldn't have to get you out of bed. I've been deputised to take care of you.'

'Deputised?' She frowned. 'By whom?'

'Your sisters.'

'You were at the theatre?'

'Yes, I called in to see how things were going.'

Aoife forced herself not to ask. He'd only accuse her of hovering again.

'So I'm at your disposal.'

She relaxed back against the pillows and concentrated on trying not to slurp her soup.

When they'd both finished eating, he took the empty cartons and put them back in the bag. 'I'll make tea. And I'll bring you up some more water.'

'Thanks, but you don't have to do that. I can stagger as far as the kitchen.'

'Nonsense,' he said bossily. 'That's what I'm here for.'

'But … don't you have to get back to work?'

He shook his head. 'I've taken a few days' leave to deal with this crisis.' He waved vaguely to her.

'They shouldn't have made you do that,' Aoife said crossly. 'You don't want to waste your leave looking after me. And I'm not so far gone that I can't make myself a cup of tea.'

'They didn't make me do anything. I offered, when I heard you were laid up.'

'You did?'

'Yes. I'm part of Team Halfpenny Lane, so I'm doing my bit for the war effort.'

'All the more reason you shouldn't be here. We don't want the whole team coming down with this.'

'I'm dispensable,' he said cheerfully. 'You and your sisters are not. So, no more arguments. I'm going to make that tea.'

Aoife obeyed meekly and sank back against the pillows as he left the room, a little dismayed but oddly comforted by his taking charge so forcefully. Then she looked around and panicked as she took in the mess in her bedroom. She quickly grabbed the pile of magazines, books and clothes that were strewn at the foot of the bed and leaned out to stuff them underneath. Then she swept the detritus from the top of the nightstand into one of the drawers. She plumped up the pillows and straightened the duvet as she listened to the sounds of Jonathan moving around downstairs. She felt like Jane Bennet waiting for a visit from Mr Bingley while she was recuperating at Netherfield Hall.

Jonathan appeared again carrying a steaming mug. He set it on the nightstand and sat down on the edge of the bed. Aoife's heart hammered. This suddenly felt as intimate and inappropriate as if she actually was a regency miss entertaining a gentleman in her boudoir.

'Careful, it's hot,' Jonathan said as she picked up the mug.

She took a sip and recoiled. 'Ugh! I don't take sugar in my tea.' She put the mug down again. 'Sorry, I should have said,' she added, realising she was being rude when he'd meant to do something nice for her.

'It's honey. It'll be good for your throat.'

'Oh.'

'So, drink up.' He lifted the mug and handed it to her, watching as she took another cautious sip. It was gross. Why couldn't all things that were good for you taste as good as tom yam soup?

When she'd finished her disgusting tea, Jonathan left and Aoife managed to go back to sleep. But every time she woke up, he seemed to be there, offering her tea or water, insisting it was important she keep her fluids up. She woke in the late afternoon to find him striding around the room spritzing water into the air from a spray bottle.

'What are you doing?' she asked, struggling to sit up.

'I'm adding moisture to the air,' he said, not stopping. 'Dry air can make your symptoms worse.' He fished something out of his pocket. 'Now that you're awake, have one of these.' He handed her a packet.

'Elderberry lozenges?' she said, reading the wrapping.

He nodded. 'Take them four times a day. Studies show they can reduce the symptoms of colds and flu and shorten your recovery time.'

'Oh my god, you totally Googled how to treat a flu patient, didn't you?'

He gave her a crooked smile. 'Why not? I'm a firm believer in taking advantage of all the resources we have at our disposal.' He looked pointedly at the packet of lozenges in her hand.

Aoife did as she was told and took one.

25

THE FOLLOWING days passed in a fug. Aoife slept for hours, and when she was awake, Jonathan was there feeding her hot sour soups that spiked her appetite and cool creamy yoghurts to soothe her scratchy throat. In the evenings her sisters stood in the doorway and filled her in on what was happening in the theatre, always maintaining a safe distance and wearing face masks for good measure.

Apparently the auditions were running smoothly, the show was almost completely cast, and a photocall had been arranged for Saturday for publicity images. The shoot would take place in the grounds of a stately home in Wicklow, and Mimi had even organised a bus to transport everyone there. Aoife wondered if they were giving her the full picture, frustrated that she couldn't go and see for herself. But for now she'd just have to take their word for it.

They were full of stories about the auditions, telling her about the actors who'd been cast and how brilliant they were. Aoife was pleased to hear Margaret Brennan would play Anfisa, but daunted at the same time about the scenes she'd have with her. Mimi and Sive raved about how insightful Lorcan was and how thrilling it would be to work with everyone. But their excitement and enthusiasm only made Aoife more frustrated that she was missing it.

After four days in bed, she was over the worst and her temperature was back to normal. She was able to get up, but she still felt weak and her sisters continued to bar her from the theatre.

'There's no need,' Mimi told her when she joined her sisters for breakfast in the kitchen. 'Everything's taken care of. We want you completely fit for the photocall on Saturday.'

'Besides, you might still be contagious. We don't want to risk anyone else getting this,' Sive added.

Aoife couldn't argue with that. So she agreed to stay home for another couple of days, even though she was itching to get back to Halfpenny Lane. Apart from worrying because she wasn't there to see what was going on and sort out any problems, she hated that she was missing out on the excitement. It wasn't fair! It was their first – and possibly only – production at Halfpenny Lane, and she didn't want to miss a moment.

'If you feel up to it, you could use the time to study your part,' Mimi said, probably sensing Aoife's impatience to get back to work. 'Get Jonathan to run lines with you.'

'I think Jonathan can stand down as my nurse at this stage.'

As if conjured by his name, they heard him come in the front door.

'Oh, you're up?' he said to Aoife, appearing in the doorway.

'Yes, I'm feeling much better.'

'But still not great,' Mimi added.

'Not well enough to go into the theatre,' Aoife said. 'But I don't need you to nurse me anymore. So you can get back to work.'

'I've got the rest of the week off,' Jonathan said, moving into the kitchen.

'We were saying you could run lines with her,' Mimi told him.

'Sure. Whatever you need, I'm at your service.' He gave Aoife a little bow.

'You can keep her out of mischief and make sure she doesn't sneak out,' Sive said with a cheeky smile in Aoife's direction.

Aoife thought it would be awkward spending so much time with Jonathan, but she was surprisingly relaxed around him. They watched television, and played cards, and he ran Aoife's lines with her. But they could also sit comfortably in silence together. She was pleased to discover that he could read without moving his lips – a skill her time in O'Brien Sweeney had taught her not all adults had. Liz would insist on reading articles out to her, even if Aoife told her she'd already heard the news or read the piece in question herself. She would also relay accounts of TV programmes she'd watched in grinding detail, forcing Aoife to listen to the gory details of a true crime documentary she'd deliberately avoided because she knew it would be unbearable. She really didn't miss working with Liz.

Jonathan was infinitely preferable company, and she learned a lot about him during the time they spent together. She knew that he could guess the murderer in Midsomer within five minutes, that he was uncannily good at answering the questions on Pointless, that he preferred mustard to ketchup, that he read mostly non-fiction but occasionally thrillers, that he'd broken up with his last serious girlfriend when he left London … and that she was falling for him – hard.

On Saturday, she returned to the theatre for the publicity photoshoot, hoping she'd still have time to sort out any details that had been forgotten and pick up whatever balls had been dropped in her absence. Sive and Mimi had gone ahead earlier and insisted she have a lie-in and only come in time to get ready for the photoshoot. Aoife had no choice but to agree. She didn't want it to look like she didn't trust them to handle things themselves. And she did trust them, she told herself. It was just that she knew accidents could happen and everyone made mistakes, no matter how competent they were.

She braced herself as she entered the stage door, expecting to find the place in chaos, but prepared to take charge, iron out any problems and soothe frazzled nerves. There was a strange air of calm that did nothing to put her mind at rest as she made her way up the narrow stairs to the dressing rooms. It was unnaturally quiet, the backstage area devoid of the air of bustle and panic she'd anticipated. Instead as she walked along the corridor, knocking on the dressing room doors, she found the whole cast present and correct, quietly going about the business of getting ready. She entered the main dressing room to find Sive and Mimi sitting at the dresser in costume, putting finishing touches to their hair and make-up.

'Aoife!' Sive turned to her as she entered. 'You're just in time. I was beginning to worry that you weren't going to make it.' She stood and waved Aoife to the seat beside Mimi. 'Hurry up and get changed. The photographer will be here in half an hour.'

Aoife sat in a daze. 'What were you going to do if I

didn't turn up?' she asked, starting to panic that they'd have let the photoshoot go ahead with just two sisters.

'Oh, we'd already thought of that. We were going to get Cara to stand in for you, and get the photographer to shoot the three of us from the back, maybe standing with our arms around each other. It would have been pretty effective, I think.'

'That's a great idea,' Aoife said approvingly. Cara, the stage manager, was a similar height to her.

'Anyway, you're here now,' Sive said, clapping her hands together. 'I'll go and check on everyone else, make sure they're all ready to go.'

'What came over her?' Aoife asked, turning to Mimi as Sive left the room.

Mimi gave her a sidelong glance as she applied a final lick of lipstick. 'I don't know. Maybe she was finally allowed to take responsibility for something and she stepped up.'

Aoife sighed. 'Yeah, you're right.'

'She's always had it in her, you know.'

'I just never gave her credit.'

'You never gave her a chance to try.' Mimi smiled at her kindly. 'But you're learning.'

By the time Aoife had changed into her costume and finished her hair and make-up, Sive had assembled the whole cast in the corridor and was ushering them down to the street, where a bus was waiting to take them to the stately home in Wicklow where the photoshoot was being held. She was holding a clipboard and ticking the actors off on a list as they went.

'Well done, Sive,' Aoife said to her as she stepped to the front of the line. 'You've done an amazing job.' It may look like a simple task, but Aoife knew how difficult it was to marshal a group of actors like this, and get everyone ready on time. It was like herding cats.

Sive put an arm around her and gave her a squeeze. 'Thank you.'

'Sorry I couldn't help. But you obviously didn't need me.'

'We'll always need you. But I've enjoyed it! It's kind of fun bossing everyone around, isn't it?'

Aoife couldn't say she felt the same. She was too much of a worrier, too anxious about something going wrong. She needed to relax more and trust in other people. It was like Jonathan said, she didn't have to keep the world turning all on her own.

Mimi came running down the corridor towards them, grinning, her eyes sparkling. 'This is so exciting! I can't believe we're finally doing this!'

'Me either,' Aoife murmured as it sank in. They'd dreamt of this day for so long, and now it was finally here. They were really going to do *Three Sisters* together at Halfpenny Lane. Whatever else happened afterwards, they'd always have that.

'It's so exciting!' Sive squealed, beaming at her sisters.

Margaret, just ahead of them, turned around. 'Detta would be so proud of you girls,' she said, smiling kindly, and Aoife's eyes welled up.

'Okay, everyone!' Sive raised her voice, lifting her chin to be heard over the remaining throng in the corridor. 'Let's go! The buses are waiting outside.'

Aoife swallowed the lump in her throat as she lifted her skirts and followed the rest of the cast towards the stairs.

26

REHEARSALS for *Three Sisters* began the following week. It was all new and thrilling to Aoife, and from the moment she stepped into the rehearsal room for the first time, she knew this was what she wanted, what she'd been missing without even knowing it. The energy was electric and seemed to fizz through her veins. This was how she wanted to spend the rest of her life – doing this creative, collaborative work with talented people like these. It seemed to fill an empty space inside her that she hadn't been aware was there.

Lorcan began with some games and exercises around the theme of the play, which Aoife loved and threw herself into with abandon and a lack of self-consciousness that surprised her. But her nerves started to kick in when they did the first table read and she looked around at all the famous actors, people she was used to watching from a distance. She struggled not to let it overwhelm her and tried to act as if she belonged among them, to see herself as one of the players rather than a wannabe. But she couldn't help feeling out of place, like the new girl on her first day of school.

They spent the next couple of days taking a deep dive into the play, discussing their research and doing a close reading of the text so that everyone understood the meaning of the play and their roles and aims as actors. She loved the work, but it was on another level from the amateur dramatics she'd taken part in at college, and she immediately felt out of her depth.

She was envious as she watched Sive and Mimi engage in the process so effortlessly, impressed at how they held their own in such distinguished company. They blended in seamlessly as they took part in exercises, made suggestions, riffed off the other actors and played with the script as if it was second nature to them – which she supposed it was. That was what two years at acting school did for you – not to mention all the extra classes, workshops and professional acting jobs they'd had since.

She thought back to when they'd been in acting school and they'd come home brimming with excitement about techniques they were learning or new insights they'd had, and dying to tell Aoife about it. It was all they could talk about sometimes. She wished now that she'd paid closer attention, asked them to teach her, to share what they were learning about movement and voice and stagecraft. As the week went on and rehearsal proper began, she felt more than ever like an imposter.

But when she suggested to Sive and Mimi that they replace her – for the good of the play, she said, hoping to appeal to their sense of professionalism – they wouldn't hear of it.

'We're non-negotiable,' Mimi said. 'We've said that from the start. We'd sooner fire Lorcan than get rid of you.'

'It was always the plan to do this play together in Half-penny Lane. You can't bail on us now that our dream is finally coming true.'

'But the idea was that I'd go to acting school first.' That had been *her* idea anyway. It occurred to her now that maybe she'd never shared that with her sisters. In fairness, the dream had always been light on details.

'We don't have time for that now,' Mimi said. 'This might be our only chance to do it.'

'But I can't just insert myself into a company of profes-sionals. I don't know what I was thinking agreeing to this. I'm not good enough. It's just not right. We can't make this a vanity project.'

'It's not a vanity project.' Mimi rolled her eyes. 'And of course you're good enough. We'd tell you if you were shit,' she added.

That reassured her somewhat. She wasn't so sure about Sive, who was nodding earnestly in agreement, but she believed she could trust Mimi to be brutally honest.

'If I thought you weren't ready, I'd be the first to replace you,' Mimi continued. 'You might think we'd just let you continue out of sisterly loyalty, but it wouldn't be a kindness to let you go on if you were rubbish. That would be embarrassing for all of us, not just you. But you're as good as anyone in the cast – and I include myself in that, so I don't say it lightly,' she added with a smirk. 'You deserve your place.'

Aoife smiled. Mimi wasn't given to throwing out compliments profusely, so it really meant something when she did.

'Okay, maybe you're a bit rough around the edges on the finer points,' she continued. 'But that's all. Acting school would give you a shine, sure. But you can't polish a turd, and we can work on some of the bells and whistles with you.'

'Yes, we'll help,' Sive chimed in.

'Just no more nonsense about quitting, okay? We need you to commit to the process.'

Aoife was impressed. She'd never seen Mimi so serious.

'Okay,' she said. 'I'm all in.'

She returned to rehearsals the next day with renewed confidence, and as the days passed, her self-belief grew stronger. She began to forget her doubts and to feel like a real working actress and a worthy member of the cast. She realised her sense of inadequacy had been all in her head. The other actors had accepted her as one of them from the start. No one spoke down to her or treated her like a newbie, and Lorcan seemed happy with her performance. He didn't give her any more notes than he did anyone else.

Nevertheless, she still thought she should voice her concerns to him, and offer him an out if he wanted to replace her. After all, he'd been given no choice in casting her and her sisters. He was the director and should have the final say, whatever Mimi might think.

She lingered behind the following night, as everyone gathered up their stuff and trailed out of the rehearsal room. Mimi and Sive were going to the pub with some of the others, and she told them to go ahead and she'd catch up. 'I just want to ask Lorcan something.'

'If it's is he single, I think you're out of luck,' Sive whispered. 'I'm pretty sure he's taken.'

'And even if he's not, you'd be at the back of a very long queue,' Mimi said. 'No offence, but I don't fancy your chances.'

Aoife laughed. It was true half the cast were in love with Lorcan. Clever, talented and astonishingly beautiful, he could have been intimidating if he wasn't also so kind and friendly. But he was a total sweetheart and a joy to work with. 'It's not that. I just want to clarify something about one of his notes.'

Mimi gave her a nod of approval, and they left.

When they'd gone, she turned back into the room.

'Aoife.' Lorcan smiled at her as she approached him shyly.

'Could I just have a quick word?'

'Of course.' He nodded to the bench behind him and they sat side by side.

'What's up? Great rehearsal today, by the way. Did I say that already?'

Aoife beamed. 'You did. But thanks. I can't hear that often enough.' Lorcan was demanding, but generous with his praise. 'That's kind of what I wanted to talk to you about, actually.' She took a deep breath. 'I think you know I didn't go to acting school.'

'Right.' He nodded. 'I knew that, yes. What *did* you do?'

'Up until a couple of weeks ago I was an accounts technician.'

'Seriously? Gosh! That's quite the career change.'

'Yeah. The point is, I'd trained to be an accounts technician, and I'd had lots of experience. I was good at it. That's not the case with acting. This is my first real acting job.'

'So you're throwing yourself in at the deep end.'

Gah! Why was she finding it so hard to say what she wanted to? *Just spit it out.* 'The thing is, I know I was foisted on you. I mean, the three of us were – me and my sisters. But it's different with Mimi and Sive. They're professionals. I'm not, and you weren't given any say in casting me. So if you want to replace me, it's fine. I'd completely understand.'

'Replace you?' he asked, startled. 'Why would you think I'd want to do that?'

'Well, because I'm not a real actress, like everyone else. I've never trained—'

Lorcan shrugged. 'That doesn't matter. But you *are* a real actor, Aoife. Believe me. What do you think you've been doing here every day? I'm sorry if I've made you feel—'

'No, no!' She hastened to reassure him. 'It's nothing you've said or not said. You've never made me feel I was on a different level from the others or like I didn't belong. But—'

'So why the lack of confidence? You're a great actor, Aoife. I wouldn't say that if I didn't mean it. Is this just about not having gone to acting school?'

She shrugged. 'I suppose so.'

'Well, let me put your mind at rest about that. Training to be an actor isn't the same as qualifying to be an accountant or whatever—'

'Accounts technician.'

'Okay, accounts technician.' He frowned. 'I don't even know what that is. But I imagine it's not something a person might just be able to do naturally – an innate ability you could be born with?'

'No,' Aoife said with a light laugh.

'Well, acting's not like that – as you should know. As you've demonstrated here every day.'

Aoife smiled, teary with gratitude. His praise meant so much to her. 'Thanks.'

'And you know, there are lots of famous actors who never went to drama school. Ian McKellen … Jennifer Lawrence … Ben Kingsley … Tom Cruise.'

They both laughed. 'So you're saying I could be the next Tom Cruise?'

'If you play your cards right. Work hard. Join the Moonies or whatever.'

'Get my teeth capped.'

'Make *Top Gun*.'

'Perform all my own stunts.'

'Yeah, maybe Tom Cruise is reaching. But you could definitely be the next Ian McKellen.'

After that, Aoife shook off her insecurities and threw herself completely into rehearsals. By the end of the first week, she had that old feeling of soaring and she knew there was no going back. She was an actor now. She might take accounting jobs from time to time, but Mimi was right – deep down in her soul she was an actor first and always.

Her new-found confidence seemed to seep into other aspects of her life too. She stopped fretting so much about money. If funds were running low, she could always take temp jobs for a while or find freelance accountancy work online. She felt capable and resourceful, ready and able to cope with whatever came her way. The idea that things could work out without her worrying was novel and very freeing.

Her sisters could take care of themselves – thrive even – without her help. Things could happen without her constantly driving them forward. She even started to believe that perhaps she could relax and stop resisting her crush on Jonathan – just give into it and see what would happen. Maybe things could work out between them. It might be really good. Mimi and Sive were okay with it. They'd warmed to Jonathan, and even though they knew they might lose Halfpenny Lane because of him, they didn't seem to resent him anymore. If they could get past it, surely she could too.

So she didn't even pretend to herself that she wasn't excited about it when he asked her to meet him for lunch on Monday, or that she didn't make a special effort to look nice. They met outside his office building, and got sandwiches from a nearby deli to eat outside. It was a hot, sunny day and the banks of the canal were crowded with office workers sunning themselves on their lunch break and picnicking on the grass, but they managed to find an empty bench overlooking the water.

'How are rehearsals going?' Jonathan asked her as he unwrapped an over-stuffed Reuben.

'Great!' Aoife beamed. 'I'm really enjoying it.'

'I can see that,' he said, watching her face intently. He smiled. 'I like this new, confident Aoife.'

She raised her eyebrows. 'You didn't like me before?'

'Oh, I did. Very much. But I'm … pleased for you, I suppose. I like seeing you like this. You seem so much happier, and it suits you – gives you a glow.'

She laughed. 'Thanks. I must say, it does feel good. I could get used to happiness.'

'I hope you do.'

They looked at each other for a moment that stretched for an uncomfortably long time. Aoife looked away first. She took a bite of her Cajun chicken panini, and concentrated on chewing. When he'd asked to meet, Jonathan had said he wanted to discuss the crowdfunder with her. But she was starting to wonder if that had just been a pretext, because they'd said all they needed to on that subject while they were queuing in the sandwich bar.

Jonathan crunched up his empty sandwich wrapping and brushed his hands. 'Anyway, there was something I wanted to ask you. A favour.'

'Oh?' She turned back to him.

'I have this thing I have to go to. A company dinner, next Saturday – the summer ball, actually. I was wondering if you'd come as my plus one.'

'Oh! You don't have anyone else to bring?' As soon as the words were out of her mouth, Aoife wanted to kick herself. Why was *that* her automatic response? She hated the thought of him going on a date with someone else, so why put the idea in his head?

'I don't have anyone else I'd *rather* bring,' he said, and Aoife felt a flush of pleasure.

'Next Saturday?' She nodded. 'Okay. I mean, thanks. I'd love to.'

'Really?'

He looked so surprised, Aoife couldn't help laughing. 'Were you expecting me to say no?'

'Well, yeah, I can't say I was sure of myself. But I'm very glad you didn't.'

'Will it be very fancy?' She suddenly realised she'd have to find something suitable to wear.

He nodded. 'It's black tie. So pretty fancy, I guess.' He put a hand into his jacket pocket and pulled out an invitation, handing it to her. It was printed on thick cream card with embossed gold lettering. The McWilliams summer ball was being held at the Marker Hotel, beginning with a drinks reception at six-thirty.

'I'll get a cab and pick you up at six?' he said as she handed him back the card and he put it back in his pocket.

Aoife nodded. 'Okay, great. It's a date.' Oh god, it *was* a date. She was going on a date with Jonathan Hunt. How weird was this? But first she had other things to worry about – like shoes and a dress and … possibly a bikini wax?

27

Even though they'd given her permission to like Jonathan, Aoife was still nervous about telling Mimi and Sive she'd agreed to go out with him.

'So, um, I've … got a date for Saturday night,' she said, broaching the subject obliquely at breakfast the following morning.

'Oh?' Mimi paused in buttering her toast, and Sive put down the cup that had been raised halfway to her lips. Suddenly she had their full attention, both of them looking at her expectantly. Damn, she should have gone on dates more often, so that it wasn't such a big deal to them.

'Who with?' Mimi asked.

'Where are you going?'

'Do we know him?'

'Ooh, is it Mitch?' Mitch was the actor playing Vershinin, who Sive maintained she'd caught eyeing up Aoife.

She shook her head. 'No, it's not Mitch, yes, you do know him.' She counted their questions off on her fingers as she answered them in reverse order. 'We're going to dinner at the Marker. It's a company bash. With Jonathan.'

Mimi merely raised her eyebrows in response, and resumed buttering her toast. Aoife wished she knew what she was thinking.

Sive gave a delighted squeal. 'This is great! I knew you were sweet on each other. I called this from the start.'

Aoife smiled. 'You did. So … you don't mind?' She looked between them, wincing.

Mimi shook her head, her mouth full.

'Of course not! We already gave you our blessing, remember.'

'You're the one who had a problem with it,' Mimi said when she'd swallowed and could speak again.

'We like Jonathan.'

Aoife frowned at Sive. 'You called him our arch-nemesis.'

Sive waved her hand dismissively. 'That was at the beginning, before we got to know him.'

Aoife looked to Mimi.

'I admit he was a slow burn, but we do like him. He was very good when you were sick.'

'And he's been so helpful with the fundraising when he didn't have to be.'

'He *has* thrown himself into it,' Mimi allowed.

'And Marlowe slow-blinked him,' Sive said. 'So it's unanimous!'

'Marlowe'll slow-blink anyone,' Mimi scoffed. 'He's a tart.'

'That doesn't mean his opinion counts for nothing.'

'You're right.'

'We mustn't slut-shame Marlowe,' Sive said solemnly.

'Anyway,' Mimi said, 'Detta obviously cared about him, or she wouldn't have left him Halfpenny Lane. If

Detta loved him, who are we not to take him to our bosoms?'

Aoife breathed a sigh of relief and grabbed another slice of toast. She could enjoy her breakfast now that the hard part was over.

'So, tell us everything. How did he ask you? Was he nervous? I bet he was nervous!'

'Sive, it wasn't a proposal,' Mimi said dryly.

'Still, I want details! We've been starved of romance around here for too long.'

'Doesn't say much for you and Ben.'

'Oh, Ben and I are practically Darby and Joan. It's lovely and everything, but it hardly counts as romance at this stage.' Ben had grown up across the road from them, and had gone to the same school. Sive had started going out with him when she was fifteen and they'd been together ever since.

'I think he *was* pretty nervous, actually.' Aoife smiled. 'It was sweet. He didn't expect me to say yes. And he said—'

'Yes?'

'I asked him did he not have anyone else he could take, and he said he did, but there was no one else he'd *rather* take.'

Sive gave another squeal.

'I have to hand it to him, that's a pretty decent line,' Mimi said, smiling.

'So, a company dinner at the Marker,' Sive said. 'Sounds fancy.'

Aoife nodded. 'It's a ball, actually – black tie. So yeah, it'll be fancy.'

'A ball!' Sive gasped. 'Get you, Cinderella.'

'And with a proper man – Detta would be so proud.'

'What are you going to wear?' Sive asked.

'I have no idea.' Aoife's smile faded, replaced by a worried frown.

'You should go for something long,' Mimi said, musing. 'There's that red dress I wore to the IFTAs last year. Or Sive's dark-green chiffon – that colour would be gorgeous on you.'

'Or how about that Halston dress of Detta's?'

'I'm not sure I'd have the nerve to wear that.'

Luckily they were all more or less the same size and could wear each other's clothes – and Detta's too, though they sometimes required a little alteration, especially for Mimi, who was bigger in the bust than her sisters.

'Well, there are lots of options,' Mimi said. 'We'll go through our wardrobes tonight and see what we've got. Then there's still time to go shopping if we can't find anything suitable.'

'And I can do any alterations, if need be.'

Aoife smiled at them gratefully.

'Yay, a project!' Sive clapped her hands. 'We'll be your fairy godmothers.'

'You *shall* go to the McWilliams ball!'

Aoife was surprised how jittery she felt as she got ready for the ball on Saturday night. But she supposed she was just out of practice. She'd broken up with her last boyfriend, David, almost a year ago by mutual consent when he'd decided he was too young to be in a serious relationship and wanted to enjoy being single for a while. He'd since cut a swathe through most of their friendship group and acquired a reputation as a bit of a player. She'd missed him sometimes, but she hadn't been heartbroken.

She hadn't gone out with anyone since, and she couldn't remember when she'd last been on a date. In fact, now that she thought about it … apart from that single disastrous (and very expensive) night out with Matthew, had she ever been on one? She and David had met at college and morphed seamlessly from friends who studied together and chatted over coffee into friends who kissed and held hands and slept together. Ludicrous though it seemed, she had to conclude that at twenty-seven years of age tonight would only be her second real date.

She was jumping in at the deep end – a black tie event with a 'proper man'. Maybe the butterflies in her stomach weren't so much excitement, as fear that she was out of her depth. She'd certainly never felt this shivery, nervous exhil-aration about seeing David. But then, she didn't think they'd ever really gone beyond friendship emotionally.

'How are we doing?' Mimi asked, sticking her head around the door.

Aoife nodded. 'Okay.' She was sitting on her bed in her dressing-gown and had just finished drying her hair.

'Your dressers have arrived,' Sive called, appearing beside Mimi.

They came into the room and Mimi handed her a glass of white wine. 'To steady your nerves.'

'Thanks.' Aoife took it from her gratefully. 'I need it.'

'It's been a while,' Mimi said. 'But you'll be fine.'

'Sit.' Sive nodded to the dressing table, and Aoife got up from the bed and sat in front of the mirror. Her sisters came to stand behind her, surveying her reflection.

'Now,' Mimi said, grabbing a brush, 'hair up or down?'

Half an hour later, when her sisters had left the room, Aoife stood in front of the mirror. Despite her misgivings, Sive and Mimi had somehow persuaded her to wear Detta's Halston dress, and she was surprised to find that it boosted her confidence. It was the sort of thing she'd never have envisaged herself wearing, and she'd worried that it would make her feel fake and awkward, but she had to admit it looked good … more than good.

A floor-length cream Grecian-style gown, it was simple, elegant and very sexy – the sort of dress, Mimi said, that would immediately make men imagine what you'd look like with it off. With a high neckline and soft folds of fabric falling to her feet, from the front it looked understated and demure. But it was completely backless, exposing the entire length of her spine to just above her bum. She ran her hand down the skirt, loving the texture of the soft jersey fabric. Mimi had done her hair in a messy upstyle, tendrils falling softly around her face. She looked sophisticated and glamorous, but was reassured to find she still felt like herself – just an elevated, polished version of herself.

She could tell what Jonathan thought as soon as she opened the door to him.

'Wow!' His eyes widened appreciatively. 'I mean … wow!' He seemed at a loss for words. 'You look amazing!'

'Thanks. So do you.' Behind him, a cab waited at the kerb and she ushered him inside for a moment while she gathered her bag and a shawl in case it was cold later. Her heart was hammering already as he brushed past her and she caught the woody scent of his aftershave. He was movie-star handsome in his black suit and snowy white shirt, and he literally took Aoife's breath away.

Gratifyingly, he seemed to feel the same. He couldn't take his eyes off her, his gaze constantly flicking across to her as they sat in the back of the cab and drove to the hotel. She couldn't stop thinking about what Mimi had said – was Jonathan imagining her naked? Thinking what it would be like to take her dress off – undo the clasp at the back of her neck and let the fabric fall to her waist? Lay her down across the seat of the cab and …

'Hot, isn't it?' Jonathan ran a finger under the collar of his shirt.

She gulped and nodded. 'Very muggy.' Her voice came out husky and low. The car did feel stifling and airless, but it had nothing to do with the warm, humid night.

'There's thunder and lightning forecast later,' the cab driver informed them, rolling down the windows. It made very little difference.

Aoife was glad she'd gone all-out when they walked into the reception and she checked out what the other women were wearing, relieved that she'd judged it just right and had achieved what Detta used to call the 'Goldilocks look' – neither underdressed nor overdressed. She didn't feel at all out of place, and she was pleased she'd made such an effort for Jonathan's sake.

The ballroom was beautifully decorated with balloons and vast banks of flowers, and waiters stood at the entrance with silver salvers of champagne adorned with strawberries. Jonathan took a couple and handed one to Aoife, then led her through the throng, introducing her to friends and colleagues. It was interesting seeing him in this setting. He was clearly popular and highly regarded, and she was proud to be his date.

They were a friendly crowd. Everyone was warm and welcoming to Aoife, and she found them easy to talk to. But she was barely aware of what was being said, too conscious of Jonathan's hand on her back as he guided her from one group to the next, her skin seeming to tingle wherever he touched.

'So you're the actress we've heard so much about,'

Olivia, a tall, angular woman with short, spiky hair said to her.

'Now I see why you don't bother hanging out with us anymore,' Philip said to Jonathan with a grin.

'Shut up.' Jonathan had mentioned Philip to Aoife a few times, and she knew he was his best friend in the firm.

'I think you know we have the partners to blame for that,' Olivia said. 'Jonathan's working his fingers to the bone to get back in their good books. Poor Aoife probably sees as little of him these days as we do.'

Philip nodded. 'He does have a lot of ground to make up with them.'

Aoife caught Jonathan frowning at his friend, giving an almost imperceptible shake of his head. She wondered what that was about. She couldn't see Jonathan as someone who'd be in trouble at work.

'That dress is amazing,' Alice, another of his colleagues said to her, drawing her attention away from Jonathan. 'Do you mind me asking where you got it?'

'Thanks. It's vintage. It belonged to my Great-aunt Detta.'

'Is it … I mean, it looks like a Halston,' Olivia said. 'Circa nineteen-seventies?'

Aoife nodded. 'It is. That's very impressive.'

'Olivia's our resident fashionista,' Alice said.

'Wow,' Olivia breathed. 'Lucky you! Good old Great-aunt Detta, eh?'

There followed much gushing by the women in the group over Aoife's dress, and she flushed with pleasure as she caught Jonathan watching, his face suffused with pride.

'How's the crowdfunder going?' Alice asked her.

'Oh, you know about that?'

'We've all invested,' Olivia told her, circling a finger to indicate the group.

'Gosh, thanks.'

'We'd never hear the end of it from this one if we didn't,' Philip said jovially, jerking his head towards Jonathan.

'Sorry.'

'No, don't be,' Olivia said. 'It's a great project. We're happy to support it.'

There were murmurs of agreement from everyone.

'It's going great so far,' Aoife said in answer to Alice. 'But we have a way to go yet.'

Jonathan excused himself to go to the loo, asking Aoife if she'd be okay. She told him she was fine.

'Don't worry, we'll look after her,' Philip said.

'What did you mean about Jonathan needing to get into the bosses' good books?' Aoife asked Olivia when Jonathan was out of earshot. 'I always thought he'd be the golden boy.' She smiled fondly.

'Oh, he used to be, believe me. Until very recently they thought the sun shone out of his arse.'

'So what changed?'

'They were very put out when he turned down the offer of partnership – especially since he'd made so much noise about wanting it. Pretty much from the day he joined, he made it clear he was interested. Then when they offer it to him, he turns it down. So now they're worried he's looking elsewhere and some other firm are trying to poach him. He's got great contacts and brings in a lot of new business, so they don't want to lose him. But they also don't want to invest in someone disloyal who's got one foot out the door.'

'*Is* Jonathan looking elsewhere?'

'Apparently not. He just changed his mind about partnership.' She shrugged. 'So now he's launching a massive charm offensive, working late, volunteering for all the crap assignments, to win back their approval and convince them he's in for the long haul.'

Aoife was glad to find Olive and Philip were seated at the same table as them for dinner. The food was sublime, the meal a procession of exquisitely presented courses with paired wines. Afterwards there was a rousing speech from one of the senior partners and a performance by a well-known stand-up comedian, followed by dancing. It came as no great surprise to Aoife that Jonathan wasn't keen to shake his booty, but she joined Alice and Olivia on the dance floor.

By the time she returned to Jonathan, the crowd was starting to thin out and he was alone at the big round table. His eyes were on her as she made her way to him, and she wondered if he'd been watching her the whole time.

'Having fun?' he asked as she collapsed in the chair next to him.

'Yes, but I'm pooped.' She looked back to the dance floor. Olivia and Alice were still giving it loads to Lady Gaga. 'I like your friends.'

'Yeah, they're great,' he said, following her gaze.

'Can I ask you something?'

'Of course.'

'Olivia said you were offered a partnership and turned it down.'

Jonathan nodded. 'Yes.'

'Why?'

He glanced away. 'It just wasn't the right time. I decided I don't want to be tied down to the firm just yet. I'd rather keep my options open.'

That sounded reasonable. 'Because you might get a better offer?'

'Exactly.'

'Are you looking around? Planning to jump ship?'

'Aoife?' He took her hand, his fingers curling around hers.

'Yes?'

'Let's not talk about work, okay?'

'Okay. What do you want to talk about?'

His eyes raked over her. 'You. That dress.' His gaze dropped to her lips, and there was a heavy-lidded look to them. 'I'd rather not talk at all, actually. I'd much prefer to kiss you.'

She nodded breathlessly, her heart hammering. 'Same.'

He leant in and kissed her, his lips warm and firm on hers. She put her hands in his hair and breathed in the warm, woody scent of him as she kissed him back. Oblivious to everyone around them, he pulled her onto his lap, his hand warm on the bare skin of her back. His breathing became jagged as his tongue slid into her mouth.

Their hands roamed, reaching for each other restlessly as they tilted their heads to find the perfect angle. Jonathan's lips slid to her neck and she felt him hardening against her leg as he pulled her in closer. Everything else seemed to disappear until nothing existed but his mouth and hands on her skin, the warmth of his body against hers. She suppressed a moan as his hand brushed tantalisingly against her breast.

They were both breathing heavily as they pulled apart, blinking dazedly into each other's eyes, and there was no doubt in Aoife's mind that they wanted each other. *We can't do this here*, was her only coherent thought, no doubt in her mind that *this* was going to happen.

'Shall we go?' he asked.

She nodded. 'Your place?' Since he lived alone, it seemed the obvious choice.

He frowned. 'Your house is nearer.'

'Okay. To Ranelagh, then.'

'To Ranelagh and as quickly as possible.'

It was after two when they got out of the cab, and Aoife was relieved to see that the house was in darkness. Sive and Mimi were obviously already in bed. She opened the door quietly, putting a finger to her lips to shush Jonathan as she ushered him inside.

'I don't want to wake Sive and Mimi,' she whispered. She hoped they were asleep as she took Jonathan's hand and they tiptoed upstairs to her bedroom.

She closed the door softly behind them, and then they fell on each other, mouths mashing together, fingers clutching as they shed their clothes silently. It only took the loosening of a couple of ties and Aoife's dress fell in a pool at her feet. Jonathan groaned and she clamped a hand over his mouth.

'Ssh, we have to be quiet.'

He kissed her palm and nodded, his eyes burning into hers. When she took her hand away, he didn't make a sound. There was something incredibly hot about trying to be quiet, their frenzied movements contrasted by their hushed gasps and stifled moans, the silence only broken by their ragged, heavy breaths and the sound of soft, wet kisses in the darkness.

28

THE NEXT MORNING, Aoife stayed in bed as long as possible, reluctant to go downstairs and face her sisters. She and Jonathan lay side by side propped up against the pillows, the sun already blazing through the gap in the curtains.

'Can we get up now?' Jonathan whispered.

Aoife cocked an ear, listening to sounds of movement in the kitchen. She'd heard Mimi's bedroom door open and footsteps going downstairs a few minutes ago.

'Not yet,' she whispered. 'Let's give it another while.' She was hoping Mimi would just make herself a mug of tea and go back to bed. She often did that on Sundays.

'But I'm starving,' Jonathan complained.

'You should have thought of that when you insisted on coming back here instead of going to your house.'

'I didn't know we'd be in a siege situation here. Are you afraid they'll be cross with you for sleeping with the enemy?'

'No, of course not. And you're not the enemy. It's just … embarrassing.'

'Do you want me to sneak out?' he hissed.

'No. Anyway, she'd hear you.'

'I could shin down the drainpipe and make a run for it?' He nodded to the window.

Aoife giggled. 'Don't be silly. Just wait another few minutes.'

'Okay, but I'm warning you now, if she starts cooking bacon, I'm breaking cover and throwing myself on her mercy,' he said as the smell of toast drifted through the house.

But Aoife was starving too, and hunger won out in the end. When there was no sign of Mimi going back to bed, she decided it was time to get up and face the music.

When they'd both showered and dressed, they went downstairs, Jonathan still wearing his suit trousers and white shirt from the night before, looking incongruously formal for a Sunday morning.

Mimi was sitting at the table eating a toasted bagel, a paperback propped open in front of her. She looked up as they appeared in the doorway.

'Hi, Jonathan,' she said after a moment's silent scrutiny, her voice barely registering surprise. Her eyes flicked to Aoife. 'Last night went well, then?'

Aoife nodded happily. 'It was fun.'

'Last night was perfect.' Jonathan gave Aoife's hand a squeeze and they moved into the room.

'No Sive?' Aoife asked as she got out mugs and flicked on the kettle.

Mimi shook her head. 'She's at Ben's. He's home for a few days between trips.'

Jonathan stretched and yawned, and Aoife nodded for him to sit. He pulled out a chair opposite Mimi.

'Tea, coffee?' she asked him.

'Coffee, please.' He rubbed his face, his eyes bleary.

'There are bagels,' Mimi said, nodding to the bread bin.

Aoife felt deliciously weary and limp as she got breakfast ready. 'It's such a lovely morning,' she said, looking to the window. 'Why don't we eat outside?' The sun was already hitting the little patio outside the kitchen door, and she could do with the fresh air to wake her up.

'Sounds good,' Jonathan agreed.

'What time did you get home last night?' Mimi asked. 'I didn't hear you come in.'

'It was after two. We tried to be quiet, so as not to wake you.'

Jonathan turned around at that and gave her a secretive smile, and she blushed as she thought of their muted urgency as they reached for each other in the dark.

'Can you take this out?' she asked Jonathan when she'd loaded up a tray with orange juice, coffee and bagels. He stood and took it from her, and she opened the kitchen door for him, nodding to the little bistro set on the patio. 'I'll just make another coffee and then I'll join you.'

'So last night went *really* well?' Mimi asked quietly, as Aoife closed the door behind him and returned to the coffee machine.

'Really, really well.' Aoife grinned. 'Never better, in fact.'

'Seriously?'

'Never. You were right about that dress, by the way.'

'Go Halston,' Mimi said, raising her mug in salute.

. . .

'Any plans for the rest of the day?' Aoife asked Jonathan as they ate a leisurely breakfast in the garden. 'You can stay here, if you like.'

'I'd love to, but I need to go home and change into some normal clothes. Stupidly, I'd already arranged to meet Philip and Olivia for brunch and a debrief about last night. Why don't you come with me? I'm sure they'd love to see you.' He smiled. 'You were a big hit.'

Aoife was glad. She'd liked them too. 'Thanks, but I'm too knackered.' She closed her eyes, tilting her face up to the sun. 'All I'm fit for is lazing around for the day. But you could come back for dinner?'

'Unfortunately I'm having dinner with my rotten brother.'

'Sam's lovely,' she said, opening her eyes.

'He has his moments, I suppose,' he said with an affectionate smile.

When Jonathan left, Aoife and Mimi got out the sun beds and spent the rest of the day lying in the garden, reading and dozing in the sun. Sive came home around lunchtime and joined them, all agog as Aoife filled them in on the details of last night, talking them through the dinner course by course.

'And then to top it all she had the best sex of her life,' Mimi finished, and Sive squealed with delight.

'I'm so happy for you,' she said, giving Aoife a squeeze. 'Yay Jonathan!'

It was a blisteringly hot day, and Aoife felt drunk on sensuous overload, as happy and sated as the fat bees that buzzed in the flowerbeds. Later Mimi made Aperol spritzes and they had dinner in the garden, chatting late into the evening over big bowls of pasta with chilli and garlic.

It was still bright outside when she went to bed,

exhausted but still hardly able to sleep for excitement as the events of the weekend replayed endlessly in her head.

In the days that followed, Aoife couldn't remember a time when she'd been happier. She was in a permanent state of bliss, in love with everything – with acting, with Jonathan, with the beautiful summer days. She bounced giddily from one high to another, getting up every morning excited to go to work and coming home in the evening excited to see Jonathan, to kiss Jonathan, to touch Jonathan. Life was wonderful.

The only thing harshing her mellow was the crowdfunder. Donations had been tapering off for the past couple of weeks, and as the deadline drew nearer, it looked increasingly unlikely that they'd reach their goal. She tried not to be bitter about it, but it was hard not to be. They'd worked so hard, put everything they had into it, and all for nothing.

But it wasn't for nothing, she reminded herself. They'd have *Three Sisters*; she'd got to work with wonderful people; she'd had a taste of being a professional actress; she'd discovered what she really wanted in life; she'd learnt lots and had valuable experience under her belt. Best of all, she had a new-found confidence in herself and the people around her, a sense of security and self-belief that she felt was here to stay. And she had Jonathan. It wasn't nothing.

It seemed inevitable now that they'd lose Halfpenny Lane, and she tried to come to terms with it. She knew what she wanted most now – acting and Jonathan – and she didn't need Halfpenny Lane to have those in her life.

29

'Aoife?' Sive called from the kitchen when Aoife got home on Friday evening. 'Come here, quick.'

Aoife threw her jacket on the stand in the hall, then went to join Sive.

'We've got a problem,' Sive said urgently, beckoning her over to the table. She was staring at her laptop, open on its surface. 'Have you looked at your social media today?'

'No, I didn't have time. I hardly had a minute all day.' She'd had a costume fitting at Halfpenny Lane in the morning and a dental check-up in the afternoon, followed by a private voice coaching session. She had a creeping sense of dread as she crossed the room. It usually wasn't good news when people told you to check your social media. 'What's up?'

'It's the crowdfunder. It's sort of … gone viral!' Sive said, dismayed. 'It's all over Twitter and Facebook and Instagram!'

'What? But that's great!' She couldn't understand why Sive seemed so troubled. Aoife bent to peer over her shoulder as Sive pointed to the screen. It was open on Twitter, and the hashtag #SaveHalfpennyLane was trending in Ireland.

'This is brilliant!' Her face split into a grin as she pulled out a chair and sat beside Sive. 'How did it happen?'

Sive turned to her. 'Rocco,' she said, her brows pinched together in a worried frown.

'Rocco?' Aoife's smile faded.

Sive nodded. 'He tweeted about the campaign, and then everyone started retweeting him and sharing his post on Facebook. It's got loads of traction. He even put a little video on Insta, talking about Detta and how much the theatre meant to him, and of course that practically broke the internet.'

'Oh no!' Aoife whimpered, leaning an elbow on the table and cupping her chin in her hand. 'I mean, it's great in one way,' she said uncertainly. 'But ...'

'Exactly. How's Mimi going to react?'

'She hasn't seen it yet?'

Sive shook her head. 'Not as far as I know.'

Rocco Agnew was currently the hottest new thing in Hollywood – a rapidly rising star, massive heartthrob and the great love of Mimi's life.

They'd met in their first year at the Gaiety School of Acting, and became inseparable almost instantly, moving in together after just a few weeks. Aoife had been alarmed at how fast the relationship was moving, fearing for her sister's impetuous heart. But her worries had been laid to rest as soon as she'd met Rocco and seen the two of them together. He was clearly every bit as smitten as Mimi, and their devotion and commitment to each other was completely mutual. It was soulmates at first sight and would have seemed almost fated, if you believed in such things.

Aoife had envied Mimi. She knew how rare it was for two people to fall into a relationship so easily, to be instantaneously in sync. Neither had the upper hand; there was no power imbalance, no games, no insecurities. Mimi had never experienced a moment's anxiety about Rocco, never paced her room waiting for him to call, never fretted about his eyes straying to someone else or wondered whether she loved him more than he loved her.

It had been Mimi's first serious relationship, and she'd had no idea how lucky she was. She'd taken it for granted, assuming that was just how it worked. You fell in love with someone, they fell in love with you, and that was that – simple. Aoife had been happy for her, glad it had come so easily to her after her earlier struggles. She'd already got over her rebellious phase and was applying herself diligently to acting school, but Rocco was a further calming influence and the relationship stabilised her even more, giving her a sense of peace she'd never had before. She'd become positively domesticated. Aoife and Sive had loved Rocco too, and he'd quickly become an integral part of their lives, one of the family.

But then Hollywood had beckoned. He'd gone to LA to audition for the lead role in what had since become a major film franchise. He didn't get it, but he'd returned to Dublin full of Hollywood energy and ambition. He wanted them both to move there, where the action was. It was the first time he and Mimi weren't on the same wavelength. She'd been horrified by the idea. She was just starting to establish herself and build a career on the Dublin stage. She didn't want to go back to square one, being a tiny minnow in the vast, sparkling aqua pool of Hollywood.

Aoife hadn't thought for a moment that Rocco would go without her. But when it seemed he would, she'd tried to persuade Mimi to go with him, even though she hated the thought of her moving so far away. She couldn't fathom Mimi's reluctance. She was usually the fearless, impetuous one. Now Aoife was the one trying to persuade her to take a chance – to go to Hollywood and give it a year. If nothing happened they could come back to Dublin and take up where they'd left off. Besides, she argued, it would be fun to live in LA for a while, even if she did end up waiting tables for the entire time. What did she have to lose? Just Rocco – and Aoife never believed Mimi would risk that when it came down to it.

But that was what happened. They'd had their first and last big row, Rocco had left for LA, and Mimi had stayed in Dublin. She'd been shattered, utterly devastated. Sive and Aoife had been frantic with worry about her. Overnight their lively, vivacious sister had been replaced by a zombie, stumbling blindly through life in a haze of misery. She'd barely eaten for weeks, and her work had suffered. She was dull and listless, and her enthusiasm for the theatre seemed to have vanished along with Rocco.

But after a few months of moping around like a lost, agitated ghost, she'd pulled herself together. Aoife and Sive were beyond relieved to have their spiky, spirited sister back. But Rocco's name was never spoken in their house again. Aoife and Sive had carefully avoided any mention of him at first, lest they upset Mimi's fragile equilibrium. By the time she was back to her old self, they'd been tiptoeing around the subject of Rocco for so long, the elephant in the room had taken up permanent residence – always there, never acknowledged. If one of his movies came on TV, they quickly switched it off, and if his name came up in the media, they ignored it and pretended it wasn't happening. Rocco Agnew was as dead to them as if he was buried six feet under.

But there was no way they could pretend he didn't exist

now, Aoife thought, watching in dismay as Sive scrolled through the hashtag on Twitter. It was massive. Several major Hollywood stars who'd worked with Rocco had retweeted about the crowdfunder, and their combined gazillions of fans had taken up the call.

Sive paused on Rocco's video message, and Aoife leaned in to watch. He really was an astonishingly beautiful man, and he knew how to work it without ever appearing in the least vain. He talked fondly about Halfpenny Lane and Detta, and Aoife's heart wrenched as he made a heartfelt plea for support for the crowdfunder. She missed Rocco. He was good-natured, funny and friendly, and she'd liked him being part of their family.

Their eyes flew guiltily to the door as they heard the front door open, and Mimi's step in the hall.

'Hi!' she called breezily as she swept into the room, her smile quickly fading as she took in Sive and Aoife's expressions. 'Oh god, what's wrong?' Her gaze flicked to the laptop.

'Nothing.' Sive quickly closed the lid.

'There's no point trying to hide it,' Aoife said to her. 'She's going to find out anyway, so we might as tell her.'

'Tell me what?' Mimi's hand flew to her chest. 'Has someone died?'

'No, nothing like that.'

'It's actually good news,' Sive told her.

'It doesn't look like it.'

'Well, there's good news and bad news,' Sive said. 'Which do you want first?'

Mimi rolled her eyes. 'I want you to cut the codswallop and tell me what's making you two look like Marlowe just let off one of his silent-but-deadlies in your face.' She walked around to stand behind them, grabbing the laptop and turning it towards her. Aoife watched her face carefully as she took in what was happening on social media. She was clearly trying to keep her expression bland as she watched Rocco's video, but Aoife saw the slight hardening of her jaw, the brittle edge to her eyes.

'Our crowdfunder has gone viral!' Sive said brightly. 'Everyone's retweeting it and sharing it on Facebook and Instagram. Helen Mirren even posted about it. Did you know she'd worked with Detta once?' She was babbling nervously.

'Well, this is great,' Mimi said tightly, turning the laptop back to Sive.

'Yes, isn't it?' Aoife said. 'The total's doubled in the last couple of hours! We could make the goal after all.'

'So, what's the bad news?' Mimi frowned.

'Well …' Sive fiddled nervously with her sleeve. 'It's thanks to Rocco.'

'He who shall not be named,' Mimi said wryly. And just like that, the eggshells they'd all walked on for the last two years were crushed to pieces under their feet.

'It was very nice of him,' Aoife said tentatively.

'If he'd really wanted to help, he could at least have taken his shirt off,' Mimi said waspishly. 'Well, I've had a bloody awful day. I'm going to bed.'

'It's six-thirty!' Sive said.

'So? Consider me one of the great eccentrics.'

'But what about dinner?'

'I'm not hungry.' With that, she turned on her heel and left the room without another word.

Aoife and Sive listened in silence to her making her way up the stairs. When they heard her bedroom door close, they turned to each other.

'Well, that went …'

'Well?' Sive said uncertainly.

'I wouldn't say well, exactly. But it went, so that's something. We've spoken Rocco's name in this house, and the world didn't come crashing down around us.'

'Do you think she's okay?'

Aoife frowned. 'I don't know. But it's probably a good thing. She's been forced to acknowledge him now, and we can all admit that Rocco Agnew is a person who exists in the world.'

'Oh! Does this mean we can watch *Passing Strangers* now?' *Passing Strangers* was a massively successful streaming TV series that had given Rocco his big break. They seemed to be the only people in the world who'd never seen it.

'I think it might be a bit soon for that. But maybe one day.'

'Oh, look!' Sive turned back to the laptop, where tweets were still stacking up under the hashtag. 'Al Pacino has tweeted about it!'

Aoife read the tweet. He'd been in one of the handful of Hollywood films Detta had made, and said he had very fond memories of working with her.

Mimi didn't come out of her room for the rest of the night. It wasn't like her to be so quiet or to keep her feelings to herself, but Aoife respected her need for space and privacy. However, she couldn't help worrying, and when she went up to bed later that night, she knocked softly on her door.

'Just saying goodnight,' she called through the door. 'Are you okay?'

'Yes, I'm asleep.' Mimi's voice was hoarse, and it was obvious she'd been crying. But she clearly didn't want to be disturbed. 'Goodnight.'

'Goodnight. See you in the morning.'

. . .

Mimi seemed to have recovered the next morning, and was back to her old self – almost.

'I don't want to talk about it,' she announced when she joined them for breakfast, and Aoife and Sive nodded readily in agreement, both happy to do whatever was necessary to avoid another meltdown. Aoife had been scared last night that Mimi would ricochet back to her old ways. But her sister was more mature than that now – she should trust her not to go off the rails at the slightest upset.

'It was very good of Rocco,' Mimi said, and Aoife saw the effort it took for her not to flinch as she spoke his name. 'He made a very generous personal donation too, and I appreciate it. But let's not speak of it again.'

'Agreed.' Aoife was happy to draw a line under it, relieved that Mimi wasn't going to go into a spiral of wondering what it could mean, and whether Rocco might still have feelings for her. She'd avoided all that angst while she was in the relationship. It would be a shame if she had to go through it now.

'We'll have to respond, though,' Sive said. 'Publicly, I mean,' she added hastily.

'You're right,' Aoife said. 'We can't have all these people promoting our cause and not at least say how grateful we are.'

Mimi gave a tight little nod. 'Of course.'

'But we can do it from the Halfpenny Lane accounts,' Aoife said. 'We can just write a blanket thank-you to everyone who's helped. There are too many people now to thank them all individually anyway.'

'Good idea,' Mimi said, her features relaxing. Her relief was obvious.

. . .

Aoife spent the following day composing and posting messages of thanks on social media in breaks from rehearsals. Jonathan was working late, but came over after dinner.

'What's happened to the campaign?' he asked her when they were alone in the living room. Sive and Mimi had made themselves scarce and gone to the pub to give her and Jonathan some privacy. 'It's suddenly blown up. How did all these big movie stars get involved?'

'Rocco started it.'

'Rocco Agnew? Does he have some personal connection to the theatre? He's too young to have started out there.'

'He used to be with Mimi.'

'With? You mean …'

She nodded. 'They were in a relationship.'

'How come I never knew that?'

'It was before he was famous. They met in acting school. It ended when he moved to LA.'

'Oh. So I guess they're still friends, then?'

She shook her head. 'No, it ended really badly, actually. They haven't spoken since.'

'It was very decent of him to help, in that case. He's drummed up a lot of support.'

'Yeah.' Aoife plucked at her skirt. 'I guess he still cares about Mimi. He knows how much this means to her.' She felt a little stab of envy that even Mimi's ex, someone whose heart she'd broken, still cared so much about her and would do anything for her. She couldn't help wishing she could inspire that kind of fierce loyalty and passion.

'Well, he's done wonders for the crowdfunder,' Jonathan said. 'Have you seen the balance today?'

Aoife nodded, grinning. 'We're almost there. I think we'll hit our goal by the end of the week.'

30

THE FOLLOWING SATURDAY, Mimi's friend Catherine was home from London for the weekend and came for lunch. She arrived early, and Mimi got up to answer the door to her while Aoife and Sive stayed at the kitchen table, hulling strawberries for Eton mess.

'Girls, girls,' Catherine said breathlessly, rushing into the kitchen and waving hello. 'Wait until I tell you what I heard.' She unhooked her cross-body bag from around her neck and flopped into a chair opposite them. She was officially Mimi's friend, but they were all fond of Catherine – a tall, striking girl with a strong Galway accent and no filter.

'What?' Mimi sat beside her, avid for gossip.

'It's about your so-called partner.'

'Who?' Mimi frowned, confused.

'You know – whatsisname. Jonathan Hunt.' Catherine grabbed a strawberry and popped it in her mouth. 'It's as you always suspected,' she said, nodding at Mimi. 'He's completely evil.'

'I didn't think he was evil—'

'Yes, you did. You said so – no soul, dances with the devil, et cetera. Anyway, the good news is it turns out you were right.'

Aoife went cold. She could sense Sive and Mimi throwing her wary glances. She tried to ignore them and concentrate on chopping strawberries.

'How is that a good thing? I mean even if it was true,' Mimi added, her eyes flicking to Aoife.

'Because … now you're justified in hating him and you don't have to feel bad about it. He deserves it.'

'I'm sure he doesn't,' Sive said.

'You won't think that when I tell you what he did.'

Aoife felt herself blushing. She really didn't want to hear this, whatever it was. But she knew Jonathan now. Was there anything Catherine could say that would alter her opinion of him so drastically?

'And we don't hate him,' Mimi added. 'In fact, now that we've got to know him, we all like him.'

'He was really good to Aoife when she was sick,' Sive said.

'And he's been very helpful with the crowdfunding for Halfpenny Lane,' Mimi said.

'Hmm,' Catherine drawled. 'I bet he has.'

'Why do you say it like that?'

'From what I hear, he's very good at helping himself when it comes to money.' Catherine punctuated this zinger by helping herself to another strawberry while she let it sink in.

'I can't see him doing anything underhand,' Sive said.

'Well, listen to this.' Catherine grabbed another strawberry. They were disappearing as fast as Aoife hulled them. 'So I bumped into Sophie Barron last night in the Duke.'

'Who?'

'Sophie Barron. She was in our year at school, remember?' She waved her hand dismissively as Mimi looked blank. 'Anyway, we were chatting away, and your name came up, so I was telling her about Halfpenny Lane and the whole crowdfunder thing. I mentioned you having to buy Jonathan out, and it turns out she knows him. She used to go out with his brother.'

'Sam?'

'Yes.' Catherine nodded vigorously. 'They were engaged and everything. So obviously she knew Jonathan, and she said he was absolutely vile.'

'Well, that's not so strange, is it?' Mimi said, throwing a glance at Aoife. 'I mean, Jonathan is sort of … well, an acquired taste.'

'It took us a while to warm up to him,' Sive said.

Catherine shook her head. 'No, listen. So, Sam and Sophie were engaged. Then Sam and Jonathan's father died. Everything was left equally between the two of them, of course, including the family home. They had this great house in Sandymount. Well, we all know what houses in Sandymount go for. It would have been worth a million at least.'

Aoife had a horrible feeling she knew where this story was going. 'The house Jonathan lives in now.'

'Exactly. So obviously they needed to sell it to split the proceeds. The other option was for one of them to buy the other out, and that's what happened. Jonathan didn't want to sell, so he bought Sam out, but Sophie said he only gave him a pittance for it – nothing like what his share was worth.'

'Gosh!' Mimi exclaimed, as Aoife's mind scrambled around for extenuating circumstances.

'Right? Apparently Sam needed the cash quickly because he and Sophie wanted to get a place together. So he signed over his rights to Jonathan for a hundred grand.'

'A hundred grand!'

'Jonathan claimed he couldn't afford to give him any more, but everyone knows he's loaded. So he got to keep the house, and now if it's sold, all the money is his.'

'Oh my god! That's awful!'

Catherine nodded. 'So you see, he has form. This isn't his first time swindling someone out of their inheritance.'

'Well, he isn't swindling us out of Halfpenny Lane, to be fair,' Mimi said. 'Detta left him a share in it fair and square.'

That gave Aoife hope. Maybe Sophie was as given to hyperbole and over-dramatisation as Mimi could be at times. Perhaps she'd made it sound worse than it was because she was pissed off that Sam didn't inherit as much as she'd hoped. There could be some perfectly reasonable explanation. There had to be.

'And what happened with Sophie?' Sive asked. 'Did they split up?'

'Yes. She blames Jonathan for that too. They'd been going to buy a house when Sam got his inheritance, but then they couldn't afford it. They couldn't get a mortgage and Sam was always skint. Sophie said it ended up driving a wedge between them. They were always fighting about money—'

'But I don't see how Sam was broke, when he'd just got a hundred grand?' Aoife said, feeling something about this story didn't add up.

Mimi gave her a pitying look. 'I know you want to think the best of him, but–'

'It's not that. I'm just trying to understand. Okay, I get that Sam expected more, but a hundred grand is still a lot of money – enough for a deposit on a house at least.'

Catherine shrugged. 'I don't know. Sophie didn't seem to understand it herself. She said Sam was kind of vague about it, and he got angry if she questioned him about it. She tried to persuade him to fight Jonathan for it, but he refused to do anything. So Jonathan had the house in Sandymount, and meanwhile Sam was living like a pauper. He never had the money to go out or do anything fun. He quit the gym; he even cancelled his Netflix subscription. It ended up ruining their relationship. One of Sophie's friends was getting married in Italy, and he said he couldn't afford the flight. She had to go on her own. I think she'd lost all respect for him by then anyway because he wouldn't stand up for himself.'

Aoife had to admit it did sound damning.

'So she and Sam broke up. Apparently he now lives in this crappy little flat in Rathmines, while Jonathan lords it up in his house in Sandymount. And now he wants to get his grubby mitts on Halfpenny Lane too.'

She sat back, clearly pleased with herself for being the bearer of such a juicy piece of gossip. But her smile died away as she took in their dejected expressions and realised her story wasn't getting the reception she'd been expecting.

'What?' she asked, looking at each of them in turn. 'What's wrong? I thought you'd be delighted.'

'It's just we'd got to like him,' Sive said.

'Some of us more than others,' Mimi said, and Aoife caught her swivelling her eyes in her direction.

Catherine was silent for a beat. 'Oh no!' she gasped then, clapping her hands to her mouth as the penny dropped. 'Have I put my size nines in it? You *like* like him?' she asked Aoife, leaning across the table and grabbing her hands. 'I'm so sorry. I shouldn't have said anything. Why didn't you tell me to shut up?'

'It's fine,' Aoife shrugged.

'I'm sure there's some reasonable explanation,' Mimi prompted Catherine.

'Yes. It's probably not even true. You know, Sophie was always a spoiled brat – thought the world owed her something. I wouldn't put it past her to have made the whole thing up. Honestly, nothing would surprise me with that little madam.'

'It's just hearsay anyway,' Sive said. 'There's probably more to it.'

'Exactly,' Catherine said. 'Two sides to every story. Forget I said anything.' She cast her eyes around the room, clearly in an agony of embarrassment and desperate to change the subject. 'So, Eton mess for dessert, is it?' She waved to the bowl of strawberries. 'If you have enough left, ha ha!' she said as she reached for another. 'Bet you're glad you invited *me*.'

Aoife smiled at her. 'There's plenty.'

'We're eating in the garden,' Mimi told Catherine, standing. 'Come outside and say hello to Marlowe. I'm sure he's dying to see you. Sive, could you grab the bottle of Cava in the fridge?' She picked up a bowl of salad from the counter, and Sive and Catherine followed her outside.

'I'll be out in a minute,' Aoife called after them. 'I'm just going to whip the cream.' She hung back and sat dumbfounded as she finished preparing the strawberries, absentmindedly popping several in her mouth as she went. They tasted like sawdust.

31

THE NEXT DAY Aoife invited Jonathan to dinner, while Mimi and Sive went out with Catherine. Overnight they'd discussed Catherine's story and rationalised it among themselves, determined to give Jonathan the benefit of the doubt. They were hearing it third-hand from someone who had an axe to grind with him. There was probably no foundation to it. Besides, Sam and Jonathan seemed close. Why would Sam still be friendly with a brother who'd cheated him out of his rightful inheritance? It didn't make sense. Sophie was probably just a bitter ex spreading vicious rumours about someone she didn't really know.

She decided to put the whole thing out of her head and enjoy an evening alone with Jonathan. She made vegetable lasagne and salad and they ate outside, sitting in the garden drinking wine until the sun went in and it got chilly. They moved inside for coffee and sat close together on the sofa.

'So it looks like the crowdfunder is going to go over its target,' Aoife said, smiling as Jonathan pulled her onto his lap.

'Hey, you don't have to look so happy about it.'

'Of course I'm happy about it. Why wouldn't I be?'

'Because that means you can buy me out and be rid of me,' he said teasingly.

Aoife smiled. She knew he was joking and she tried to laugh it off. But she couldn't help the little niggle of irritation she felt at the reminder that he was still expecting them to hand all that money over to him. She knew she was being irrational and unfair – he was entitled to it, and it was what they'd agreed to. She couldn't expect him to just give it up for her sake. But she realised now that a little part of her had thought – hoped – that he'd change his mind now that they were together and let them put all the money they'd raised into the theatre. It wasn't as if they couldn't use every penny they could get their hands on. Why couldn't he be happy to be a co-owner with them?

'Well, I hope you're not just sticking around for your money,' she said, a slight edge to her voice.

'Of course not.' He grinned, not picking up on her tone – for which she was grateful. She knew she was in the wrong, but she couldn't seem to help herself. 'But there'll be no more campaign meetings and fundraising activities,' he continued. 'I've kind of enjoyed being part of it all – hugger-mugging with you about budgets and strategies.'

'Well, that doesn't have to end just because the fundraiser's over. You could still be involved in the theatre and hugger-mugger with me to your heart's content.'

He frowned. 'What do you mean?'

'Well, we don't have to buy you out, you know,' she said, playing with the buttons of his shirt.

'You mean I could give up my share in the theatre?'

'No, I mean you could keep it and be a joint owner with us. There'd be no end of hugger-mugging to do then, I can assure you.'

His smile faded slowly and was replaced with a frown. He looked at her intently. 'Are you serious?'

'Yes, why not? What have you got to lose?'

'Er ... half a million euro?'

'It's just money,' she said airily.

'Just money!' He laughed harshly, tipping her off his lap. He leaned forward and rested his arms on his knees, pinching the bridge of his nose. 'You're actually serious, aren't you?'

Aoife couldn't believe how quickly the atmosphere between them had changed. 'It's just a suggestion,' she said nervously, fidgeting with her sleeve. 'I mean, you were saying you were going to miss being part of it. I was merely pointing out that you still could be,' she said stiffly.

'But we agreed – buying me out was built into the goal for the crowdfunder. I thought the whole point was that the three of you would own Halfpenny Lane outright.'

'Yes, you're right. Forget I said anything.'

'I'm finding it hard to. Have you been thinking this all along – hoping I'd have a change of heart and hand the lot over to you?'

'No! I told you, I'm not talking about you handing over anything. I just thought you might want to remain a joint owner with the three of us. Clearly I was wrong. Please forget I said anything.'

'Well, it's hard to when you're looking at me like that. You're annoyed with me, aren't you?'

Aoife sighed. 'Yes, I am. Sorry.' She tried to tamp down her irritation, but it burst out anyway. 'I just—' She broke off in frustration.

'What?'

'I don't understand why you're being so mean about it!'

'*Mean?*' He looked wounded, and Aoife instantly regretted saying it.

'Well, it's not like you need the money.' She seemed unable to back down now that she'd started.

'Oh, don't I?'

'You've got a good job—'

'So do you. At least you had until you gave it up.'

'But I have to look after my sisters too.'

'Right. Of course. And I don't have anyone to look after, I suppose?' His voice was tight.

'Well, you don't, do you? Though I suppose you could have if you wanted to,' she added under her breath.

'What are you talking about?'

'I know what happened with Sam.'

He frowned, rearing back in shock. 'You do? What do you know about it?'

'I know you bought him out of your parents' house and that you didn't give him anything like the market value.'

'Right. I see.' He nodded. 'So this is what you think of me?' He looked at her aghast.

'It's not an opinion. I know you don't need the money from the theatre. You have a good job and a big house in Sandymount.'

'And you don't have a big house in Ranelagh?' he said, looking around the room pointedly. 'This place must be worth at least a million.'

'But it's our home,' Aoife said indignantly. 'It's where we live.'

'And my house is what – just an asset?'

Aoife shrugged sullenly.

'You could sell this place if the theatre is so important to you – find somewhere cheaper to live.'

'Like rent a crappy flat in Rathmines?'

A look of horror passed across his face. He obviously didn't expect her to know that he'd consigned Sam to living in squalor. At least he had the decency to look ashamed.

'What's that supposed to mean?'

'You know what it means. Your brother—'

'You know nothing about me and Sam.'

'I know you cheated him out of part of his inheritance. And you were responsible for breaking up his engagement—'

He gave an incredulous laugh. 'Who told you that?'

'A friend of Mimi's met his fiancé, Sophie.'

'That mercenary cow! He's a lot better off without her, believe me.'

'That's not your call to make. It's not up to you to decide how someone else is going to be happy, what relationships they should have—'

'You have no idea what you're talking about. But by all means believe second-hand gossip from a bitter ex rather than ask me what happened.'

'Okay, then. What did happen?' They were both rigid with fury now as they faced each other, breathing heavily.

Jonathan shook his head. 'Forget it. Believe whatever you want.' He surged to his feet and picked up his phone from the coffee table. 'I had no idea you had such a low opinion of me.' He grabbed his jacket from the back of the sofa and started to pull it on, his movements jerky with anger. 'But you need to get over yourself, Aoife. You're no saint. You're just scared to take any risks. You have plenty of options if you want to keep the theatre. You could sell this place and you could all live somewhere else. Your sisters are old enough to look after themselves, but you can't accept that because then you wouldn't be the one making the world turn. And you really like to feel in control, don't you?'

'No! I—'

'Yes you do.'

How had they got here, she wondered. A few minutes ago they'd been so companionable. How could he have got her so wrong?

'Poor downtrodden Aoife, bearing the burdens of the world on your shoulders. You know, there are lots of things you could do if you wanted it that badly. Your sisters could get decent jobs that pay more, take some of the responsibility for putting food on the table and making ends meet. But you couldn't have that, could you? You have to be the heroic martyr, everyone's saviour, the lynchpin that holds it all together. Because what would you do if they took charge of their own lives? What would be the point of you then? Maybe you'd have to face up to the fact that the only one stopping you pursuing your dreams is you.'

'That's not—'

'Mimi made it happen, didn't she? And Sive? Do you think they'd be doing anything differently if you weren't stepping in, filling the gaps? Look at Detta! She never had a bean, but it didn't stop her. They'd find a way.'

'How? You have no idea what it's like not to have money, to—'

'Oh, don't I? Tell me more, because you seem to know a hell of a lot more about my life than I do.'

'Look, forget it. Like I said, it was just an idea. I thought you might want to change your mind, but clearly you don't. So we'll proceed as planned. Thanks to Rocco, we'll be able to buy you out soon.'

'Oh yeah, Rocco – the hero of the hour swooping in to save the day! Forget the hours and days we've put in, the nights I've worked until all hours on this, the sacrifices I've —' He stopped abruptly.

'What sacrifices have you made?'

'None,' he said, shaking his head. 'You're right, forget

it. I'm just a mean, selfish bastard – that's what you think, right? Well, you won't have to put up with me much longer. You'll buy me out, and then you'll be shot of me for good.' He heaved a sigh, raking a hand through his hair. 'I should go.'

'That might be best,' Aoife said tightly, tears burning in her throat. She couldn't understand how they'd come to this. Everything had been great just an hour ago. She tried to think of a way to make things all right again, something she could say to smooth things over. But Jonathan was gone before she could even draw breath, and she was still sitting dazed on the sofa, the sound of the door slamming echoing in her ears.

She pummelled the arm of the sofa in impotent rage. It wasn't fair! How dare he imply that she was controlling, that she wanted her sisters to be flaky and helpless just so she could feel needed? She'd thought they were getting closer, but he didn't know her at all! Anyway, she had nothing in common with such a cold-hearted, uncaring mercenary as him. She wouldn't expect him to understand her. And suggesting they should sell their home! She fumed, burying her head in her hands.

'What's wrong?' Mimi took one look at Aoife's face when she got in a few minutes later and rushed over to sit beside her on the sofa. 'What happened? I saw Jonathan outside and he barely said hello. He looked furious.'

'We had a blazing row.' She swiped tears from her face. 'He left.'

'What did you fight about?'

'Money.' Aoife sniffed. 'I was talking about the difference Rocco made to the crowdfunder and he could tell I was annoyed with him for wanting us to buy him out.'

'But that's what we agreed on.' Mimi put a comforting

arm around Aoife and hugged her close. 'That's the whole point of the crowdfunder.'

'I know, I know.' If Mimi was siding with Jonathan against her, she knew she was very definitely in the wrong. 'I was being unfair. And then one thing led to another, and it got out of control. I said some really mean things to him.' He'd said some rotten things to her too, but she was beginning to wonder if she'd deserved them. Did she secretly like other people being dependent on her?

'We can't expect Jonathan to forego that kind of money. We have no idea what he might need it for. I know he seems rich to us, but at the end of the day, he's just a solicitor. Yes,' she added quickly as Aoife opened her mouth to protest, 'he's a high-powered one and he earns loads and has a big fancy house in Sandymount. But it's still just a normal job. It's worlds away from the kind of money Rocco has to throw around. He's a movie star. He can afford to make grand gestures. We can't expect an ordinary mortal like Jonathan to compete with that.'

'You're right.' Aoife nodded. 'I was being ridiculous. Instead of being happy that we've almost reached our goal, I was annoyed that we have to hand a big chunk of it over to him.'

'It's what Detta wanted him to have.'

'I know. I was totally in the wrong, I get that. I just thought us being in a relationship might change things – that he'd want to be in this with us … with me.'

'But you wouldn't really want that, Aoife.' Mimi stroked her hair soothingly. 'If you think about it, would you truly be happy with him owning the theatre with us – gifting it to you like some patronising benefactor? We want to own the theatre outright, but only if we can do it standing on our own two feet – not because some bloke as good as bought it for us.'

Aoife smiled wearily. 'You're right.' She really wouldn't want them to own the theatre that way – for Jonathan to keep his share just as a favour to her, when his heart wasn't in it. She'd always be beholden to him. And what if things didn't work out between them? Where would they stand then? It would be super-awkward at best. At worst, the theatre would be in jeopardy again and they'd be right back where they started.

'We'd have to include him in every decision,' Mimi said.

'We wouldn't be able to do plays at a loss just because it was something we wanted to do.'

'He'd probably make us put on a panto.' Mimi widened her eyes in horror, and they both laughed.

'I don't know what came over me. I had such a go at him. And we'd been having such a nice evening too.'

'Silly sausage.' Mimi pouted.

'Where's Sive?'

'She just stayed on for one more with Catherine. I'd had enough.'

'I suppose I should text Jonathan and apologise.' Aoife picked up her phone, but then hesitated.

'Maybe you should leave it for tonight – give you both a chance to calm down.'

'Yeah, that's probably a good idea.' She was too tired to deal with it now. Their fight had left her weary and deflated.

'What's going on?' Sive asked when she got home a short while later and found Aoife and Mimi huddled together on the sofa.

'Aoife had a row with Jonathan,' Mimi told her.

'Oh no! What about?' She joined them on the sofa, eyeing Aoife with concern.

'Everything.' She still didn't understand how it had got

quite so out of control. 'I had a go at him about wanting the money from Halfpenny Lane. And I told him what Catherine heard about how he treated Sam.'

'But we don't even know if that's true.'

'He said some horrible things to me too,' she said defensively. 'I'm not controlling, am I?' she asked her sisters.

Sive laughed. 'Well—'

'What?' Aoife reared up indignantly, and caught Sive and Mimi exchanging a look. It was meant to be a rhetorical question.

'I wouldn't say controlling, exactly,' Sive said. 'Not in a coercive control kind of way at least.'

'But in some way?'

'In a very caring way,' Mimi said soothingly.

'God, you really think I'm controlling?'

'We know it's just because you love us,' Sive said.

'So you both think this?' She looked between the two of them. 'You've discussed it between the pair of you?'

'No. Well … sometimes. But it's not like we're talking about you behind your back.'

'It sounds like you're doing exactly that.'

Sive shook her head. 'You know we're always telling you that you don't have to do everything, that we can look after ourselves.'

That was true. They *were* always telling her that. But it didn't mean Jonathan had been right about her. It wasn't as if she enjoyed shouldering all the responsibility. She'd be more than happy to let someone else take over for a change.

But she thought again about what Jonathan had said as Sive and Mimi went to the kitchen to make tea. Her sisters were capable, resourceful people who knew what they wanted in life and were laser focused on achieving it. They didn't let anything stop them, and they'd have found their way with or without her help. They loved this house, but Jonathan was right – they could be perfectly happy living somewhere else as long as it didn't mean giving up their dreams and ambitions. They'd all still have each other, and that was the most important thing. If Aoife had sacrificed anything for them, it had been her decision alone. They hadn't asked or expected it of her.

But who would she be if she wasn't the caretaker? If she hadn't taken on the role of parent, would she have done anything differently? Or was Jonathan right and her sisters were just an excuse because she was scared to take a chance, clinging to the idea that she didn't have a choice because it was too hard to try and risk failing?

She was in bed later that night when she heard Mimi locking the doors and coming upstairs.

'Mimi?' she called through the half-open door of her bedroom.

'Yes?' She stood on the threshold.

'What would you have done if I'd gone to acting school? If I hadn't done accounting and taken the job at O'Brien Sweeney?'

Mimi moved into the room and sat on the edge of the bed. 'What do you mean?'

Aoife sat up, leaning on her elbow. 'I mean, would you still have gone into acting?'

'Of course.' Mimi frowned. 'Why wouldn't I?'

'But what about money? How would we have managed?'

'I don't know. We'd have worked it out. We'd be poor as church mice, but we'd manage.'

'We're already as poor as church mice as it is.'

'Then we'd beat church mice at their own game.'

Aoife smiled.

'Did you text Jonathan?'

'No. I decided to leave it until tomorrow.' In truth, she'd been hoping he'd text her and be the first to apologise, but that hadn't happened.

'Better to do these things in person anyway. Why don't you go over to his place tomorrow and surprise him?'

It occurred to Aoife that Jonathan never invited her to his house. 'I've actually never been to his place.' She frowned. 'He always comes here. Why do you think that is?'

'I suppose it's close to his work. And at first he was coming here to see the three of us – or at least he let on he was,' she said with a smirk.

'Yeah, I guess that makes sense.' Aoife still thought it was a bit weird that they never went to his place. He lived alone, after all, whereas here there was always the danger of being interrupted by one of her sisters.

'Or maybe he has a mad wife hidden in the attic.'

'True.' Aoife grinned. 'That's probably it.'

'Or the bodies of all his former wives stashed behind a locked door.'

'Now you're making me nervous. I'm definitely going to go over to his.'

'Good idea. If he *is* some sort of modern Bluebeard, best you find out now before you get in any deeper.'

32

WHEN SHE STILL DIDN'T HEAR FROM Jonathan the next day, Aoife dug out the copy of Detta's will that Patrick had emailed to her and put his address into her phone. She finished rehearsals at six and got the bus to Sandymount, hoping that Jonathan would be in. He'd been working late a lot lately, so she might have a wasted journey.

She found his house easily with the satnav on her phone – a double-fronted villa-style house set back from the road with a short gravel path leading to the dark blue door. She rang the bell and heard footsteps in the hall, but her heart sank when a woman she didn't recognise opened the door. She was tall and pretty, with voluminous honey-coloured hair piled on top of her head in a messy bun. She looked a little older than Aoife, in her mid-thirties perhaps, well-heeled and sophisticated in an expensive-looking trouser suit. Aoife felt incredibly gauche and foolish as the woman looked at her expectantly, with a friendly smile. Oh god, this was worse than she'd thought – much worse. Was this Jonathan's girlfriend? No wonder he'd never invited Aoife here.

'Hello. I was looking for Jonathan.'

'Jonathan Hunt?'

'Yes. Is he … home? I just wanted to, um … give him something.'

The woman frowned. 'He doesn't live here.'

'Oh! But isn't this—' Aoife fished her phone out of her pocket. She checked the address again and looked up at the number over the door. It was the same. Perhaps she'd taken it down incorrectly. 'Sorry to bother you,' she said to the woman with an apologetic smile. 'I must have made a mistake. I thought this was his house—'

'Well, it is. But he hasn't lived here for a while. He's the landlord.'

'You're renting from him?'

'Yes. I've been here … just over a year now. But I have an address for him if you'd like?'

'That'd be great. Thanks.'

'Just a moment.' The woman held up a finger indicating for Aoife to wait, then she disappeared into the house.

She came back with a handful of envelopes. 'Some of his mail still gets delivered here. If you're seeing him, could you pass these on to him?' She handed the sheaf of envelopes to Aoife.

'Sure.'

'I'm Annie, by the way.' She took a piece of paper out of her trouser pocket and gave it to Aoife. 'That's his address.'

Aoife thanked her and left. She shoved the post in her bag as she walked out the gate, then looked at the piece of paper in her hand. Somehow she'd expected the address to be nearby, but it wasn't. It wasn't in Sandymount at all, but an apartment complex in Rathmines. She frowned, puzzled. That sounded like where Sophie had said Sam was living. Surely that couldn't be right. Why would he be getting his post sent to his brother's place? She pulled out her phone and searched her email for some correspondence between Patrick and Jonathan that had been copied to her, but the address on that was the same. How odd. Well, if she didn't find him there, she'd just have to give in and call him.

She decided she'd wasted enough time already, so she got a cab to Rathmines. The apartment was in a nice modern block behind the main street and not the dump his ex had made it sound like he was slumming it in. It wasn't as fancy as the family home in Sandymount, but it looked like a perfectly nice place to live, six four-storey buildings grouped around a well-kept central courtyard with a grassy area planted with trees and shrubs, and a neatly raked gravel path between the buildings.

As she'd expected, she found Sam's name on the bells at the entrance to the block, and she was just about to buzz when somebody came out and held the door open for her. The lobby area was clean and well lit. There was a small lift, but Aoife took the stairs to the second floor and walked down a short corridor to No. 11. She pressed the bell and waited, and the door swung open.

'Aoife!' Sam's face split into a wide smile. 'Hi! This is a surprise. It's lovely to see you again.' He stood back, holding the door open. 'Come in.'

'Thanks.' She stepped past him into a narrow hallway. 'I was looking for Jonathan, and the woman who's renting his house gave me this address.'

'Oh, you went to Sandymount?'

'Yeah. I thought—' She felt awkward admitting she didn't know where he lived.

'He's not here at the moment,' Sam said, leading her

into a large, airy open-plan living/dining room. 'But he should be home shortly, if you want to wait.'

'Oh, right.' She was confused by his referring to this as 'home' for Jonathan. But it was where Sam lived, so she supposed it was just how he thought of it. It was nicer than she'd expected as she stood in the middle of the floor looking around her. She'd been in plenty of flats like it and recognised the standard furniture of cheap rentals – low-grade laminate flooring, flimsy flatpack furniture, cheap IKEA rugs and paper lampshades. It wasn't the dump she'd been imagining from Sophie's description, but it was still a far cry from Jonathan's house in Sandymount, and it didn't look like somewhere he belonged. She couldn't imagine him getting dressed in his expensive suits here in the morning, getting ready to go to his big shiny offices.

'Have a seat.' Sam waved her to a sofa by the window. 'Would you like a glass of wine? I'm having one,' he added when she hesitated.

'Yes, please, then.'

'White okay?' He went to the table and lifted a bottle.

Aoife nodded. 'Lovely, thanks.'

'Is Jonathan expecting you?'

'No. I just decided to call over on the spur of the moment.'

Sam handed her a glass of wine and sat beside her on the couch.

'So, Jonathan is … staying with you at the moment?'

'Well, we live here – the two of us.'

'Oh. I'd, um … heard you were living in Rathmines, but I didn't know Jonathan had moved.'

'He didn't tell you?' Sam frowned.

'No. I suppose it never came up.' But she couldn't escape the feeling there was more to it than that – that it was a deliberate omission on Jonathan's part.

'Well, yes. This is where we live in fraternal bliss.' Sam grinned and clashed his glass against hers. 'Cheers.'

'Cheers.' Aoife smiled. Sam was so open and friendly compared to his aloof brother. How could two people in the same family be so completely different? But then, look at her, Sive and Mimi.

'This is nice,' she said, looking around.

'No need to sound so surprised.'

'No, it's just … a friend of ours met your fiancé,' she admitted dazedly. 'Ex-fiancé,' she corrected herself.

'Oh god.' Sam threw his head back against the sofa with a groan. 'You've been talking to Sophie?'

'Not me. Our friend Catherine.'

'I bet she had some choice things to say about me.'

'She had a lot of choice things to say about your brother.'

'Really?' Sam grinned, seeming deeply amused. 'What did she say exactly?'

'She said that you were living in a dump in Rathmines after Jonathan—' She broke off, biting her lip. 'I mean, not that this *is* a dump. I'm just repeating what she told Catherine.'

He shrugged. 'It's not bad. Not quite what Jonathan is used to, but we call it home.'

Aoife tried to hide her bafflement as Sam prattled on. He seemed to think she knew more about Jonathan's life than she actually did. But she was perplexed. Why was Jonathan living here? Why had he never said anything when she'd mentioned his house in Sandymount? And – oh god, she thought, her stomach churning – had he thought she knew when she accused him of letting Sam live in a dump? She'd been talking about this place, she realised, her face flushing with mortification.

'How come Jonathan doesn't live in his house in Sandymount anymore?'

'He didn't tell you?'

'No. The woman there just said she was renting it from him.'

'Ah! Typical of my brother – preserving the family honour,' he said with a grin.

'Oh, don't feel you have to divulge any family secrets,' Aoife said hastily. 'Forget I asked.'

'He needed to economise … downsize,' Sam said unabashed. 'The rent on this place is less than half what he gets for his house.'

Aoife was sorry she'd asked. She didn't feel he should be telling her Jonathan's private financial business.

'He hasn't mentioned any of this to you? Or explained why he wants you to buy him out of the theatre?'

'No.'

Sam huffed a laugh. 'That's Jonathan. He's the stoic type – stiff upper lip, take it on the chin sort of thing.'

Aoife felt a twinge of guilt. She'd obviously badly misjudged Jonathan. But he hadn't told her any of this because for whatever reason he didn't want her to know, and she should respect that. 'You don't have to explain it to me,' she said to Sam. 'He'd have told me himself if he wanted to.'

'Don't worry, it's my secret to tell. It's all my fault, I'm afraid,' Sam said cheerfully. 'I got into some serious debt – owed a lot of money to some very scary people. They were threatening all sorts if I didn't pay up – breaking my legs, you know, the usual stuff.'

Aoife really didn't know, and perhaps she'd lived a sheltered life, but she didn't think there was anything 'usual' about people threatening to come around and break your legs.

'So Jonathan rode to the rescue and saved the family jewels, so to speak. And I got to keep these intact.' He patted his jean-clad thighs. 'Which was a relief, because I'm quite attached to them. He had to come up with the money fast or I literally wouldn't have a leg to stand on,' Sam finished with a chuckle.

But Aoife didn't find it funny. She felt awful. She thought of all the things she'd said to Jonathan, accusing him of being mean and greedy, of not understanding what it was like to be responsible for anyone else. And he hadn't said a word to defend himself because he didn't want to shame his brother.

'So what else did the fair Sophie have to say?' Sam asked. 'Or should I say the foul Sophie? "Fair is foul, foul is fair" …'

That answered the question as to whether Sam still harboured feelings for his ex.

'She said she blamed Jonathan for your break-up.'

'Well, he did help me see the light about her. And for that I'm forever in his debt. I dodged an Exocet missile there.'

'She also said he'd cheated you out of your inheritance – that he bought you out of your parents' house for a fraction of its worth.'

Sam rolled his eyes. 'Hardly. The truth is my debts accounted for most of my share, and he paid them off directly. Which is just as well because if I'd got my hands on it I'd just have used it to dig myself an even deeper hole.'

'But Sophie didn't know any of this?'

'No, and I didn't bother to enlighten her. I suppose I should have, but she dumped me pretty quickly anyway when she realised I wasn't coming into any money – at least none that I hadn't already spent several times over.'

Aoife wondered how someone his age could have blown through that much money in such a short space of time.

'I had a gambling problem,' Sam said, answering her unspoken question.

'Oh, I'm sorry.'

'I'm okay now. I dealt with it – did therapy, Gamblers Anonymous, all that. And straightened out my finances with the help of my brother.'

'That's great. Good for you.' Aoife drained her wine quickly, suddenly acutely aware that she shouldn't be here when Jonathan got home. He'd be embarrassed to find her invading his privacy, with Sam washing their dirty linen in front of her.

'I'll just leave these with you – it's some mail his tenant asked me to pass on.' She took the post Annie had given her for Jonathan out of her bag. But as she held them out to Sam, something in the corner of one of the envelopes caught her eye and she pulled them back. She frowned down at it, turning it over in her hands. It was from Detta's nursing home, rubber-stamped with their official logo. But why would they be corresponding with Jonathan? He wasn't Detta's next of kin. Unless … Something Sam had said once suddenly came back to her and hit her like a brick. *I wouldn't have been the fairy godson you were to her.*

'Sam, was Jonathan … was he paying Detta's nursing home bills?'

'Why?' Sam frowned, looking at the envelopes in her hand. 'Is there a problem? Has he missed one?'

'No, no. It's fine. Everything's fine.' She handed him the sheaf of mail. 'I should go,' she said, standing.

'Aren't you going to wait for—'

Sam was interrupted by the sound of a key in the door, and, a moment later, Jonathan was standing in the living

260

room, looking at them with a mixture of emotions on his face – horror, shock, and something else Aoife couldn't quite fathom. She cringed as she thought of the things she'd said to him the last time they'd been together, the horrible things she'd accused him of.

'Aoife!' He frowned. 'Hi.'

He looked so out of place here in his sharply cut suit, his shirt sleeves pushed up to reveal strong tanned forearms lightly dusted with dark hair, his expensive gold watch gleaming on his wrist.

'Did you want to see me?' He dropped his keys on the table. 'You should have called—'

'Not everything is about you, mate,' Sam said, looking up at him with a cheeky grin. 'She could have come to see me.'

Jonathan was clearly shocked to find her here – and not pleased, judging by his expression. Hardly surprising given what she'd said to him when they'd fought. 'Right. Well.' He stood for a moment, hands on hips, seemingly at a loss as to what to do.

'Um, I was just going,' Aoife said. 'Thanks for the wine,' she said to Sam.

'Don't be silly,' Sam said, standing. 'I should be the one to make myself scarce. I'm getting some serious fifth wheel vibes here.'

'Have you been here long?' Jonathan asked her. She couldn't tell what he was thinking, but he was clearly uncomfortable.

She glanced at her watch. 'Only about fifteen minutes.'

'Long enough for me to show her all the skeletons in our closet,' Sam said.

'You're not staying for dinner?' Jonathan asked Sam as he pulled on a jacket.

Sam hesitated. 'What is it?'

'I got prawns – thought I'd make a Thai green curry.'

This got stranger and stranger. Jonathan was coming home from a day at the office and setting into cooking his little brother's dinner? And he'd had a go at her for molly-coddling her sisters! She tried to suppress the smile that was twitching at the corners of her lips.

Sam looked torn.

'Well, don't let me interrupt,' Aoife said to Jonathan. 'I just wanted a quick word with you, but it can wait for another time.'

'Stay to dinner,' Jonathan said to her. 'Both of you. I can make enough for three.'

Sam hesitated, his jacket half on. 'Well, it *is* my favourite.'

'Thanks,' Aoife said. 'But I don't want to intrude. Sorry, I should have called first.'

'It's fine. You're not intruding.'

'And Jonathan does a mean green curry,' Sam said.

'You can help, if that's any inducement,' Jonathan said to her.

'Okay, then.' She smiled at him. 'I mean, thanks.'

'You won't be sorry,' Sam told her as he removed his jacket and flopped back onto the couch. 'His Thai green curry is epic.'

'You could start on the prep while I get changed?' Jonathan said to her.

She nodded readily. She wasn't good at being a guest and was much happier being given a job to do. Anyway, Sam seemed to have the guest thing covered, she thought, as he sat back down on the sofa and picked up the TV remote.

'Come on and I'll show you where we keep the knives,' Jonathan said to her with a mocking glance at his brother.

He led her into a small kitchen, which she was glad to

see was completely separate from the living room, and closed the door behind them. She wanted to have a chance to talk to Jonathan in private, without his cheeky little brother butting in. He provided her with a knife and chopping board and a pile of vegetables to prepare, and left her to it as he went to change.

33

WHEN JONATHAN RETURNED to the kitchen, he was dressed casually in black jeans and a T-shirt that flattered his long legs and lean torso, and Aoife felt a pang of longing. She was relieved that the hostility of last night seemed to have evaporated on both sides, but she still needed to say her piece and apologise properly for the things she'd said.

Jonathan set up another chopping board on the counter beside her and began slicing chilli and ginger.

'I came over because I wanted to say sorry for last night,' she said in a low tone, not wanting Sam to overhear. 'I'm sorry I had a go at you. I was completely out of order. I've no right to be angry with you because you don't want to be involved in the theatre. It's your inheritance, and it's none of my business what you do with it. Detta wanted you to have it, and that's all I need to know.'

'Aoife,' he said softly, 'it's not that I don't want to be involved. If it was up to me—' He broke off. 'It's complicated.'

She held up a hand to stop him. 'It's okay. You don't have to explain yourself to me. I really wish I hadn't said what I did and if I could take it back, I would. I was just tired and—'

'I said some awful things to you too. I didn't mean them, and I'm sorry.'

'You were right, though. I knew nothing about you and Sam, and I shouldn't have listened to stupid gossip. He told me about his gambling problem.'

'He did?'

'I wasn't prying or anything,' she said hastily. 'He volunteered the information. It sounded pretty scary.'

'It was,' he said grimly. 'But he got through it and he's getting back on his feet.'

'Thanks to you. So that's what you needed the money from Halfpenny Lane for – to pay off Sam's gambling debts.'

Jonathan nodded. 'They're mostly paid off now, but we're still dealing with the fallout.'

'I wish you'd said.'

'Sam's pretty ashamed of himself as it is. I didn't want to humiliate him – and it didn't feel like my secret to tell.'

Aoife was glad Sam had decided to tell her himself. She'd have gone on thinking the worst of Jonathan. She'd been so unfair to him, and she wished there was something she could say to make it better. If only she'd trusted her own knowledge of him instead of listening to spiteful rumours.

'Anyway, I'm sorry,' she said, even though it seemed hopelessly inadequate. 'None of the stuff I said was true.'

'I'm sorry too. Can we put it behind us?'

She turned to him and smiled. 'I'd like that.'

He leaned over and gave her a soft kiss on the lips as if to seal the deal.

As they cooked, they moved around each other easily,

and Aoife enjoyed the comfortable atmosphere between them.

'How did you know where I lived anyway?' he asked her.

'I went to your house in Sandymount and your tenant gave me your address. But why all the subterfuge? Why didn't you tell me you were living with Sam?'

Jonathan gave her a crooked smile. 'Maybe I didn't want you to know I was living in a grotty flat in Rathmines.'

'Oh god,' she closed her eyes. 'I'm sorry. I was only repeating what Sophie said. But it's not grotty. Why would she even say that?'

'Because she's a bitter wagon who hates me and blames me for breaking up her relationship?'

Aoife laughed. 'Well, at least it explains one thing. I never understood why you always wanted to meet at my place with my sisters around all the time – not to mention Marlowe barging in on us.'

'Yeah.' Jonathan rolled his eyes. 'I figured even Marlowe giving me stink-eye was infinitely preferable to my obnoxious little brother showing up at any moment.'

Aoife giggled. 'Sam isn't obnoxious. But I can't believe you had a go at me about mollycoddling my sisters. Talk about the pot calling the kettle black.'

He frowned questioningly as if he had no idea what she was talking about.

'Here you are, coming home from a long day at the office to cook your brother's dinner. While he lounges on the sofa watching TV.' She pointed a knife towards the living room.

'Oh,' Jonathan said, looking shamefaced. 'I suppose you're right. I'm no better.'

It occurred to Aoife that they had a lot more in

common than she'd realised. They'd both been orphaned at a young age, they were both the eldest in their family and had to grow up fast, and they'd both taken on the role of parent to their younger siblings.

'You hadn't even thought about it, had you?' she asked him. 'You're still treating him like a kid. Why do you do that?'

He frowned. 'I don't know. Force of habit, I suppose. After Mum died, I took over cooking for all of us. I guess I just never thought to stop.' He paused as he stirred coconut milk into the pan. 'But you're right, I have spoilt him. Maybe it's my fault he expects everything to come so easily – for opportunities to just fall into his lap.'

'Cut yourself some slack. We're not actually their parents, remember?'

'How about we both start treating our siblings like the adults they are?'

Aoife sucked air in through her teeth. 'Just cut them adrift? Let them make their own way in the world?'

'Scary thought I know. But we have to cut the apron strings sometime.'

When the food was ready, she helped Jonathan carry it through to the dining room.

'Grub's up,' Jonathan called to his brother, who was still reclined on the sofa.

Sam pointed the remote at the TV, shutting off *Friends* and joined them at the round glass table.

'Well, isn't this nice?' he said as he poured them all wine. 'Have you two patched things up?'

Aoife blushed and said nothing as she spooned fragrant jasmine rice into her bowl. She wondered had Jonathan told him about their argument.

'What makes you think we'd fallen out?' Jonathan asked him.

'Just a wild guess based on the mood you were in when you came home last night.'

'Well, not that it's any of your business, but we have.'

'It's my business when I have to live with you.'

'This is lovely,' Aoife said as they began to eat. 'You were right,' she said to Sam. 'He's a great cook.'

'You helped,' Jonathan said to her. Then he turned to his brother. 'But Aoife pointed out to me how ridiculous it is that I'm coming home from work and making your dinner while you lounge around watching TV. I'm not your mum.'

Sam's face fell dramatically. 'I'm starting to go off you,' he said to Aoife. 'You mean you expect me to start cooking my own dinner?' he asked Jonathan.

Jonathan shook his head. 'Not just your own dinner. Mine too.'

'Well, I'll give it a go,' Sam said gamely. 'But on your head be it if I burn this place to the ground.'

'I'll take my chances.'

'Seriously? You'd risk dying in a fire rather than let me off cooking dinner?'

'Yep,' Jonathan said implacably. 'Nothing you say will make me change my mind.'

'You used to be such a lovely mum. What's happened to you?' Sam shook his head. 'This'll be your influence,' he said to Aoife.

Aoife smiled. 'I certainly hope so.'

'But how will I live without your Thai curry?' Sam made puppy-dog eyes at Jonathan.

'Don't worry, you won't have to. I'll give you the recipe.'

Aoife laughed.

'So, Jonathan tells me you've hit the target on the crowdfunder,' Sam said.

'Yes. We've gone over it, in fact.'

'So you'll be able to keep the theatre. That's exciting.'

She nodded. 'It is.'

'Well, if you're ever looking for a barista or foot soldier or ... the back end of a horse, I hope you'll think of me.'

'Horse's ass – the part you were born to play,' Jonathan said, and Sam gave him a playful thump on the arm.

'I was the leading light of the drama society at uni, I'll have you know.'

'Well, I'll certainly keep you in mind,' Aoife told him. 'In the meantime, we could give you a job as an usher, if you're interested – checking tickets, doing the safety announcement, that sort of thing.'

'I'd love that.' Sam beamed, like she'd just told him he'd won the lottery.

'Great. You can start for *Three Sisters*.'

'It's a pity this comes too late for you,' Sam said to his brother.

'What do you mean?' Aoife's head whipped around to Jonathan to find him frowning and shaking his head at Sam. 'Too late for what?'

'Sorry, I thought you'd know. Don't you two ever talk? Jonathan was going to buy into a partnership at his law firm with the money from Halfpenny Lane.'

'Oh.' Aoife was floored. So he'd turned down the partnership not because he wasn't interested, but because he couldn't afford it. 'And it's too late?'

'It was a time-limited offer,' Jonathan said evenly. 'But it's no big deal.'

'But if you'd had the money from the theatre—'

'Chances are the sale wouldn't have gone through in time anyway.'

She got the feeling he was playing it down for her sake. Maybe if they'd put the theatre on the market immediately, if he hadn't agreed to give them more time … 'But couldn't you have got a short-term loan? You were getting the money eventually either way, whether from the sale or the crowdfunder.'

He shook his head. 'Borrowing isn't an option.' Something flickered across his face, and he seemed very uncomfortable with the conversation. 'I'm not a good loan risk,' he said finally, as if the words were being dragged from him. 'My credit rating is terrible.'

'Wow! That doesn't leave much hope for the rest of us.'

'That's my fault,' Sam said cheerfully.

'Unfortunately, I was stupid enough to give my little brother access to my credit card once upon a time and he racked up a mountain of debt in my name.'

'And then he had to practically bankrupt himself to bail me out.'

Aoife couldn't help feeling Sam should be more contrite. Instead he seemed almost proud of what he'd put Jonathan through. It was as if he was boasting about the sacrifices Jonathan had made for him – giving up the chance of partnership at his firm, and renting out his beautiful house to move into an apartment with his brother.

'I'm sorry you missed making partner,' Aoife said later when they were alone. Sam had left shortly after dinner, saying he'd give them some privacy as they clearly had a lot to talk about, and they'd moved to the sofa.

'It's fine, honestly. There'll be other opportunities. And that wasn't the main thing I wanted the money for.'

'What *was* the main thing?'

'I wanted to buy a place for Sam – with cash. If my credit rating's bad, his is even worse. He'll never be able to get a mortgage.'

Bloody Sam! This was all his fault. And he seemed the least put out by it of all of them. 'Sam doesn't seem very repentant about all the trouble he's caused you,' she said. 'In fact, if anything he seems almost boastful about you having to bail him out, as if it's something to be proud of.'

Jonathan frowned thoughtfully. 'I think he *is* kind of proud of it, in a way.'

Aoife looked at him quizzically.

'It's hard to explain. But I think he's proud that he has someone who'd do that for him – someone who'd be on his side no matter how badly he messed up.' He sighed. 'He didn't get a lot of unconditional love growing up. Our father was very hard on him – on both of us, I suppose, but I had Mum around for longer to offset it. Dad was very demanding, and nothing Sam did was ever good enough. He was always berating him, telling him he was useless, he'd never amount to anything. No matter what he achieved, he could have done better. So if it seems like he was boasting, it's probably because he was.'

Aoife nodded thoughtfully, absorbing this. It certainly put Sam's bragging in a completely different light.

'I know it probably sounds daft,' Jonathan said.

'No, it doesn't. It makes sense.' She wished she could go back to the start and begin again with Jonathan, knowing what she did now – understanding how truly good he was. She would have been a better ally to him. 'He's very lucky to have you,' she said softly.

They were quiet for a moment, both lost in their own thoughts.

'I wish Detta could have known – about us,' Aoife said finally.

Jonathan smiled, his eyes crinkling at the corners. 'You think she'd have been pleased?'

She nodded. 'Definitely. She was always talking you up, you know, telling me what a lovely man you were.'

'Same.'

'She told you I was a lovely man?'

He grinned. 'She often said she wished we'd got to know each other better. She was always trying to get me to talk to you at parties and stuff when we were kids.'

'I wish you had. Why didn't you?'

'You and your sisters were always so … self-contained.'

'Unapproachable you mean?'

'No, but it was like you had your own little world. You seemed so happy together, just the three of you.'

'We were. We *are*. That doesn't mean we don't want other people around too.'

'It also didn't help that you were never on your own. It was hard enough to muster up the courage to talk to a pretty girl at that age without doing it in front of an audience.'

Aoife was amazed he'd thought of her like that back then. 'Well, Detta brought us together in the end anyway.' She played with his hand, entwining her fingers with his. 'Maybe that's why she left you a share in Halfpenny Lane – so that we'd be thrown together.'

'You think she's matchmaking from beyond the grave?' He rubbed his thumb against hers. 'I like that idea.'

'That's not it, though, is it?' She looked up, meeting his eyes.

'Not what?'

'You said once you knew why she put you in her will.'

He shook his head. 'I said I had my suspicions.'

'Is it because you were paying for her nursing home?'

He frowned and looked away. 'How do you know that?'

'Sam told me. Don't blame him,' she added as Jonathan opened his mouth to speak. 'I guessed. He just confirmed it. He thought I already knew.'

'I didn't expect her to pay me back. Honestly, it never occurred to me she'd do that. I was as surprised as anyone when I saw the will.'

'I believe you.'

'But I can't say it wasn't welcome, coming when it did.'

'I'm sure it was. And then I accused you of being mean. I wish you'd told me.'

'I didn't want you to feel indebted in any way. If you'd known, would you have kept fighting for the theatre?'

She thought about it. 'No, probably not.'

'Definitely not,' he said softly. 'You'd have felt honour bound to sell.'

He was right, she would have. 'But why didn't Detta talk to *us* if she was running out of money?'

'She didn't want to burden you with it.' He huffed a laugh. 'It was bad enough that one of you had already been forced into a life of accountancy just to keep body and soul together.'

Aoife gave him a crooked smile. 'So she burdened you with it instead.'

'She didn't know about my money troubles.'

Of course, because he'd never have breathed a word about them.

'Anyway, it all worked out for the best in the end.' He squeezed her hand. 'I'd hate you to have lost Halfpenny Lane on my account.'

Knowing what she did now, she was glad he hadn't agreed to keep it for their sakes. 'So, the crowdfunder ends tomorrow.'

He nodded. 'You'll be able to buy me out.' She

couldn't help thinking he looked a little sad. 'And you can get on with your lives.'

'Well, I hope you'll still be in it – my life, I mean.'

He smiled and turned to her, his eyes lingering on her face. 'I'm counting on it,' he said, his voice husky as he bent to kiss her.

34

Tech week began on the third Monday in September, and there was a chill in the air as Aoife made her way to Half-penny Lane for rehearsal. Today for the first time they'd run through the show with all the technical elements in place – sound, lighting, sets, costumes and make-up. Any problems with the practical aspects of the performance would be ironed out by the dress rehearsal on Friday.

At the theatre she found Mimi and Sive in the dressing room already in costume. Mimi was sitting at one of the dressers fiddling with her hair, and Sive was at the adjoining mirror, her back to Aoife as she entered. She was bent over a chair and appeared to be putting make-up on one of the other actors.

'There, done!' she said, straightening. She spun the chair around to face the mirror, and Aoife caught Jonathan's – heavily kohled – eye in the mirror.

'Sive! What on earth are you doing?'

Sive turned around to face her, blowing powder off a blusher brush. 'What does it look like?'

'It looks like you're giving Jonathan a makeover. And

not a very good one.' Though Aoife had to admit, the kohl did great things to his eyes.

'It's stage make-up – it's not supposed to be subtle. But doesn't he look lovely?' She beamed at his reflection in the mirror, admiring her handiwork.

'Why on earth are you putting stage make-up on him?' Aoife glanced at the clock on the wall. 'We haven't got time for messing around.'

'Because he's going on as Vershinin,' Sive said as if stating the obvious. Jonathan was unable to speak for himself as she turned his chair back to face her and he clamped his mouth closed as she applied lipstick.

'What! No he damn well isn't. Where's Mitch?'

'Calm down. It's just for the first scene. Mitch is on his way, but he's been delayed. He got knocked off his bike.'

'Oh no! Is he all right?'

'He's fine. He walked away from it, but he'll be a bit late. And in the meantime, Jonathan very kindly agreed to help out.'

'Isn't there anyone else who can do it?'

'Not really.'

'And he knows the play because he's run lines with you so many times,' Mimi said.

'I've told them acting isn't my thing and I won't be any good,' Jonathan said as Sive finished his lips and released him. 'But they said it doesn't matter.'

'It doesn't,' Sive insisted. 'He doesn't have to be off-book. We just need someone to speak the lines and hit their marks.'

Aoife couldn't suppress a smile. 'You know damn well he doesn't need full make-up for that.'

Sive gave her a cheeky smirk. 'I thought it would be more fun if we were all in make-up.'

'More fun for *you*, you mean.'

'Well, that too. But it's a full dress rehearsal, so we should all be in full dress, and that includes make-up.'

'What does Cara think about this? And Lorcan?'

'They're fine with it. We just need a body.'

'How do I look?' Jonathan asked, turning to Aoife with a grin.

Aoife laughed. 'Not bad, actually. The eyes are good, but I don't think that lipstick is really your shade.'

'I'll bear that in mind next time I find myself at the Bobbi Brown counter.'

'Well, stop dawdling there in the doorway admiring him,' Sive said to Aoife. 'You need to get into your costume. Chop-chop!' She clapped her hands.

Aoife blushed and moved into the room, shrugging off her jacket.

'I'll leave you to it,' Jonathan said, rising from the chair and picking up a copy of the script. He looked incredibly handsome in Vershinin's military uniform and boots. 'See you on stage.'

Jonathan had been vastly over-stating his talents when he said he wouldn't be very good. He was, in fact, appalling – worse than Aoife could have imagined possible. He was more wooden than Nottingham Forest, delivering his lines as if he was reading the instructions from a particularly dull boiler manual. There had been an almost audible sigh of relief from the whole company when Mitch skidded onto the stage halfway through the first act and took over, putting Jonathan and everyone else out of their misery.

'Don't give up the day job,' she said to him afterwards, laughing as she walked offstage and joined him in the wings.

'What? I thought I did okay. I didn't mess up any of the lines, did I?'

'No, you didn't. You read them very well.' She gave him a reassuring pat on the arm. 'And you hit all your cues. You were very … accurate.'

Jonathan laughed. 'What more could you ask? No one said I had to emote. That's not really my forte.'

'No kidding! Seriously, though – thanks for stepping in. I know it's outside your comfort zone.'

'I'm so far from my comfort zone right now, I may never find my way back.'

'Well, it was really helpful. I appreciate it – we all do.' He'd looked so ill at ease out there, it had been all Aoife could do not to crack up laughing every time he had to deliver a line.

'Have I earned one of those post-rehearsal suppers I've heard so much about?'

'You certainly have. But do you mind if we don't stay out late? I could do with an early night.' There had been so many stops and starts that the rehearsal had gone on for almost four hours, and she was exhausted.

'Not at all. If you'd rather go straight home, I don't mind.'

'No, I'd like to go out. I'm starving. Besides, I wouldn't want you to have got all dolled up for nothing,' she said, waving a hand in the area of his face.

'Dream on! I am *not* going out like this. Show me how to get this stuff off, please.'

'Sive put it on. Let her take it off again.'

'Right. I'll see you out front in ten minutes?'

'See you there.' Aoife grinned as she watched him stride off in search of Sive.

35

'THAT WAS FUN,' Jonathan said later, linking Aoife's arm as they walked along the quays.

'It was.' They'd gone to a pub on the other side of the river with several of the cast and crew. Jonathan had got equal amounts of good-natured teasing about his performance and sincere thanks for stepping up in their hour of need, while Mitch had received copious amounts of sympathy and an endless supply of pints on the back of his traffic accident. Most people had left early, tired after the long rehearsal, but there were still a few stragglers when Aoife and Jonathan called it a night.

There was a cool breeze off the river as they walked across the Halfpenny Bridge and Aoife leaned into the warmth of his body.

'It's beautiful, isn't it?' Aoife breathed, pausing halfway across the bridge and looking down towards the Custom House, the lights of the city glinting in the water. She loved Dublin on nights like this. It may not have the majesty and grandeur of Paris or London, but it had a scruffy charm that for her made up in authenticity what it lacked in splendour. It was like Irish men, she thought, glancing at Jonathan. They may lack the suave sophistication of their Continental counterparts, but their gruff declarations were heartfelt. Maybe she was biased, but on a night like this with the light just so and the right man by her side, it felt like the most romantic place in the world.

'It's gorgeous,' Jonathan said, turning to her. Their eyes met and held, and Aoife's stomach flipped in the most delicious way as his gaze dropped to her mouth and she knew he was going to kiss her. The white clouds of their breath mingled in the air as he bent his head to hers. He wrapped his arms around her, pulling her up on her tiptoes as he deepened the kiss. Aoife buried her hands in his soft, thick hair, her lips clinging to the soft warmth of his mouth.

'Get a room!' a rough voice called as a drunken youth strode past in Aoife's peripheral vision.

Jonathan lifted his head and quirked an eyebrow as he looked down at her. 'Not a bad idea.' He cocked an eyebrow, a smile playing at the corner of his lips. 'What do you think?' He jerked his head towards the Clarence behind him. 'Shall we?'

She didn't hesitate for a second. Sive and Mimi had left the pub early and would be home by now. Sam would be at Jonathan's place. 'Yes, let's,' she said breathlessly, the impulsiveness of it making it all the more thrilling.

Jonathan grinned happily at her enthusiastic response. He grabbed her hand and they tripped across the bridge to the gleaming lights of the Clarence. The lobby was warm and welcoming, and the receptionist who checked them in was studiously unjudgy, not batting an eye at the fact that they had no luggage and were obviously checking in for a spontaneous shag.

Once they were in the lift on the way to their room on the second floor, Aoife turned to Jonathan and collapsed in giggles. She felt like a naughty schoolgirl, giddy with the reckless spontaneity of the moment.

Jonathan pulled her into his arms and they kissed all the way to their floor, then staggered down the corridor in a knot of limbs made weak with lust.

'Well, last night was a revelation,' Jonathan said the next morning as they lay side by side in bed.

'We discovered you can't rock a red lip, for one thing,' Aoife teased.

'I'm told not everyone can pull it off.'

'I think with your complexion, you should go for more peachy tones. Just being honest.'

'Thanks. I'll bear that in mind.'

'We also discovered you can't act for toffee.'

'Act for toffee! Where do you come up with these expressions?'

Aoife shrugged.

'Well, I hope you discovered I have other talents?' He gave her a wicked grin.

'Oh yes, definitely,' Aoife nodded. 'You're excellent at memorising lines.'

'Right. What else?'

'Um … hitting your mark?' Aoife raised her eyes to the ceiling as if she was trying to think of something. 'I think that's it really.'

'Seriously? That's all? Clearly I need to try harder.' He bent his head and kissed her thoroughly before pulling away. 'Well?'

'Hmm.' She licked her lower lip, enjoying the way Jonathan's eyes darkened. 'There's something there. Maybe you just need more practice.'

'No problem.' He leaned closer, his breath warm on her face. 'We don't have to check out until twelve.'

'Hungry?' Jonathan asked an hour later, laughing as Aoife's stomach rumbled embarrassingly loudly.

'Just a bit.'

He sat up and grabbed the room service menu from the nightstand. 'Let's have a huge breakfast, check out at the last minute and then go for lunch.'

Aoife laughed. 'We can't afford a huge breakfast here,' she said looking at the menu. 'Have you seen the prices?'

'Sod the prices!'

'I thought you were supposed to be broke?'

'Not broke. Just not rich enough to forego half a million euro. The cost of a hotel breakfast doesn't amount to a hill of beans in the crazy world of bailing out my brother or saving Halfpenny Lane.'

'I guess you're right.'

'What made you so convinced I was rich in the first place?'

'I don't know. You took us out for that lunch in the Saddle Room. You ordered champagne like it was sparkling water.'

Jonathan smiled. 'It was one lunch. I wanted to do something to honour Detta's memory. And you girls looked like you could do with a treat.'

'Yeah, it was kind of a rotten day. Sorry,' she added, realising it was he who'd made it rotten for them.

'It's fine. But being able to afford a blowout lunch once in a while doesn't exactly make me Rockefeller.'

Aoife nodded. 'I get that. But there was also the fact that you have a really good job. And you just look rich. You wear fancy suits, and you have an expensive watch—'

'Goes with the territory. I have to keep up a certain level of professionalism. And the watch was a gift.'

Aoife wondered who from. Had an ex-girlfriend given it to him? 'I also thought you were still living in your house in Sandymount. How's the house hunt going, by the way?' She tried to sound super casual. They'd bought Jonathan out of Halfpenny Lane with the crowdfunding money and he and Sam had started looking at apartments.

'Good. I've put an offer in on a place we saw at the weekend.'

'That's great. And will you be moving back to Sandymount?'

'Yeah. As soon as Annie's lease is up.'

'Not that it affects me in any way, of course.'

'Of course not.' Jonathan grinned. 'But it's nice having the place to ourselves, isn't it?'

'It's lovely.'

'So it's a good thing the lease is up soon, because I couldn't afford to check in here every time we want to be alone.'

'Are you sure about breakfast? It really is quite expensive.'

'I may not be loaded, but I think I can stretch to breakfast.'

'Even if I have the eggs royale?'

'Stick with me, baby,' he said in a sleazy gangster voice, 'and it'll be eggs royale all the way.'

Aoife giggled.

'Full disclosure, though,' he said, his expression suddenly serious. 'I may not be working at McWilliams much longer.'

'Oh no!' Aoife frowned. 'Are they kicking you out because you didn't take the partnership?' Jonathan assured her he wasn't bothered and he mightn't have had the money in time anyway, even if they'd put the theatre on the market straight away. But she still felt guilty that he might have missed out on it because he'd given them more time.

'No, they're not kicking me out. It's good news actually. Philip and Olivia have been talking about leaving to start their own firm and they've asked me to join them.'

'Oh, that's exciting! Are you interested?'

'Very. So it turns out it's a good thing I didn't buy into the partnership when they offered it to me.'

'So keeping Halfpenny Lane was the right thing for all of us in the end. I'm so glad.'

He nodded. 'If we'd sold it straight away, I might be locked into McWilliams for the foreseeable future.'

'And just think, the world would never have seen your *Vershinin*. Now *that* would be a real tragedy.'

36

Opening night finally arrived. In the afternoon, Aoife, Mimi, Sive and Jonathan went to Halfpenny Lane to take a final tour of the theatre before anyone else arrived. There had been enough excess in the crowdfunder after buying Jonathan out to do some more work, and the place looked amazing.

The brass handrails and door plates were polished to a shine, and the new carpet was thick and soft underfoot. Newly restored and reframed photographs of previous productions hung along the walls, and a stack of freshly printed programmes stood by the door to the auditorium. Aoife picked one up and flicked through it, breathing in the smell of fresh paper and ink. Jonathan had done a great job of pulling in advertising. There was a piece about the history of the theatre, and Sir Peter Bradshaw had written a very moving tribute to Detta. And there in the centre was the cast list, with her name printed alongside her sisters'. She could scarcely believe it was real.

They moved into the auditorium, the heavy wooden doors opening with a satisfying suck. Aoife walked down the aisle, running her hands along the backs of the seats and breathing it all in. It was a real theatre working theatre.

'I wish Detta could see this,' she said, tears stinging her eyes as she looked around.

'She'd be so proud of you,' Jonathan said at her side, his voice thick with emotion.

'She'd be proud of us.' She took his hand. 'All of us. It wouldn't have happened without you either.'

'I'm not so sure about that, but I'll take it.'

'We did good, didn't we?' Mimi said, smiling.

'We did great,' Sive agreed.

The theatre was bustling with activity when they returned in the evening to get ready for the show. Sive had baked cupcakes for the green room, and they'd bought small gifts for all the cast and crew – copies of the print of Halfpenny Lane that they'd used for the crowdfunder, inscribed with tonight's date to commemorate the occasion.

Aoife gave Lorcan his. 'I also wanted to say thanks personally,' she said, 'for everything. For making my first time so easy.' She blushed to the roots of her hair as she realised how that sounded. 'I mean—'

'I know what you meant.' Lorcan grinned. 'It's been a privilege, Aoife. And now I can brag that I got to direct *the* Aoife Carroll in her stage debut. Because, believe me, you'll be a *the* one day.'

Aoife smiled, flushed with pleasure. She didn't know what to say, so instead she threw her arms around him and gave him a hug.

'Just do me a favour,' Lorcan said when they broke apart. 'Be sure to mention me in your Oscar speech.'

'I'll remember!' she called as she headed for the dressing-room, already on a high.

She was giddy with nerves and excitement as she and her sisters got dressed. The dressing room was already filled with flowers and gifts from well-wishers and the rest of the cast and crew. Jonathan had delivered a huge bouquet of lilies personally, a dusting of yellow pollen on his dark jacket as he handed it over.

As the five-minute call came over the sound system, Aoife took her sisters' hands, and they stood in a circle communing in silence for a moment, too overcome by emotion to speak. But Aoife knew they were all feeling the same way, thinking the same thing.

'We made it,' she whispered finally, squeezing her sisters' hands.

'Moscow,' Mimi breathed.

'Moscow.'

Act One beginners to the stage, please, Cara's voice came into the room.

'That's us!'

Aoife's heart pounded as they took their places on the stage. On the other side of the curtain, they could hear Sam putting his all into making the safety announcement, even throwing in a few jokes and turning it into a performance in itself. He really was a natural, and seemed to be enjoying himself hugely. Maybe they could let him try out in a small role in their next production.

Then a hush fell over the audience, the curtain pulled back and Aoife forgot about Sam and Halfpenny Lane and what play they might do next. She forgot herself entirely. She was Olga Prozorov now, a spinster school teacher, and her sisters were Irina and Masha. She beat her wings and began to soar.

COMING SOON – ACT TWO

Catch up with Aoife, Mimi and Sive in the second part of the Halfpenny Lane series …

STAGE KISSES ON HALFPENNY LANE

Mimi and her sisters have saved their beloved Halfpenny Lane Theatre, but keeping it afloat is still a challenge.

So when Hollywood heartthrob Rocco Agnew wants a part in their upcoming production of *Private Lives* it promises to be a lifesaver. Rocco sets hearts racing and ticket sales soaring wherever he goes.

The only problem: Rocco is Mimi's ex and she's slated to play opposite him in a role that will bring them far too close for comfort.

They can't say no to Rocco. Mimi can't say no to the part. Will the little theatre be big enough for both of them?

ALSO BY CLODAGH MURPHY

Lightning Source UK Ltd.
Milton Keynes UK
UKHW040401290722
406540UK00002B/299